A Silver Path

Emma Jo Renner

Emma Jo Renner

Elk Mountain Books, Wilsonville, Oregon

A Silver Path

Emma Renner

Published by:

Elk Mountain Books
PO Box 21
Wilsonville, Oregon 97070
info@elkmountianbooks.com

ISBN Print Edition: 1453699473
EAN-13: 9781453699478

Elk Mountain Books titles are available for special promotions and premiums. For details contact:
sales@elkmountainbooks.com

Special thanks to

First of all: Thank you Father God and Jesus, my Lord and Savior and Blessed Holy Spirit for your help and guidance not only for this story but in all of my life.

My Sister Ruby Wallin and my Sister-in-law Lelia Olson were the first to read this story. They both insisted that I get it published. My Daughter Della Mae Leftridge and son Arthur Renner were next, again telling me to get it published.

My sons Robert, (Bob), and John and Daughter Kandi Kirkland and Granddaughter Charity Hess all have been bugging me. The rest of my family echoed that and have pressured me to get published. My friends Helen and Deryol Anderson also read it and encouraged me to get published.

THANK YOU ALL!

My dear friend Perry P. Perkins, who heard of my book and offered to get it published and has been so wonderfully helpful, and is getting it to happen.

The rest of the page could be filled with, "THANK YOU PERRY"...and it wouldn't be enough!

And, although I'm Thanking God again. I'm not putting Him last, but acknowledging that He is the beginning and finisher of all good things in my life. You should be able to see where God has had influence in the writing of this novel.

He has spoken to me through it and I hope that He'll speak to you. He is threaded through out the story. He has had a great part in my life. Without Him, I'm nothing.

May God richly bless each reader in the special ways that you need.

This, my first novel, is dedicated to my sisters - who are both jewels, my brothers - good men who loved me, and finally to my children, grandchildren, and great-grandchildren - whom I love very much and who have made my life so very, very good!

CHAPTER ONE

Eva opened the sliding glass door and stepped out on the deck of her upstairs apartment. The view overlooked a sliver of town, and above was Mt. Rainier.

She stood looking at the mountain.

"You're beautiful this morning, as always," she said, admiring the mountain. "You seem closer today. Maybe I'll paint you again." She put her arms up, hands outstretched, as if to embrace the view.

"It's going to be another beautiful day!"

She stood searching out the mountain promontories that she'd come to know so well in the last few months.

Each hour you change, revealing some of your hidden folds and seams. Like folds and creases in a full garment draped around you. That's what you do, don't you, wear the upheavals of creation like a garment. Wearing the tree covered hills like robes with meadows and pastures like skirts 'round about; displaying each part in the revelation of the changing light. Wearing a great crown of sparkling white snow and icy glaciers, and showing your glory a part at a time.

As time passes, revealing to us more of you, like secrets, as the light reveals them, because your full beauty would be overwhelming for us to see all at once.

That is the way with God. It is impossible for us to comprehend all at one time, the beauty and magnificence of the awesomeness of God. Yet that awesome God is the loving Father of His children.

"Thank you Father," Eva whispered, "thank you for your care over me. Thank you for this apartment and safety that I've had here."

She'd felt so closed in, moving into the apartment, sheltered behind two locked doors. She was learning to appreciate the relative safety.

Henry can't even get into the building, much less though my door.

She was still afraid that Henry might come to try to see her, to talk to her. He'd told some of the kids that he wanted to see her, to hug her.

She remembered that his hugs had never been pleasant.

He'd liked to catch her unawares from behind, pulling her suddenly off balance, and with a quick squeeze, knocking the breath out of her.

Then he'd laugh, like he thought it was funny.

He thought that if he could talk to her now, he could convince her to come back, he'd told them.

Why did he want her back?

Twice during that last summer, she'd gone to the doctor, and once to the hospital with unexplainable symptoms.

Wanting her back was just 'show and tell' for the kids. It was a bid for sympathy, a disclaiming of fault. His ego was bruised that she'd left him.

The *she* had left *him* – HIM.

It was almost two years since she'd fled her home to escape the verbal abuse and fear of her husband of forty-seven years.

Years that she'd tried to make a good home for her children and for him, too…years of pretending. Pretending that everything was all right. Of course, there had been many good times too, with her children.

Henry had been handsome when he was young, and was still a good-looking older man. He'd been a good worker, seldom missing a day of work, and was never late. He was talented, able to do many things, and do them well. Almost a perfectionist in everything that he did, he expected others to be able to do things as well as he could, especially his children and Eva.

He was impatient when they didn't meet his expectation.

Yet, there had been times when he was hesitant about his own abilities, often as he started a new job, but Eva had encouraged him, telling him that if anyone else had done it, he could, and even better…and he often did.

Henry had a gift for improving on the way to do things on his jobs, improvements which those companies often incorporated into their system. Eva had been proud of him; maybe that was why it was so devastating when she discovered he was 'fooling around'.

She'd always been true to him. He'd been the only man in her life since 'that day'.

Henry had ways of making it seem as if she were at fault, not him.

He played nearly as hard as he worked. If he played ball, he fought to win. When he went fishing, he caught fish with single minded, grim determination.

When he went hunting, he got his game, taking pride in his abilities. He was able to figure out ways to get the advantage, to be able to win. Even with people, to be able to make others think that he, Henry, was right and they were wrong.

When he *was* wrong, he promptly forgot it.

Eva had asked the Lord to give her a love for Henry, and God had given her the love, a love that forgave. A love that overlooked and helped to hide some of the things, some of the times, from others, even from his own family.

However, love needs to be returned…love needs to be cared for and nurtured, to survive.

Henry apparently couldn't love her.

She had kept hoping that he would change, that he could care for her, could be true to her, to the marriage vows. She wanted and needed his love. She'd hoped for it, longed for it, prayed for his love.

When she finally realized that she would never win him, never be his only love, the only woman in his life, she gave up trying to woo him. Still, she stayed, continuing to pretend, acting like everything was fine, yet feeling that she'd failed.

It was devastating, and her love for Henry finally died.

The verbal abuse grew worse with time. She finally realized that Henry not only didn't love her, he must hate her, or at least despise her, to treat her that way he did.

He must have been unhappy in a marriage that he hadn't wanted. Had they lived together all those years with both unhappy? Had Henry had any happiness?

Her happiness was in her children. She'd stayed, not wanting her children to know and be hurt. They became what was most important to her.

Finally, she knew that it had to come to an end. She'd slipped outdoors and walked out to the beach, climbing into a hummock of beach grass.

She'd been sheltered there, from eyes and the wind, as the Pacific Ocean calmly swept the sand with gentle waves leaving it smooth. The clear blue sky gave the water a deep blue cast to vie with the emerald green in the depths of the waves. The sun had touched the sea with sparkles like a thousand diamonds and rubies, dancing in the spray.

The beauty of the sky and water and the sound of the gentle waves had done little to calm the turmoil of her thoughts.

"I can not do anything more, Lord." Eva has whispered, "Henry is beyond my help." She raised her hands as if she held him within, "I give him to you Lord, I release him. He is in your care from now on."

There were no more tears, just trust in her Lord. She heard the Him speak:

"Go, my daughter, leave him to me. If you are between, I can do nothing. He has kept you between himself and the Lord. Go quickly my daughter; he will be in my care."

She had fled, fearing Henry, fearing for her life, but trusting the Lord. She knew that it was the only way, the best way.

Maybe Henry would be happy now, could find some happiness at last. The divorce became final, and Eva began making a new life for herself. She quickly learned that she enjoyed the freedom, and the peacefulness living alone in the small town near her siblings.

She enjoyed her little apartment, with the view of the mountain. She stood there on the deck, looking at the beauty of the changes that the sun was showing on the mountain.

"I love this place," she thought. "I love my mountain. I think that I like the fall here as much or better than spring."

Voices coming closer caught her attention.

"No, I don't know everyone who lives in these apartments."

"No, I don't know who the person is that you're looking...

"Well, I'm sure that she lives here."

Eva looked down from her balcony....she could see the two men. *That voice!*

Yes, it was....Henry.

He's here...he's looking for me! Oh, Lord help me.

Fear griped her, turning her cold. She slipped back into the apartment and closed the door. She grabbed up her purse and started to flee.

No – stop and think! She told herself. *Think! What to do? Call Sis...*

"...Jewel, he's here! Oh God, he's here!"

"Who? Who's here?"

"Henry! He's out in the parking lot."

"You're sure?"

"Yes, I saw him."

"I'm come over....Eva, I'm on my way!"

"No! You mustn't! He'll see you. He'll know for sure that I live here if he sees you! I don't know what he might do to you. "

"I'll call the police! I'll call Deputy Ryan and tell him," Jewel cried, "then I'll call the church and see if I can get some help. Don't go near the deck or a door where he might see you."

Eva shuddered.

"Okay…Jewel, I'm scared!"

"We'll get you out through someone else's apartment. Stay put until I call you back, or come to get you. Pack some clothes, enough for a few days. Can you do that? Are you okay?"

"No, I'm shaking."

Jewel prayed, "*Father help us and calm Eva right now, Amen.* Now do as I say, Eva, and I'll be there as soon as I can. Be careful!"

"You too!"

"I'll call you back as soon as I can."

"Okay."

The phone went dead in her ear.

Eva started to pack. She didn't have a large suitcase, and usually hung her clothes up in the car when she went anywhere for a few days. She packed medication and vitamins in one bag, personal items in another bag. Then she took a kitchen bag to put some towels in it.

Ten minutes later, her sister called back.

"Deputy Ryan and Owen from church are coming with me. We're coming in from the other side through a patio door, and we'll take you out the same way. Deputy Ryan is going to keep Henry busy while we get you out from there. We'll be there in just a few minutes."

"Okay…"

A half-hour later, Owen, Jewel, and Eva were driving into the mountains on an unnamed country road.

"My Grandson has a cabin that I'm going to take you to,

for right now anyway." Owen assured her, "You'll be safe. There's no way that anyone will find you there."

The cabin apartment was half of a duplex overlooking a lake. Mount Rainier soared in the background. Owen's grandson, Steve, was doing laundry and packing when they arrived. Owen introduced them, explaining the need of secrecy. Steve would be leaving in a few days for college and would not be returning to the apartment for some months.

"Eva," Owen asked, "do you have enough things to get by for a few days?"

"Yes, I think so…but I didn't bring any bedding."

"I have extra sheets and blankets," Steve said. "The bed in the extra room is made up, clean, and ready. You can use it as it is, Ma'am."

"That will be wonderful, thank you."

They carried her things in and put them in the second bedroom. Jewel helped her to hang clothes up, while Owen checked with Steve, "How about food?"

"There's some, but since I'll be leaving soon, I haven't bought much."

Owen looked in the refrigerator and cupboards. "I'll bring some things out. Eva, if you'll trust me to do it. I'll get some help and bring your personals out here. I own this place, and since Steve is leaving, you can stay here as long as you'd like to."

"Really?" Eva's shoulders slumped in relief. "That would be wonderful. God bless you, Owen! I just hope that Henry can't find me here."

"We'll do everything we can to make sure of that," Jewel assured her. "I'll go with Owen now, but I'll be back later."

Jewel turned to Steve, her voice shaking a little despite herself, "Are...are you going to be here all night?"

"Yes, Ma'am." He replied, "I don't leave for two days. The couple who live next door are good folks, and they'll watch out for Eva too. They usually get home around five."

"Eva, do you want to give me your keys?" Owen asked.

She gave him the keys, but asked "What about my car? Henry knows my car and he might follow it if he seen it goes somewhere."

"We'll leave it there for a few days. We're not going to bring it out here until we are sure that Henry's given up and gone home," Owen assured her, then turning to Jewel, "If you'll supervise, I'll recruit some help and move Eva's things out here in the next day or two."

"We can do that." Jewel replied, wrapping her arms around her sister's shaking frame. "Eva, everything is going to be just fine. I think you'll like it here. This apartment is nice...and look, you still have your view of the mountain. I'll bring some more of your things as soon as I can."

After Jewel and Owen had gone, Steve asked, "Have you had breakfast?"

"No, but I'm not hungry." Eva replied. In truth, she was simply exhausted, yet she didn't want to be along. Steve sensed her fear, and nodded.

"I'll make some coffee," he replied, "I want some, too."

Steve made toast. "I had a half of a cantaloupe, how about you eating the other half?"

"Thank you, I love melons."

They talked, Steve telling her about going to college in Oregon on an athletic scholarship.

"You play football, don't you? I recognize your name as being a football star in the high school here."

Steve grinned, "More infamous than famous in some games. I'm about to go from being a big fish in a little pond, to being a guppy in the ocean!"

They discussed the last game of the season, and of his school taking the championship.

Steve walked Eva out to the boat dock to see the view.

"This is my boat." He said with evident pride, "It'll be here for you to use if you want. It's not much of a boat, and there's no motor, but if you row out there," he pointed, "anchor and still fish and you can catch fall the trout you want. It's not far to row. Brandon uses the boat too, and maybe he'll take you out sometime too. Do you like to fish?"

"Yes, I love fishing," Eva replied, "but I haven't been for ever so long. It sounds like fun to try again. What a view of the mountain there is from here!" She exclaimed.

"Isn't it something?" Steve grinned, "I'll sure miss the mountain, and the lake, when I leave."

"When you have a holiday from school, why don't you come home here and stay with me? That is, of course, if I get to stay here." Eva replied.

"Say…I might just do that! I think that granddad is planning on you staying, if you like it here, and want to."

"I think I'll like it here." Eva said, gazing at the distant mountain, "It's beautiful and quiet, being out here at the lake with the mountain – so peaceful. I…I need that."

"Yes, it is. It's been a good place for me; a quiet place to hit the books and study. I hope that I can concentrate in a dorm with a roommate. I've been alone for a year now."

"I've spent a lot of hours sitting here on the dock. That's why I built this bench."

"I'll remember that when I come out here and I'll pray for you that you can study well at school."

"Thank you, I'll probably need that." He laughed.

They sat on the boat dock and talked awhile, before going back to the apartment.

"I feed some wild birds here near the deck, and I have a couple of humming bird feeders hanging in the trees. The humming birds come late in February and leave in August, so they've already gone for this season."

"I'd love to keep feeding the birds."

"Before spring I'll fix a place to hang the feeders on or near the deck so that you can see them better."

"I'll like that. I love humming birds. They are such little beauties and so interesting to watch."

Steve made sandwiches and they ate at the picnic table on the deck, enjoying the birds, which swooped in to get crumbs.

A squirrel set up chatter in a tree near by until Steve brought some peanuts for him. Eva felt something run across her foot. It was a chipmunk trying to get some of the peanuts and crumbs. Steve tossed him a crust of bread. The chipmunk stuffed as much into the pouches on the sides of his face as he could, then carried the rest away in his paws.

"This place is a wildlife haven," Eva exclaimed.

"That's not all, there's a doe has twin fawns. Sometimes in the evenings, she brings them here, even up on the deck. They're so curious, checking out everything."

"This sounds like a wonderful place to live."

"Yes I think it is, if you don't prefer the town or city life."

"Not me. I love the country, the mountains, and the woods, and I love the Ocean too. I love to see the handiwork of God, as untainted by man as possible. Yet, I like people too. I guess it's more the simple way of life that I like. I was happy in town too, but it is a small town. I don't mind a shopping trip to Tacoma, but it's nice to come to a quiet place."

"I think so too," Steve agreed. "That's the one thing I've worried about most…living in a big town, on campus, with a bunch of people. Here, I've been able to get away for a while each day. I love football, and football is going to help me to go to college. I want to get a good education."

"You're a good boy, Steve," Eva smiled, "come home here when ever you can. I have three boys and two girls and I miss them terribly. I don't get to see them very often. Of course, they are working and busy with lives of their own."

"I will. I'll come home here. Thank you. It'll be nice to have someone to come home to, too."

*

And, he did.

Whenever he had time to get away from school, and just like that, Eva had another friend, almost like a son or grandson.

A friend who knew Jesus.

CHAPTER TWO

Jewel and Owen arrived at almost at the same time that evening. Jewel appeared at the door with a cooker full of food items out of Eva's refrigerator and her pillows.

"I know that you like your own pillows," Jewel smiled.

Owen brought several bags of groceries, "To keep you going until you can go shopping."

Brandon and Billie, the young couple from next door, arrived soon and they met them on the deck, Steve introducing them. Jewel and Owen explained what had happened and the need for security for Eva.

"I'll be leaving in a few days," Steve said, "so Eva will be here alone. You'll like her, she's nice people."

"We'll do our best to watch out for her. You've been a good friend, Steve; we'll miss you. It'll be nice to have someone else nice here," Brandon told him.

Eva and Steve talked about her car, and what to do about it. Steve asked if he could go look at it. He took the keys and checked it over. When he came back, he told Eva that he'd checked the Blue book on both cars, hers and his. The value was about the same.

"Shall we trade cars?" he asked after he'd explained about checking on them. "That way you'll still have a good car and yours will be out of town. Your Ex will never know that this is your car."

She agreed and, just like that, they traded.

Owen, true to his word, moved Eva's things out to the apartment at the lake a few days later. Jewel helped to get her settled.

Before the others left, Owen said, "Eva, we're going to pray with you, that Henry can't find you. God can, and will, protect you. God doesn't bring fear to His children, but brings grace, perfect peace, and joy."

Even with the different car, Eva stayed home for several days, not wanting to take a chance on meeting up with Henry.

Deputy Ryan stopped by, reassuring her that Henry had returned to his home in Oregon. And so, Eva 'settled in' at the new apartment, adjusting well in a short time, considering the unexpectedly hurried move. Because of the different car, she was soon able to go to church again, shopping and out and about.

"And I still have my mountain, A little bit different angle of view, but still my mountain," she'd said.

The fact that Brandon and Billie were close and at home each night was comforting. They talked to her every evening. Sometimes Eva was up in time to wave goodbye to them as they left for work.

They soon became good friends.

By late fall, Eva had settled into a quiet routine. Steve was gone back to school. Jewel was busy. She hadn't heard from her kids for a while. They were busy of course.

She felt cut off, isolated.

It had been raining off and on all day, and it grew darker and darker. The storm picked up force and lashed the rain at the windows, howling around the eves. Bits of tree branches danced wildly across the deck. The lake was rushing madly at the dock. White caps were blowing off the tops of the waves but the little boat was resting safe and snug upside down on the bank, as though waiting for spring.

The power kept going off, and on, and finally off. It really wasn't cold but Eva put on a sweater, and sat watching the stormy windows.

Suddenly, she burst into tears, sobbing.

"Lord," She cried out, "what has happened to my life? I had plans, hopes, - things that I wanted to do, things that I needed to do. The years have fled by and I've done nothing. I've wasted my life, and have nothing to show for it. I've just wasted all those years. I kept waiting to do things, waiting for the right time to do something, and I didn't do them.

Your word says to walk in wisdom, redeeming the time. I've lived and knew, and didn't know. The time that I had hoped for to do things has slipped past and now I'm growing old and still the things are not done. Forgive me, Lord!" she cried aloud, with great sobs and groaning.

She slipped to the floor, her head on her arms resting on a small table, next to her Bible. At last the sobs slowly stopped. She continued to sit thus, washed with tears, the storm spent inside her as well as outside.

Finally, she was quiet and heard the word of the Lord come to her:

"Why are you cast down, my daughter? Speak to thy self and ask why are you disquieted? Hope thou in God. I am the Lord thy God that divided the sea, whose waves roared: The Lord of Hosts is His name. I have put my words in thy mouth, and I have covered thee in the shadow of my hand. Thou art mine. Fear not; for thou shalt not be ashamed: neither shalt thou be confounded; for thou shalt not be put to shame; for thou shalt forget the shame of thy youth, and shalt not remember the reproach of thy widowhood any more."

She sat amazed.

"Thank you Lord." She whispered. She took her Bible and opened to Psalms 42. "Forgive me Father for complaining. I miss my kids and I'm lonesome."

"Yet a little while, my daughter, and I will restore you and your children, all of them."

"Thank you Father."

She sat still before the Lord. The loneliness, defeat, and despair all left, leaving peace and joy, joy in her Lord.

*

One warm evening, while Eva was on the dock tossing bread to the ducks, the sunset began to spread a cloak of glory cross the sky.

She stood a moment, and then ran for her paints and a canvas. She didn't take time for an easel, but propped the canvas on the bench. She popped the paint onto the pallet and quickly began to blend the colors right on the canvas, not taking time to mix them on the pallet.

Her strokes were sure and purposeful, bold with authority to catch the vivid colors that God was blending across the canvas of His sky.

No shadows, just a vivid blaze of colors and light, from intense blue through lavenders to rose – through pink to yellow, to blazing gold, the sun setting in a magnificent golden orange opalescent orb.

The mountain that she painted was highlighted with the same colors.

When she could add no more, she sat and watched the remainder of the sunset. Still on her knees, deeply moved by the hand-I-work of the Master Painter, the golden glow of light enveloping her. How long she sat there, she never knew, but it was almost full dark when she came to her self.

She'd truly been in the presence of her Lord and God, the painting forgotten for a while.

The next day she returned to the dock with her painting and equipment to check the way that she'd painted the mountain. It looked as beautiful as the rest.

She touched a few highlights on the snow and on the lake.

As she finished, she stepped back to look at it. "I painted that!" she almost couldn't believe that she had. "What a sunset it was!"

She turned to the mountain, "I almost couldn't see you at first, for all the glory of the sky, but God bathed you with lights and the colors of that beautiful sunset. I've caught that for you too, in my painting. You were very beautiful, bathed in golden light, roses, and lavenders with lots of gold."

On the bottom of the painting, she wrote:

The Firmament Sheweth His handiwork. Psalm 19:1.

As she stood looking at her painting, she thought, "I may never catch another sunset like that again. I wonder, will the sky put on that kind of Glory when we see Jesus coming for us?"

She dropped to her knees, lifting her face and eyes towards heaven.

"Oh Lord, you have given me a glimpse of your self, of your Glory!" She sat in awe of the Lord, in wordless worship of Him.

Later she said, "I've been in the presence of the Lord. What a marvelous God we have!"

She went to her Bible to read the nineteenth Psalm.

The Heavens declare the glory of God; and the firmament sheweth his handiwork.

Eva spent many days, that fall and winter, on the dock or the deck painting, only retreating indoors when it rained or was too cold. Then, she used the main bedroom, with all the windows, for her studio.

Of the scenes that grew on her canvas, many were of mountains and lakes in the state of Washington, The Bells, Adams, and Baker. She didn't paint St. Helens. The view was still like a raw wound after the eruption, reminiscent of the destruction.

The beach at Long Beach was a vast expanse of sky and sea, with a few fancy kites flying high above the sparkling waves.

She painted scenes of Oregon's mountains that she loved. Diamond Lake with Mt. Thielsen, Mt. Hood from Timothy Lake. The unique Mt. Jefferson – the beauty of The Sisters. She painted sunsets on the Oregon Beaches, Cannon Beach, and the Jug shaped rock at Cape Kiwanda.

The sunsets highlighting the waves, making a golden bridge like pathway off towards the sunset. The sunsets turning the sky to gold against the vivid blues shading to lavenders and lighting the ocean waves of deep blue green shades with sparkling lights on the wave caps.

The sunsets were like a promise from the God that she loved, leaving a peace and a covenant from Him, even in her paintings.

The trees around the yard and shore were posing loftily, raising plumy arms into the sky. The bushes sitting quite smugly, adding their accent. The deer and squirrels invading the scene found their places in a painting now and then.

Some days there were small boats on the lake when she went to the dock to paint. The boats made their appearance in the paintings too.

One warm sunny morning as she painted 'My Mountain' from the dock, a canoe lingered not far away, just a bit off from the shore. As she was putting highlights on the riffles as finishing touches to the painting, a man in the canoe waved to her and called, "Good Morning!"

She returned the wave and called, "Good Morning. Do you mind if I paint your canoe in my painting?"

"Go ahead," he called back. "Maybe I'll catch a fish for you to paint," he laughed. "I haven't caught one all morning."

The canoe and fisherman were soon in the painting, with him catching an opalescent rainbow fish, adding the colors of the green of the canoe, and the dark red of the jacket.

Although the distance was too far to do justice to the floppy hat that bristled with fishing flies, yet somehow Eva captured the impression, nonetheless.

Finally, she called, "Thank you, I've got it!"

"May I come and see?"

"Sure, come on."

He rowed over to her dock, climbed out, and tied up the canoe. He stood looking at the painting, comparing it to the view, taking in the details she had put in.

"You gave me a fish...even though I didn't catch one!" He laughed, "You can almost tell that it's me!"

Eva looked too. "It does look like you, although the features are really not quite distinguishable. Shall I change it?"

"No! May I buy this painting? I'd really like to have it."

"Yes," she agreed, "If you really want it. I don't have a frame for it though."

"That's all right, I'll get it framed." He pulled out his wallet. "One hundred fifty enough? I can go get you more."

"That's too much without a frame."

"Not at all. It's worth that to me. It's a beautiful painting of the mountain and the lake, and there I am, fishing, and I caught a nice fish! That's certainly one way to catch a fish," he laughed again."

Eva cautioned him, "The whites won't be dry for about three months, and don't varnish it for a year. Don't put glass over it, yet you must protect it from dust."

He introduced himself and asked, "Do you have a card? Our friends may be jealous and want a painting, too."

"Send them over, I have several paintings, or I can paint something that they would like."

"I will. Say, this is great! Tomorrow is our wedding anniversary; this painting will make a good gift. Won't my wife be surprised! Something besides perfume or candy."

"Flowers make a good anniversary gift too."

"Yes, I've already ordered some. I'm going to take this and get it framed today."

"Be very careful and tell them that it's still wet."

"I'll stand right there and watch out for it. Thank you Eva, I'm excited about this!"

She handed him the painting after he got into the canoe. He carefully set it down.

"Don't let water splash on it," she cautioned.

"I'll be very careful. Thanks again, Eva."

She watched him as he rowed across to the far side of the lake to a house, similar to one that she'd painted in the picture. She didn't paint the houses exactly as they were, unless someone wanted it that way.

Later some of those friends came and bought more of her paintings, and then *their* friends came, as the word got out, so that she sold a painting more than occasionally.

Eva had been drawing since she was four years old. In the old home, the door that led into the bedrooms, her Mother had painted a dark maroon, then had given Eva and her young brother, Sven, chalk and started them writing and drawing on that door.

They learned the alphabet and numbers, as well as drawing pictures.

Living on a farming ranch, they had many things to draw.

Sometimes the door was covered with horses and cows, the next time maybe chickens, ducks, and geese. The South Dakota Badlands Buttes, which they could see not far away, appeared on the door in their drawings.

Sometimes the old Church they attended, with friends drawn around it, or maybe the closest neighbor's house and barn. Sometimes the farm wagons and the horse/drawn buggy, with the horse hooked up.

The winters on the prairie were long and bitterly cold, too cold for small children to go out doors much of the time. The paint on the door was durable and easily erased or washed off. The children spent many winter hours at that door, happily drawing and writing, busy learning. Their sense of beauty in common every day things being enhanced to linger with them through the years.

Eva kept busy, between painting and church.

She enjoyed the place where she lived, feeding the birds, the squirrels and the chipmunks. The ducks grew more and bold to come and be fed, sometimes being noisy in begging, setting up quite a raucous. The deer came more often and seemed to accept her without fear of her.

She was happy and content. Henry had retreated from her thoughts, relegated to the parts of the past to be forgotten as much as possible.

The peace and freedom, coupled with the activities in her new life were healing balm that her Lord was orchestrating for her new life.

Christmas came.

Steve came home to her, coming in and greeting her with a hug. Eva was glad to have him there for the holidays. Henry had been with the children for Thanksgiving, and showed up unexpectedly the day before the family Christmas gathering too. He hadn't been to the family Christmas gathering for several years, always being 'too busy' to go.

Danielle called to warn her that her that Henry was there.

"He wants to see you, Mom. He thinks that you'll come for the family party."

"No I won't come if he is coming. I don't want to see him. He needs to be with you kids. You all need to see him. It's been a while since he has been with you all. Maybe someday I can be there when he is, but not yet. Have a very Merry Christmas."

Steve and Eva put up a tree and decorated it two days before Christmas. Steve spent Christmas Eve with his grandparents, and Eva spent hers with her brother Len's family. Christmas day Steve went with Eva to Jewel's house.

During the holidays, Steve was kept busy with friends and his grandparents, Naomi and Owen. Steve asked Eva if he could have some of his friends for New Years Eve.

Several came and brought girl friends. They had fixed a buffet supper with a couple of hot dishes and there were snacks for later. The young people had a good time playing games, making popcorn later. Eva enjoyed the time with them. She was proud of them, that they could have such a good time with such a simple evening. She was glad that Steve had such friends.

Steve's holiday from college was soon over and he must return. Before he left to go back he asked, "Would it be all right if I adopt you and call you my Mom?"

Eva hugged him and, with tears in her eyes, said, "Yes Steve, I'd be honored to be called your Mom."

And so, winter passed and spring was coming.

Steve came home on spring break in late March. It was a busy time for him, with friends and his grandparents. On the Sunday before he went back, he fixed dinner for his family and some friends.

It was good to have Owen and Naomi and visit with them.

"I like it out here." Owen said, "Although we own this place, we've never lived here. We could be happy living out here, couldn't we Naomi?"

Naomi agreed, "I'd probably just sit and watch the lake and the mountain most of the time."

Eva laughed, agreeing, "I spend a lot of time doing just that. It's so beautiful."

Later that evening, Steve thanked Eva for helping him, she answered him, "You did most of the work...I just enjoyed it. Your grandparents are good people, your friends too. I like them all."

They carried a bag of bread down to the dock to toss to the ducks, which came flying from all over the lake.

Steve laughed, "They sure know you!"

"Yes, we've become friends."

Later as they stepped up on the deck and sat down, Eva clicked her tongue and called, "Come Chipper, Come Chipper." Little Chipmunks came from everywhere for bread and peanuts.

"Come Reddy, Come Reddy," she called and two pine squirrels came scampering down the trees to her feet and up into her lap to take peanuts from her fingers. Steve looked his amazement. She handed him some peanuts.

"Hold one out so they can see it." He did and soon had a squirrel on his lap too. First one then another squirrel visited their laps for peanuts. "They come to you best in the evenings," Eva told him. "Some times they'll come right up to the door and stand up on their hind legs and look in, looking for me to come with bread or peanuts."

They spent a happy evening watching the animals and talking. Not long before dusk, the doe brought the twins, nearly full grown now, to get strips of carrots and apples from her.

"How did you do all this, Mom? Get them so tame?"

"You started by feeding them. I just kept on feeding them and talking to them, and they came closer and closer, until now they take things from my hands."

"Amazing!" He settled in beside her on the bench and sighed. "I have to go in the morning. I'll be coming home for the summer, and I'm going to look for a job for the summer, maybe here in town. Can I stay here or should I get an apartment in town?"

"Steve, I'd love to have you here, if you don't mind having an old gal like me around. We are good friends."

"Yes we are, and I like being here with you. It seems more like home with you here."

"Then it's settled. You come home here for the summer."

"Yes I will, thank you my Mom." He grinned and hugged her. Little did they know that her summer was to go quite a different direction, a plan that the 'Master Planer' had for her?

CHAPTER THREE

One day, Eva's brother Len called.

"Eva, Cal and Sven are here and are going to stay a few days, come join us, Jewel is coming too."

Eva promised to come, looking forward to seeing her brothers again.

Many hours were spent reminiscing about the past, reliving good and not so good events. Eva and Sven sat together reliving the years.

"Eva, remember that summer it was so hot that Mama had hung wet sheets in the windows and doorways to help cool the house. She'd mopped the floor and we took off most of our clothes and played with cars on the floor. There was a knot in the floor near the bedroom doorway. Mama seen us looking at it and told us to leave that knot alone."

"Yes I remember," said Eva Jo, "Somehow that knot got pushed out and down through the floor."

"A few minutes later Mama came and saw a rattlesnake

coiled up not far from us." Sven remarked, "She went and got a hoe that was near the kitchen door and killed the snake and took it outside. Then she pounded a cork in the hole. She said, 'that's why I told you to leave it alone. The snakes'll try to find a cool place when it's so hot like it is today.' "

"Then Mama mopped the floor again and scrubbed where the snake had been. I remember many things about when we lived there on the prairie, and us kids all together. We were happy kids," Eva smiled.

"We were grown up and married by then but remember the time when we were living in Oregon and we all packed up tents and kids and went to Gold Beach? We slept wall-to-wall people in the tents, and cooked out on the ground. I had a tomato crate to set the gas stove on and sat on my knees to cook whatever couldn't be cooked on the campfire."

"That was when I was in a body cast from that stray long rolling over me." Cal grinned, "I'll tell you what, if that ol' log hadn't bounced over me, I would have been buried right there."

"Yes, but that cast didn't stop you from going fishing," Len laughed.

"Do you remember Mother dressed in a blue silk dress, standing in the surf perch fishing? A big wave came, caught her up under her armpits, and lifted her off her feet.

I waded in, grabbed her, and got her on her feet before she fell, but she told me, 'Go get your own pole...I've got a fish on!' She wouldn't come out until she had her fish."

The siblings had quite a laugh over that.

"Mom was something, wasn't she? She must have been seventy then," Len reminded him, "and as I recall, you did get a pole and went out in the surf, too."

"And a wave came in and ran water up inside that cast and squirted water up my nose and in my eyes," Cal laughed.

Eva laughed, "I remember that the water had washed all the plaster away, and the amazing thing, you were supposed to be in a body cast for at least six months, but your back was healed. Nothing even cracked anymore. We had prayed for you when we heard that you had been hurt and taken to the hospital with broken ribs. God healed you."

"He sure did. Vi was upset with me for getting wet, she was afraid that I had done harm to myself. No one could believe that I was healed and all okay, but the x-rays showed no broken bones and the doctor confirmed it. "

"God has been good to us."

"We sure had a good time," Eva sighed, patting her sister's knee, "Your Bill and my Allan were about six months old and we wheeled those two babies around all day in a baby buggy, and they turned pink from the sun, but they didn't burn bad."

"We caught fish and cooked and ate them all. Mother caught a good-sized lingcod, and ate the whole thing. Being a *Norse*, she sure loved to catch fish."

"Yes, and she loved to eat them too!"

That brought a shared, bittersweet laugh at the remembrance of their unique Mother, an immigrant from Norway who with their father had homesteaded on the prairie.

"We had a lot of fish. We had to eat what we caught; we didn't have coolers then to keep them in, so we just ate them. We spent a lot of time enjoying each other and playing."

"We had such a good time. Remember the seaweed? We found a big long sea weed and took it back to camp and used it for a jump rope."

"Yes," Eva clapped her hands, "I'd forgotten all about that. It was long, at least twenty feet, and we swung it, but we couldn't get in to jump, then mother said, 'Let me show you.' She ran in and jumped and jumped. She turned around and around, jumping all the time, and then ran out. Then she made me do it. Then you, Cal, ran in and jumped with both feet at a time. We tried but couldn't do it very long, especially after we started laughing."

"Mama always had time to play with us."

And, so it went for long hours into the night:

"Remember the little cabin that we lived in for a couple months?"

"Remember that big dog, King, who adopted us and would lie down in front of the door and we couldn't get out?"

"Remember the day a bear came and ate all the strawberries in the garden and the deer ate the roses. The bear hung around all day and none of us could go out side all day until the men came home."

"Remember the time when Abbi and Paul were up at the spring and Paul came running with Abbi by the hand, and said that there was a 'porky pine cone' up at the spring....and it was a real porcupine?"

"Remember that day when we moved the portable sawmill and you were pinned to the ground, when the cart slipped?"

"I wonder if whose quick prayers stopped that thing from killing me?"

"God has been good to us."

"That is sure the truth."

"That was when we started working on that bigger sawmill, trying to get it to run." Cal said, his smile fading.

"It would run for a few days, and then it would shift, so that we couldn't saw straight lumber. Then we would tear things apart and try to get it straight and anchored to stay put and not shift again. It took us six weeks, but we finally got it fixed. We cut good lumber for two weeks and then the owners came, shut us down, and took the mill away from us.

They wouldn't trust us to start to pay them. They had known that the mill wouldn't stand straight for them when they came to us with the deal. That's why they wanted us to go ahead and fix it, and get it running.

As soon as we were cutting good lumber, they came and shut us down."

"They shut us out of the timber too. We had to pay for the new cat that we had working in the timber. They wouldn't let us get it out. We paid for a new cat for them as well as fixed their sawmill," Len added.

"What a bunch of wheeler-dealers. It cost us a lot of money."

Remember the time was heard many more times before heads starting nodding in sleep. There were some bad times to talk about but it is good to remember good times and exciting times from the past, from time to time. Even the tougher times were lived through and survived, leaving them all stronger people and bonded together with love.

"Those were the days, some good times and some hard times, but they all worked out for good eventually."

They had been days of love, and fellowship, and family.

*

One day Eva had a phone call from Allan, her youngest son. His oldest boy was getting married.

"Will you come to the wedding? It's going to be here in our yard, among all the flowers."

"Is Henry coming?"

"No, he said that he can't get away."

"If he is not coming, then I'll come."

She went to the wedding and had a wonderful time. She even stayed a few days and spent time with each of her kids.

The previous year she'd spent two weeks with her sons and grandsons during archery hunting season. They talked about that trip and hunting trips of the past. Another time of remembering.

"Remember Paul's first season to hunt. Dad sent him off by himself and he got a big buck deer. Dad got one too and started yelling for Paul to come help him."

"Yes," Paul laughed, "and I yelled back to come help me. I went and helped him to drag his deer down to where mine was, and then Dad took off to find a way to get our deer out."

"The next year was Jason's first year to hunt and he only had to pile off the Jeep to shoot his. That was the same year that Jason walked up on those grouse and shot their heads off, and we had them for supper. The next year they changed the season so we couldn't hunt grouse during deer season anymore."

"Remember the year that Mom got her big buck at the upper end of Buck Hollow?"

"Jason got his buck that same year in almost the same place."

"We could let all the two and three-point bucks go, there were so many deer in those days, and not nearly so many hunters. Those days are gone forever, I'm afraid."

"I think that Allan beat us all for the first year hunt. He used Mom's 308 and shot about 400 yards and got his buck, first shot."

"Well, I always was a pretty good shot," Allan grinned, polishing his nails on his shirtfront.

"That's true, you're like Mom. If you can see horns in your scope, you'll shoot."

"Did you ever see Mom miss?"

"No, that's for sure; she always gets them, and on the first shot."

"No not always," Eva laughed. "I missed the first one I that I shot at one year. I had just gotten new glasses. They were bifocals because of my work. I couldn't see the cross hairs in my scope, and I missed him clean as a whistle. I sure sent him down the hill though. I shot at him three times, but could never be sure that I got the sights on him. He ran like he'd been shot at."

"I wonder why," they joined in the laugh.

"No one else seen him and he was a dandy buck. I think that he hid out the rest of that season. I put my old glasses on for the rest of the hunt. Another year I got lost and then after I knew that I was lost, I seen a big buck and let him go. I didn't know where I was and didn't know if I'd ever find him again, after I found my way out. I just stood and admired him. He didn't seem scared of me."

"But that wasn't a missed shot."

"That's true. I didn't shoot," Eva continued.

"I've often wondered if that was the one who became the 'Gray Ghost.' Paul and I seen him across a big canyon, he ran level, no jumping. It was like a bird soaring"

"I remember that. We could hardly believe that it was a deer, but when he stopped, we looked at him in our scopes, and he had a monstrous rack of horns, almost as big as an elk. I seen him every year that we hunted there." Paul agreed.

"How about my first elk?" Allan asked. "Dad and I were coming down through Bull Arena. He was on one side of the canyon and I on the other. We hadn't seen any elk. We could hear them sometimes, but hadn't seen one. Then, all at once, it sounded like a freight train coming down the hill. Some one out on top above the canyon must have spooked them, 'cause we sure didn't. Here they came down the hillside. I looked up to see if I was going to get run over, 'cause those guys can sure move when they run. I was on a trail and a bull was coming right at me.

Thank goodness, there was a big tree close, and I jumped behind it and fired my rifle from the hip as he went by.

I didn't expect to hit him and he kept going, but about the third step he stumbled and down he went, tumbling and sliding, 'cause he was sure moving when he went past me. Then our work began. We quartered the elk and make two trips. The river was about 40 feet wide, but it was only about 18 inches deep, rather swift and rocky, so you had to walk with care. We usually had a walking stick to help keep our balance."

"I'll never forget my first elk," Eva added. "He was big and should have been a three point, but had no eye guards, just the forks. Henry and I had been hunting, with Henry just at the crest of the hill, and I just below, going along the hillside, through one hill top pocket after another.

We kept pushing out elk but could never get to see them. They would go out ahead of us and down the hill to other hunters. After pushing out three bunched to someone else, Henry sent me to the bottom.

He told me, 'You follow along near the bottom, and watch from there. I'll work the pockets (small hidden meadows) and maybe kick them out and maybe we'll get one.'

Well, the next pocket that he hunted through, he put some elk out, six cows and a bull. They came right down the hill towards me, and then turned back across the hillside, to swing behind Henry.

They were running broadside to me. I shot at the bull, but thought that I missed because he kept on running. I saw the cows all go out of sight.

When the bull went behind a big tree and stepped on that right front leg, he went down. He was out of sight and I thought that I had missed him...but when I got over there, there he was.

He was a big young bull with forks on the antlers, but no eye guards."

They had many hunting stories to relive.

Eva enjoyed her visit with her children. It had been a while since she'd seen them. The fear of meeting Henry was not as bad as it had been, and she was more comfortable being there.

*

Eva took Steve's little boat out occasionally, if the lake was calm. She caught a few fish, but didn't care much if she caught any.

She wasn't a great fish lover and didn't eat much of it. She just enjoyed rowing the boat.

Even in the boat, the ducks seemed to know her and flocked to the boat, so she would soon go back to the dock and feed them. She enjoyed sitting on the dock watching and listening to the water.

Time passed and it was spring again.

The weather warmed and Eva spent more time outdoors, painting on good days. Jewel had been keeping her busy, going someplace, to town, out to lunch. Sometimes to Tacoma or Puyallup shopping.

Sometimes they went to Tacoma to where Jewel's son Ron played the pipe organ in a pizza parlor.

Sometimes they went to help Ron when he repaired or tuned an organ.

Sometimes Alice went with them and the three had good times together. They had their favorite Chinese place where they stopped for lunch.

Jewel spent much time with Eva, all that winter, and spring.

Jewel had said, "If we keep you busy and going, you'll forget your problems." She was right, it helped.

Slowly Eva got over her fears of Henry. The bad things of the past began to loose their sting. She was happy and outgoing, making friends at church and with Jewel's friends.

"I'm becoming a whole person again," she said one day.

"I'm content here in my apartment. I love the church; we have a good pastor. The people are such good friends. I love to sit here in my living room or on the deck and look at Mount Rainier.

It's a different view than from town, but I have the lake here too. I'm happy."

Spring was coming, signs were everywhere, and the air was getting warmer every day. Many birds were back and busy about the yard, their happy voices lifted in song, filling the air with their sweet melody. They began to gather materials and building nests.

Eva often brushed her hair outdoors. One day she was pulling loose hair out of the brush and dropped some on the ground. A little bird swooped down, picked up the hair, and carried it away for her nest.

Eva sat and watched, and soon the little bird came back, fluttering around, looking at her.

Eva laughed, "I don't have any more hair for you," she told the bird. The little bird landed on her shoulder, picking at her hair, trying to get some more. Eva went to find another brush to clean the hair out to give to the bird, which came and took it from her hand. She pulled some bits of yarn apart, making thin thread like strips, which the birds took away for their nests.

It wouldn't be long until those nests would have some eggs, and soon baby birds. Eva was looking forward to Steve coming home for the summer.

"I'll clean out his room; get my painting stuff out of there so it'll be ready for him. I can paint outdoors most of the time from now on. I want a different view of Rainier to paint, maybe from the sound in Tacoma. I'm going to go look one day soon."

And before long, she did. It was to be a day that began a change in her life.

CHAPTER FOUR

Alex

Alex woke, rolled to his back, stretched and putting both hands behind his head, he smiled, enjoying the comfortable new bed.

It accommodated his six-foot plus length with room to spare. He looked over at the other pillow, 'enough room to cuddle,' he thought.

Martha had not been much for cuddling. There hadn't been much time for cuddling after the twins came, anyway.

Then two years later another boy.

In the first six years, there were four boys. All grown now and married, with two grand children.

Great Grandpa! He though, *and I'm only sixty-seven!*

It was on that sixty-seventh birthday, that he'd run into the little lady. He'd been going to Jim's place when he noticed someone on the dock. It was a small dock and no one came down there except him and Jim. So, he'd started to go around the corner of the building when it happened.

Suddenly she was against him. He caught her and held on, not wanting them to fall. She'd clung to him too. It had been a reaction that he held her closer.

It felt so right, holding her in his arms as if she belonged there. Her hair was blowing like silk against his face and lips.

He reached down and lightly kissed that silky hair.

Who was she?

He had released her, standing her on her feet, his hands still holding her arms to be sure that she didn't yet fall. He could still feel the silky hair on his lips and feel the pressure of her against him. He'd never seen her again.

She'd left in a hurry. Of course, it had started to rain.

He still wondered who she was – where she lived. He'd felt a sense of loss, a longing. He'd wondered how to find her. He shouldn't have let her go so quickly, without finding out who she was, where she lived. Something to help him find her.

It was on that same birthday that he'd decided to trade the old boat in on a bigger one. The old boat had served well for fishing in the sound for many years, but to follow the dream of making the run through the Inside Passage to Alaska he wanted a bigger boat. Big enough to sleep and live on for several weeks. He'd have to make that trip soon.

He'd sold a rental and bought this. It was big enough for several people, so maybe he'd have a crew or friends go with him. Maybe.

So far, no one could or would say that they would go with him. Except Jim.

Jim's as sold on going as I am, he thought.

Martha had been gone for six years now, but if she'd lived, she would have gone with them.

She hadn't really cared to fish, but she had gone along, and was excited when he or one of the boys had caught a fish.

Fishing hadn't been so good the last few years now, so the fishing trips had grown fewer and farther apart as the boys grew up and got busy with their own lives. Alex hadn't done much fishing, until Jim came along.

One day Alex had gone down to the dock to check on the boat as a new storm was coming in and it had been raining off and on all week. As he was fastening down the canvas, he could see a boy huddled against the building.

Alex asked, "Can I take you home?"

A short "no" was all the answer he got.

"I'm going for a hamburger here at the 'Bail 'Em Out' burger den, come and join me. I hate to eat alone."

"Don't have the money," was the short answer.

"Well, I'm inviting you so it's on my ticket. Come on, it's wet out here, and I need the company. I'd like someone to talk to."

They lingered over coffee waiting for the rain to let up, and two hours later, Alex had got the story out of Jim.

His mother had died six months earlier after a long illness, and his Dad had been killed in an accident working on the docks, just two weeks later. The money had run out and there was no more money to pay the rent. Jim would have to give up the house.

His part time job just didn't pay enough to keep it.

Alex had taken Jim to the small warehouse that he owned on the dock where the boat was moored, and offered to let

Jim live there for watching the boat.

The building had been used by fishermen years before, so there was electricity and plumbing. Alex had it upgraded with new wiring and plumbing, including a new bathroom with a shower.

The two of them had painted, and with some of the furniture from his house, Jim had an apartment, moving in within the week.

That was five years ago.

Jim had completed high school and was now in his first year at a community college. He'd worked and bought his own clothes and food, but Alex furnished the apartment as payment for Jim to watch it and the boat.

Since then Jim had been Alex's fishing partner, whenever they didn't work, which included some weekends for both Alex and Jim.

Alex lay there thinking, *"School will be out in about three weeks, and then Jim and I'll be ready to head for Alaska."*

Jim had been in on selecting the boat and making the plans for the trip. They both had to take some classes, tests, and training to be ready to make the trip. They had all the permits and license, maps, charts, everything that they needed.

They were ready to go.

Together, they'd spent the last few days putting in radios and equipment for navigation. They had seen to the installation of longer beds, that plus six-footers needed.

The bed was comfortable, more than adequate for his length. That had been Alex's excuse for them to spending the night on the boat, making sure that the beds would be comfortable for the extended trip that would require sleeping on the boat for several weeks at a time. They were going to have breakfast on the boat this morning too.

"And what a boat," he said aloud. "I guess I'm supposed to call you a Yacht!" he said patting the wall beside him.

"We'll have to give you a name yet too."

There had been some sounds on the dock for some time, but when Alex recognized Jim's voice, he finally became aware of it and listened.

Jim's talking to someone – a soft voice – a light laugh – feminine voice. Sounds like a girl. Has Jim a girl friend? Alex rose and looked out the window. *It is a girl. No, it's an older woman. She has an easel set up and is painting. A pretty good-sized painting - must be 24 inches long.*

Alex dressed quickly, put on deck shoes, and slipped out on the front of the boat to see what she was painting.

He was behind them. He was quiet; he didn't want them to know yet that he was there.

"There's something about her-"

"Do you mind my watching you?" Jim asked her.

"No I don't mind, pull up a box," she waved at some boxes next to the building. "I'm almost finished, just a few more minutes."

"Wow, that really does look like Mount Rainier."

"It's close isn't it. Rainier is hard to catch. It's almost as if he's alive. He changes all the time with the shadows from the changing light. Sometimes it's like he gathers clouds around the foothills. Sometimes he puts on a cap, or sometimes it looks like he puts on a stack of French Berets, or a stack of pancakes. Then again he becomes aloof and hides completely."

"Are you going to paint the city in?"

"No. I want it to look like it must have looked many years ago. Like the foothills are all covered with trees all the way to the shore of the sound. I'm going to put in a couple of buildings, though." She painted in some houses and a church with a steeple across the sound. Near the edge of the water, she painted in a small dock and a boat with sails furled.

Then with some quick strokes, she was adding this dock and part of the warehouse front.

"I should get Alex up, he should see this."

The soft laugh again, "Some people aren't interested in paintings, except maybe those of the old masters."

"Well, Alex will like this painting," Jim assured her.

Alex slipped back into the galley, turned on the oven, popped in some fridge biscuits, and turned on the coffee. He checked his hair, rubbed his chin, should have shaved, but – and went out on the deck.

"Alex, come see this," Jim called.

"Good Morning."

"Good Morning. Do you mind if I put this much of your boat in my painting?"

"No, go ahead. Do you mind if I watch?" He put a box closer and sat down,

A few swift strokes and the stern of the boat appeared on the canvas. "I won't make it look quite like your boat. If this was a long time ago, the boats were different, I'm sure."

Then picking up a fine brush, she painted a name on the side of the boat. "Guess that's it," she said, checking the paining against the view.

"Oh my, look at that cloud that's come! I like it." A few quick strokes and a wispy, puffy cloud appeared.

"Sign it and I'm done."

"Now, I'll go get out of here and quit bothering you. Thanks a lot, guys."

"Oh, but don't go. I put coffee on and some biscuits in the oven. Come have brunch with Jim and me."

"Yes, please do," Jim urged. "Alex is a good cook and he hates to eat alone. It's our first meal on board the boat, come join us."

"Besides, we'd like to introduce ourselves. This is Jim Dugan and I'm Alex Harmon," Alex said, holding out his hand.

"I'm Eva, Mark," She smiled. "Thank you, I'll have coffee with you. I'd love to see this beautiful boat – yacht."

Alex helped her aboard. "Jim, bring her painting things on board, - carefully."

Alex made sausage gravy for the biscuits. Eva was surprised and pleased when Alex asked the blessing on the breakfast. Two hours later, she looked at her watch.

"Oh, look at the time. I must be keeping you from other things."

"I don't have classes today, so I'm free all day," Jim said.

Alex added, "I don't have anything much to do today. Almost everything is ready for the trip to Alaska. We have been putting the finishing touches on the boat the last few days. Maybe we've kept you?"

"No, I just came to do Rainier from this side, and I think that I have what I want. I must go; I need to check my phone and call my sister."

"We'll help put your things in your car."

"Thank you for breakfast, and showing me the boat, I never dreamed that I'd get to see it when I came down here. It's a beautiful boat."

"Jim, look at the name that she put on her boat! 'THIS'N SMINE', I like that! That's her name! Do you mind if we use your boat's name for her?"

"She doesn't have a name yet? I don't mind."

"We couldn't decide on a name, but this one is it."

"I've an idea," Jim said. "I don't have classes until tomorrow – would you have dinner with us this evening? And it's my ticket this time," with a grin at Alex.

Alex looked at Eva expectantly, "Please?"

She hesitated a moment, thinking, *'what's on tonight – nothing.'* "Yes, I'd like to have dinner with you tonight, How shall I dress?"

"Just casual," Jim answered. "You can wear a dress if you want to, but not formal or what ever. We'll go to the Rafter T Steak and Lobster House, Have you been there?"

"No but I've heard that it's a good place to eat."

"It's kind of western style, with old cattle brands all around and other old ranch things," Jim added.

"Good choice Jim," Alex added, "We haven't been there since Tom's family went to California. Where can we pick you up, Eva?"

She dug a card out of her bag and wrote an address and phone number on it. "I live out of town a ways."

Alex handed her a card. "This is Jim's number here. I'll be here a while, the other number is my place. About 6:30?"

"6:30 is fine. See you then."

"Yes, see you this evening."

Eva started her car, waving at the men as she drove away.

A thrill ran through her.

Going out to dinner! I can't believe all this! Calm down girl; don't make too much out of this. After all, you're sixty-four years old and a Grandma; but that's the guy! Alex is the guy that I ran into a few weeks ago!

She'd been looking for a view of Rainier from a different angle than she'd been painting. She'd been down on the waterfront looking in several places, looking for a special place, and this was just what she wanted.

She had been standing looking across the sound at the mountain and the waterfront, trying to see it, as it must have looked years ago, before the city developed there.

"This is it!" she'd said aloud.

Then it started to rain. Rain from a little cloud – a wispy bit of a cloud. She turned and started to run to her car, ducking her head to keep the rain off her face, and 'rounding the corner of the building, she'd bumped into a man coming around from the other way.

He had caught her in his arms and kept them both from falling.

"Whoa, little Lady," he said, still holding her. "Are you Okay?"

"Yes, I'm fine. Oh! I'm sorry – I didn't look – I just ran."

He released her and stepped back.

"It was my fault too. I didn't look either. No harm done if you're all right."

"Yes, I'm fine. I just wanted to get to my car and get out of the rain. I'd better go." She'd turned and ran to her car. She had looked back after she started her car and he was standing on the boat, looking up at her.

She had railed at herself all the way home, for running into him. "Ran right into the poor man, almost knocking him down, but he kept us both from falling. Smacked right into him," she'd told herself. "Maybe that's what is bothering me the most."

She had been divorced almost two years now. Now she had a chance to have a life of her own.

Friends and family had asked her if she would find some one else. She'd laughed and said, "God will have to hit me in the face with him, I won't look."

She had laughingly gone on with a long list of requirements in a man before she would even think about it. Then she'd run smack into a man.

She hadn't been able to get him out of her mind.

When she'd gotten home, she'd fixed a quick dinner and turned on the news on television; she had watched something, she couldn't remember what.

She'd read in bed for a while, but when the light was out, she couldn't forget 'that man.' She could still see him.

He was tall- well, not too tall. Six foot two maybe. Well built, but not heavy, with broad square shoulders and blond hair, just getting white around the edges. Face somewhat tanned, but not weathered; a smooth face. Not many lines yet, and those were smile lines. He must smile a lot.

Late sixties, surely not seventy yet. Great smile. He had a rather soft voice. His laugh was musical. She smiled at the memory of his laugh.

She'd kept busy and tried not to let the memory of 'that man' creep into her thoughts if she could help it. She had driven by, but hadn't stopped because that boat was there.

She remembered seeing him standing on the boat. One day there was a different boat there, a much larger boat.

"Maybe 'He' is gone and someone else is there with a different boat," she'd thought.

So the next nice day she went down with canvas and paints to catch Rainier at his best.

That day was today, and she had her painting.

Alex had talked about the trip that he and Jim were going to take with the new boat, up the Inside Passage to Alaska. It was a dream of a lifetime.

Yes, Henry had talked about that too, maybe by ferryboat, she remembered. *The money had gone for other things, but what? There had been forty-seven years of dreams, most of them empty.*

Maybe if I can sell more paintings and be very careful of money, Sis and I can go by ferryboat, Ben too if he'd like to go. Go early in the spring before Tourist season gets started and the rates go up. Her little money didn't go far.

Well, so much for the past.

She checked the phone messages. She'd forgotten that Jewel and Ben weren't home. They had gone to Salem to a meeting and would spend the night.

How could she forget!

That was one reason that she'd decided to go paint today.

She was disappointed; she wanted to tell Jewel about Jim and Alex, and show her the painting.

Sis had laughed at her 'running into a man,' when she'd told her about it. Sis knew too, that she wouldn't go down to paint until that boat was gone, and had thought that she was being a bit silly, well more than a bit.

"Why are you afraid of him? He caught you and didn't let you fall," Jewel had asked.

"They're going to take me out to dinner! No man has even taken me even out to lunch, except family. Now two guys are taking me to dinner! Jim asked, but Alex joined in on the invitation. Oh, I'm acting like a schoolgirl – and it really isn't such a big deal, they are just nice guys being kind to me. Maybe they are lonesome too. I may never see them again after tonight."

'Breakfast' with Alex and Jim had been almost noon. She'd made an early start, as she wanted to catch the morning light for the painting.

Eva made a cup of tea and went to put the painting on a display easel to check it again.

"I did good to paint that large a painting in under four hours," she thought. There were a few places where she might touch it a bit. "Not much – just a bit here on the boat, it must look as it might have a hundred years ago."

"Well, I'd better shower and get the paint off."

When Alex and Jim returned to Jim's apartment after helping Eva put her things in her car, the phone was ringing.

It was Beth, Tom's wife. She and her daughter Betty were coming in on the plane at 5:30. She'd been trying to call him for days, and why didn't he have an answering machine.

She finally found Jim's number and asked, "Can you pick us up, and can we stay at your place for a few days?"

"Yes," He said, "and of course you can stay at my place."

He explained to Jim, "If you'll go pick Eva up, I'll meet you at the restaurant as soon as I can make it. Hope the plane is on time. I'd better go home and change and I'll see you later."

Jim started to protest but Alex didn't give him a chance.

"I could have gone to the airport," he muttered to himself.

He had been hoping that Alex would find someone, at least a friend, and this lady seemed special. They had talked.

Alex and Eva had talked. Talked almost nonstop.

"She's an artist, though she said that she just likes to play with paints, like a kid. It is a good painting. She likes baseball and basketball. She goes to church and knows the Lord."

Jim had been wishing that Alex would get more involved socially at church, or have some social life, some friends.

Most of the older adults were couples, so Alex didn't socialize much with them. In fact, Alex didn't have much of a social life at all.

When his sons move home, it'll help, Jim thought, *they'll keep him busy. Still, Alex needs friends, maybe a friend like Eva...*

Well, when we get back from the trip, Alex will have to do something. This part time 'retirement' will probably turn out to be just a vacation, and he'll go back to work at the shop. It would be great if it would work out for Alex and Eva to be friends. She's alone too."

Jim's thoughts continued on hoping and planning for his friend, planning on spending some time praying about it.

*

Eva stood looking in her closet, checking first one then another outfit.

What shall I wear? Jim said just casual, but that's what most of my pant outfits are, casual – too casual but not as casual as denim jeans. Denim is great for some gals, but not for me. Denim is for the ranch. Ranch – this restaurant has a western motif.

In the back of her closet, because she hadn't worn it for a while, hung a western outfit. A full skirt and vest with a fringe of rich brown leather with a soft silk beige blouse, almost the color of her hair…and ivory boots, just the thing!

The boots will make me two inches taller without having to wear high-heeled dress shoes. Those two dudes are both over six foot tall - and me, I'm still only five-foot-two and a quarter! She laughed. *If it was daytime I might wear the hat too, but since it's evening – better not.*

She laughed about that too.

Boy, I'm giggling almost like a school girl, but it's fun, and I'm going to enjoy this evening. Something like this may never happen to me again – that's okay, too. Today and tonight, it's been a great day already.

Eva had been ready for an hour when Jim arrived, and he was fifteen minutes early. She heard the car drive up, and Jim was looking out at the lake when she opened the door.

He was dressed in western too; a deep blue shirt with a black string tie, black pants and boots.

"How strikingly he is," she thought, *"with his black hair and dark eyes, with skin light enough to have had a scattering of freckles."*

"What a view," he exclaimed, "especially at sunset!"

"Yes. I love the sunsets on the lake. Come in. I made coffee a bit ago; do we have time for a cup?"

"Yes, we should have plenty of time. The reservations are for seven. Alex may be a little late. He has to pick up his daughter–in-law and grand daughter at the airport at six-thirty. I'm not sure if they'll join us or if Alex will take them to the house. They called just after you left. We didn't know that they were coming. You'll like them, they are good people."

Jim thought, *'they'll like Eva or I miss my guess.'*

He took his cup of coffee to stand at the window and look at the sunset on the lake.

"Alex has a great view of the sound and Mount Rainier from his house. It's built up high and he can watch the sunsets and the sunrises from his porch.

"His house is unusual; it has windows all the way around, living room, dinning room, and bedrooms, with the kitchen in the center, and daylight windows in the roof of the kitchen.

There is a view from every room. It is like one big room with a glass-enclosed hall running all the way around the outside. The bedrooms have sliding walls that can be closed off when you want privacy. Alex drew up the plans and had it built."

As Jim opened the car door for Eva Jo, he said, "Alex had this sent to my place for you." It was a corsage of three small pearl, yellow, and green orchids, with yellow and brown ribbons.

"May I pin it on for you?"

"Yes, Please. How pretty – and the colors are perfect. How did Alex know what I would wear?"

Jim laughed, "He didn't, but with Alex, you'll find that things like that'll just happen."

'If Alex doesn't fall hard for this lady, he deserves to be alone the rest of his life, but I know he will, God and I'll gang up on him,"

Eva looked up from the orchids with shining eyes and a smile.

"I didn't expect flowers too, how very nice. Thank you. I think that you guys are doing a lot for someone you just met. You hardly know me."

"That's true," Jim agreed, "but it seems like we do know you, just from the time this morning. The painting reveals a lot about you. You seem so real, no pretense, nothing fake about you. 'The words of our mouth reveal the heart,' or words to that effect. At least we want to get to get better acquainted. We believe that you're a good person, and I know that we are good guys," Jim laughed.

"So give us a chance to prove ourselves, okay?"

"Okay, that sounds good to me," she smiled.

"I know you'll like Alex, he's the best. I don't know what would have happened to me if Alex had not taken me under his wing when I was a kid. I owe him a lot. Not just money, he got me into church. He introduced me to Jesus.

He spent hours and days with me. He took me fishing, just like I was his own kid. He has been a life changing influence for me. I'm transferring from community college to the Bible College this fall. I'm going to take the summer off to take the trip with Alex, and then I'm going to buckle down and really study….and here I'm, talking your ear off!"

"Oh Jim, I'm glad that you told me. I admire you, Alex too. I believe that you're right – he is one of the best. You too."

"Well, here we are. I don't see Alex's car, but we'll go find a table and wait. Maybe Beth and Betty will be with him."

*

After the luggage was stowed in the trunk and both ladies seated in the front with him, "so we can both talk to you, Granddad," Alex headed for the restaurant.

They both told him how good it was to be back in Tacoma.

It may have been only two years, but it seemed like they had been gone half a lifetime. They kept a running commentary as they recognized stores and areas, remembering them from the past, noting changes.

"Where are we going Dad? This isn't the way to your house." Beth asked at last.

"We are going to meet Jim and a lady friend at the Steak and Lobster House for dinner."

"A lady friend? – Jim has a lady friend?"

Did that sound like a wail out of Betty? Alex wondered.

"Yes, she's a friend and I think that you'll like her."

Betty was suddenly quiet.

"Here we are."

The host showed them to a round table off in a quiet corner, where Eva and Jim were already seated and waiting for them.

Alex led the way and stepped next to Eva's chair, pulling out the chair next to him for Beth. When she'd seen the 'lady' Betty went around the other way and took the chair that Jim pulled out for her next to him.

Alex thought, *this is great, with Eva sitting. She's even pretty without the paint on her cheek.* He smiled at her as he sat down, having maneuvered his chair closer to hers.

Eva noticed that Alex, like Jim was wearing western.

Almost the same colors as mine, browns and tans," she thought. Wow he's nice looking - and so tall!

By the time introductions were over, Betty was back to her happy self again. After the waiter had taken their orders and poured coffee, Beth asked, "Dad, you know that we are moving back up here don't you?"

"Yes. I was in the office and talked with Bill and David. It's about time that Tom and Bill Jr. are back home and brought into the business. I said that I would come in to help for a few days for a week or so, if I were needed. Jim and I are making a trip through the Inside Passage to Alaska and may be gone most of the summer. We'll leave in about 3 to 4 weeks."

"That sounds exciting! I know that you'll have a good time. Tom is planning on us moving up here in about three weeks. I'm here to find a place for us by then. Betty will have to return to California and complete her courses and tests. The transfer should be no problem."

"I have to go back by Monday. Granddad, I've been accepted here at the Bible College for fall classes," Betty add excitedly.

"You too?" Jim asked. "I'm transferring to the Bible College starting with fall classes too."

Betty and Jim were exchanging information about classes, and were soon lost in a world of their own. Beth turned back to Alex, including Eva in her smile, asked, "How long have you known each other?"

"Well, not long," Eva answered, hesitantly.

"We met by accident seven weeks and two days ago," Alex added with a big grin, taking Eva's hand.

"What do you mean, by accident?" Betty asked, puzzled.

"We ran into each other...quite literally!"

Alex was still grinning at Eva Jo.

The waiter arrived with their meals and put a stop to the explanations.

"You knew that was me?" Eva quietly asked.

"Sure, how could I forget a gal that would try to run me down," he laughed.

"Oh my goodness! What will she think of me! Are you going to tell her?"

"Yes, I probably will someday...but not tonight. Don't worry, Beth will love you too, when she gets to know you."

When the last of the plates were placed, Eva reached out her hand to Jim. He took her hand with a glad light in his eyes.

"Jim," Alex nodded quietly, taking Eva's hand again.

They held hands around the table and Jim asked the blessing, thanking God for his many blessings, ending with, "Lord bless this time together and the food to use in our bodies and us to Thy service. Amen"

Eva was feeling somewhat overwhelmed, but the conversation took up again, and she began to relax.

Beth asked if there was a car that she could use to go house hunting. Alex assured her that there was, and gave her the name of a real estate office that she could call to alert them for what she wanted and the area the she would be interested in.

"And Granddad, I need to go to the Bible College registration office in the morning too."

"How about if I come by and take you?" Jim asked, "I don't have classes until afternoon."

"That would be great," Betty smiled.

The conversation continued along pleasant lines and they had a very enjoyable meal and evening, lingering over coffee.

When they were leaving, Alex handed his car keys to Jim, and whispered, "Trade cars with me. You take Beth and Betty on up to the house; I'll take Eva home.

"O...kay...I can do that."

"Jim, why don't you spend the night at the house, your room is always there, you know, and you and Betty can go to the college from the house in the morning. You can have your car back and Beth can drive my car. I'll drive the pickup tomorrow."

"Okay, Alex. That sounds like a good idea. That way I'll have a little more time in the morning. My books are in my car so I won't have to go get them."

When they got to the cars, Alex explained that Jim was taking Beth and Betty home and he would take Eva home and see them later.

"Make yourselves at home girls, you know where everything is."

Betty slipped her arm in Alex's arm and reaching up with a kiss whispered, "Better keep her if you can Gramps. See you later. Good Night Eva," she said with a hug.

As Alex was helping her into the car, Eva thought, *"Ooh, is this going right?"*

In the dark, everything seemed different.

Suddenly remembering the first time that she'd been with her former husband, and a great fear tried to attack her.

Please God don't let this be a repeat of that night," she prayed in her heart. Maybe I shouldn't have come...but Jim said that Alex knows Jesus. It must be all right, please lord."

Alex eased the car into traffic. "Jim said that you live on a lake, which road do I take?"

Eva told him the address. "It's on the north shore of Brooks Lake; do you know where that is?"

"Yes, that's easy enough to find." --

"Did you enjoy your dinner?"

"Oh yes, it was wonderful! Thank you so much. I don't often eat lobster, and I enjoyed it."

"You seem quiet, did my girls overwhelm you?"

"Oh no, they seem very nice."

"They are good people; you'll like my son Tom, too. And David, you'll meet him soon, too."

"My brother Bill and my son David run the business and Tom and Bill Jr. are coming home soon to work with us.

Bill and I both think that the younger fellows need to get in and help make it grow. They'll make a better living as well as using some of their talents to better advantage and be a part of the company. I'll help some for the next couple of weeks; then I'm off for a while – maybe until fall. I haven't had a vacation for years."

Eva listened to him talk and thought, *"He seems to be including me – meet his sons? He doesn't know me, really, and he said that 'Beth will love you too, (too?) when she gets to know you.' Does he just talk like that? Does he mean it? What does he mean?"*

"You're awfully quiet, is something wrong?"

"No. It's been a wonderful day and evening, and such a day! I'm almost overwhelmed. And I – I don't – know-"

"Don't know – what? I've been trying to fill you in on us, our lives – who we are."

"Yes, but Alex, you don't know me or hardly anything about me."

He thought, *'She sounds distressed.'*

"Well, I'm going to get to know you, if you'll let me; but I don't want to rush you. Whenever you want to, you can tell me as much as you want to. Does that sound reasonable?"

"Yes, it sounds okay. Alex, thank you for the dinner – and the orchids, they're beautiful. It is so nice of you. I love them."

"Now see, I'm trying to show you that I'm a nice guy," he laughed. "And you're very welcome"

He looked at her, "they suit you. Jo, I like your western outfit, it suits you too. It's great, but I wonder what to expect next. Here's an artist in the morning and this evening, a cowgirl, all in one day. What's next?" he chuckled.

"Well, you just never know about me, I don't know what I might do next myself. I always try to warn people," she answered with a soft laugh.

"Good. I like that idea! *Always keep 'em guessing* – who said that, Will Rogers or W.C. Fields? Someone important years ago," he laughed again. "I'm glad you're more like yourself again. I was a bit worried there for a while."

"I'm fine. Maybe a bit tired. I was up by five, anxious to catch the morning light for my painting. I couldn't sleep. The light was perfect today, especially from that angle. I'm not really tired, just savoring the evening. It's been a good day."

He asked questions and she talked about painting the rest of the way. Alex turned on the right road and drove up to her apartment.

She suddenly realized where there were.

"How did you know where I live?" she asked.

"Well, I know this area and Jim described it. When you said Brooks Lake and the view of the mountain over the lake, you had to live here."

"Will you come in? I'll make coffee, or are you coffeed out?"

"I'd like to come in. I would like to see more of your paintings, if you'll show them to me."

"Of course, come in."

She put the coffee on, and then turned on the lights in her spare room 'studio.'

"I'm not a great artist of course. It's just fun. I like to paint. It gives me something to do. It's been therapy too," she stopped *Therapy*, She thought, *I can't explain why it's therapy.'*

After looking at the paintings, they came back to today's painting.

"Do you have a frame for this one"?

"Yes, well a plain frame," she took a frame from a rack.

"Is this one sold?"

"No, not yet."

"I want to buy it. I'll give you five-hundred for it, is that enough?"

"Oh no, Alex it's too much!"

"No it isn't. I've paintings that I paid more for than that. This one will mean more to me, as I know the artist." He turned to her with a smile. "When can I take it home?"

"If I'm careful, I can put it in a frame, but the whites won't be dry for about three month. You'll have to be careful that nothing touches it."

"I'll come get it tomorrow."

They returned to the living room.

"Sit down Alex, I'll bring the coffee."

He was looking at a photograph when she returned with the coffee. "Your Family?"

"Yes." She pointed them out, naming each one. "This is my oldest daughter, Abbigail, Paul, my oldest son, and Jason my middle son. Over here is Allan my youngest son, and Danielle, my younger daughter."

"Good looking group. This one and this one are more like you. Do they live close?"

"No. They all live in the Portland area."

"That's not so far. I'd like to meet them. Do you have other family here? I remember you said something about your Sis."

"Yes, I have a brother here too, and some of their children live here in Washington. Sis...my sister Jewel's kids live here too."

"I've only one son living here now, but as you heard tonight, Tom and his family are moving back soon."

"Do you like music? I see you have some CDs and tapes."

"Yes, mostly classics and dinner music. I'm rather old fashioned. I hate the noise that they call music today. You can't hear the words, and if you could, you wouldn't want to. I like a few country-western songs and some folk music. Christian music of course – again, mostly the old songs."

"I agree. I must be old fashioned too."

They talked on; discussing music, books, and places they had been, discovering that they had many interests in common. Their talk turned to the Church, the Bible, and their experiences with the Lord, and their faith.

"We seem to be 'of like faith,'" Alex said at last.

"Yes, we both know Jesus," Eva agreed.

"That's good, I had hoped so. I must be going, so you can get some rest. It's been a long day. May we pray before I go?"

"Yes, please, Alex."

He rose and crossed to her. She stood also. He took her hands and prayed a simple prayer for her, and when he stopped, she thanked the Lord for her new friends and asked, "Lord bless them, and Lord, go with Alex and keep him safe with traveling mercies on the way home tonight."

"I'll call you in the morning, if I may." Alex asked, taking her hand.

"Yes – okay."

"Good night, Jo."

"Good night Alex."

As she closed the door, and he walked away, she could hear him softly singing, "Good Night, Sweetheart, Good Night 'till tomorrow."

What kind of a man was this?

In spite of her self- control, she felt a thrill at the soft 'Good Night Sweetheart'! Then she chided herself. – *But it's been a long time since I've had a feeling like that thrill! A long time. Did I ever, really? Like this? Was he really singing that?* She knew that he had.

She was ready for bed when the phone rang. It was her sister Jewel. "I thought you'd call me back. I left a message on your machine."

"I didn't check my answering machine. I thought that you were going to stay over in Salem."

"We came home. I called a couple of times. Where have you been?"

"Out to dinner. I've been home for a while. I forgot to check the machine. But Honey, it's late. Can I talk to you in the morning? Maybe I'll make more sense then."

"Did you go paint? You said that you were going to."

"Yes, and I think it's sold."

"But I want to see it."

"You'll get to. However, we'll talk in the morning; shush now, you'll wake your hubby. Okay, good night."

CHAPTER FIVE

Alex woke long before it was time to get up.

He lay thinking...

It's good to have family in the house again...and Jim, he's family too. But, they'll be gone again in a few days. Then the house will seem emptier than ever.

Everything is ready for the cruse. Everything...and it's three weeks until we go. There's not much reason to spend much time on the boat — or at Jim's anymore until we go.

Should take the boat on a shakedown run before we actually go, though. It's funny how Eva popped into our lives. She's something else, - Face it, I didn't realize how lonesome I am. I've been lonesome for a long time, just hadn't thought about it. Even when I worked ten-hour days, 5 or 6 days a week --- nothing to come home to, not even a dog. I'm lonesome. I wonder if Eva gets lonesome. She doesn't see much of her family, either.

I suppose I'll go back to work after this trip. Keep busy. Maybe I'll ask Tom and Beth if they want part of the house.

Alex had moved out of the master bedroom when Martha had died.

I could put in a small kitchen and keep part of the rooms in this part of the house. Tom and Beth only need two or three bedrooms. What do I need with six bedrooms now that the boys are all gone? It's been empty too long.

The house will be put in use again. I'll ask them."

"What is wrong with me, Lord?" Alex spoke. "I'm lonesome, Lord. It hasn't bothered me for a long time. When Martha was first gone, but now…is it because I don't have any projects going at the shop? But I could have if I wanted something to work on."

I wonder if Eva is awake? Well hardly at five o'clock. Wonder what time I can call her? I'll fix breakfast and clean up after. She'll be up by then. I'll talk to Beth and see what she thinks, if they would like my idea about the house. We can call Tom.

Alex got up and drew up a plan showing how they could divide off the house, and wrote a note to Beth.

*

Eva was just out of the shower when the phone rang the next morning; her hair still wrapped in a towel.

"Good Morning!" It was Jewel.

"Good Morning…it is morning, isn't it? Now are you ready to tell me – what was all that about last evening, -- going out to dinner and getting back after ten?"

"Yes, that's right. Are you sitting down?"

"Yes. Why, is it going to take a long time, or is it going to be a shock?"

Eva laughed, "Maybe both, well not so long I guess. Hey, it's only seven in the morning. You didn't lie down again after your hubby left for work."

"No. I want to hear your story," Jewel laughed, "Quit stalling!"

"Okay."

Eva told her Sis all about her day. They were still talking an hour later when she'd another call, "Hang on, I'll see who it is."

"Hello?"

"Hello Eva, this is Alex."

"Hi Alex, hang on while I clear the other line. Hi Sis, It's Alex, can I call you back later?"

"Sure, but how about meeting me for lunch?"

"Good idea, I'd love to, about noon?"

"Yes, noon at the grill."

"Hi Alex, that was my Sis on the other line. I'm to meet her for lunch."

"Great. May I come too?"

"Well – yes if you'd like."

"I'd like, I'd like! How are you this morning?"

"I'm fine, and it is another beautiful day."

Suddenly it WAS a beautiful day!

"Yes it is isn't it? I'm coming out to your place. Is that okay?"

"Ohh…yes…all right. okay! Have you had breakfast?"

"Yes. I made breakfast for the gang and now they are all about ready to take off for the day. I'm on my way. See you in a little while."

Eva called Jewel back to tell her that Alex was coming and would join them for lunch.

"He is? What gives here?"

"I don't know, but I've got to go dress, - bye."

She couldn't stay indoors and was filling humming bird feeders when Alex drove up.

"Hi. Come on in, the coffee should be ready by now…or we can bring our coffee out here, it's so nice this morning."

"Wait," he said as she stepped up onto the deck.

"Just one step and it's almost the right height. How about a hug?" He put his arms around her, holding her close.

Oh boy, now I've done it! He thought. *But…I just had to!*

"Good Morning," he said looking down at her as he released her.

"Oh!" she gasped, "Good Morning Alex," with a soft laugh. Her heart was beating wildly.

"Easy lad," Alex told himself, *"you'll scare her. She's been hurt, bad, at sometime. I hope that I can replace the sad look in her eyes with joy. Yes joy, because I've fallen for her, big time. We aren't too old to love again are we?"*

These kinds of thoughts had kept him awake. He had thought that maybe in broad daylight, he'd know.

And I know! But, I gotta must be careful. She needs to trust me, and she doesn't yet. She doesn't know me."

They talked. Talked about family and friends. Alex asking just the right questions. They talked, getting acquainted, catching up on the past years.

"Oh, it's late," Eva cried suddenly. "We're to meet Jewel in fifteen minutes at the grill. How can time go so fast?"

"Well they say that time flies when you're having fun, you know." Alex laughed.

After lunch, Jewel asked them to come to her house to visit for a while. They talked, Jewel and Alex getting acquainted.

They talked of their families. Alex told about the business that he'd worked at most of his adult life, taking over after his father and grandfather, designing and building furniture for sale. How they were expanding, putting in new equipment, and bringing two of the son's into the business.

Suddenly Alex checked his watch. "I need to go soon. I told my kids that I would have dinner at six. I like to have meals with everyone present and sitting at the table. Mom and Dad had it that way and I think it's important."

Eva and Jewel agreed with him.

"…and since I'm cook, I'd better go. Eva, would you come to dinner tonight?"

She took in a little breath in surprise. "Yes, I guess I could, if you're sure – you're not – getting tired of me."

"Never happen."

"Sis - Jewel, it's been great meeting you and get to know you."

"Yes I'm happy to meet you, Alex. Come back soon."

"I will. Maybe next time I'll get to meet your husband."

"He'll be home soon, sorry you have to go."

Alex scrubbed potatoes and put them in the oven to bake.

"I'll set the table, and then show you the house."

Alex gave Eva the tour. Hanging in the living room were the paintings that he'd told her about. She stood looking at first one then the other of the paintings.

"They're beautiful – wonderful—hours of work," she said.

She recognized the signatures of the artists.

One wall at the end of the room was lined with beautiful bookcases with leather bound books of all kinds, many of which were vintage. Near by was a roll-top desk with many little cubbyholes. The bookcases and desk had unmistakable signs of careful workmanship, having been made by Alex's father and grandfather, showing that they had been cared for and polished lovingly by his mother.

"It's a lovely home, Alex." Eva said at last. "One revealing that love has lived here." Beth came home, tired and discouraged from hours of looking at houses.

Jim and Betty came in, Betty talking excitedly about the classes that she would be taking in the fall. They were still happily talking when Alex went to the kitchen.

Eva followed him, "What can I do to help?"

"Just sit right here and talk to me. It won't take but a few minutes to broil steaks, steam some veggies, make a salad and we'll have dinner."

The meal was soon on the table with the family gathered around. Later everyone helped clean up while Alex loaded the dishwasher, and they were soon out of the kitchen.

They settled in the comfortable living room to talk.

"Dad, if you guys keep on enlarging the 'shop', you're going to have to call it a factory!" Beth said.

"Guess that could be true, but I don't want it to ever be just a 'factory'. To my dad it was a 'shop' with personalized work, and close contact with most of the customers. I'd like it to stay that way."

They continued to talk about the shop and the men coming home. Beth and Betty both anxious to get moved "back home where we belong."

"Dad, did you know that the main reason that Tom wanted to take that job in California was because of some Bible classes taught by someone he wanted to hear? He's going to take some night classes here, too"

She continued, "I asked him what he was doing and he said, 'Jesus was a carpenter. I want to know more about Him, to really know Him.' He said, 'if Jesus found carpentry an honorable profession, that makes my work doubly interesting.' "

Jim brought out the big family Bible. "Will you read to us, Alex, like old times?" After devotions and prayer, Betty went to the piano and they sang a few old hymns.

Soon Jim said, "I have an early morning class and it's getting on towards my bed time, so I'd better go home. Shall I take Eva home?" Nevertheless, Jim hoped that Alex would.

"Jim, why don't you stay on here at the house as long as Beth and Betty are here? Betty can go with you or Beth, or stay here at the house."

Alex turned to Eva, "Can you stay tonight, and I'll show you around the shop tomorrow?"

"I'd like to see the shop. But I didn't bring anything with me."

"Beth and Betty can help you with some things. There are always new toothbrushes. And I have a robe and pajamas... they'll be big on a little thing like you, but it's not like you'll be in a fashion show," he laughed.

"I guess it'll be all right, but I'll have to call my sister, Jewel."

"Sure, I'll talk to her too."

CHAPTER SIX

"I don't have an appointment until ten o'clock, so I'm doing dishes and cleaning up this morning." Beth said, the next morning at breakfast.

"After you're through, before you go out, I'd like for you to look over some plans to make me an apartment and leave the rest of the house for you and Tom," Alex said as he put the papers on the table.

"Talk to Tom, ask him what he thinks."

"I will Dad; I'll call Tom and talk to him about it."

After introducing Eva to Bill and David, Alex showed her through the shop, explaining each step, from the designing to the finished item in the showroom.

Bill's wife, Nancy and David's wife Noralee were in charge of the showroom and the office. They greeted Eva warmly.

Alex and Eva watched for a few minutes the progress on the new wing to the shop that was going up. Then they went back to the designing room.

Alex pulled up a chair at a desk with a drafting table alongside. He pulled a large paper roll out of a shelf to show her.

"This is something that I've been working on." He showed her, explaining the sketches. "When I get back from the trip, I may come in and build one to see if it's good enough to make several."

"Alex, you're a genius!" Eva exclaimed. "Do you have a book or something with pictures of what you've designed?"

"There are pictures around, but nothing in a book, but that's a good idea, a book of each one's designs. Maybe a book of all of our designs, too."

"Who designed those pieces in the showroom?"

"Bill and I worked on most of them together. Occasionally we each do something. All of the small tables are David's designs. Bill has good ideas and we hope to have more help in addition to Tom and Bill Jr., so that Bill can do more designing. David is working on some too. I'm looking forward to each one of the fellows to develop their own style and make their own line of furniture."

"It's very exciting and such beautiful furniture," Eva said.

Alex grinned, pleased at Eva's praise and enthusiasm.

As he put the sketches back, Alex said, "Let's get out of here...it's too noisy! I'll be glad when the construction is done. Of course," he laughed, "there is noise when we run saws and planers and such, but that is our noise!"

"I hope that you don't mind riding around in a pickup," Alex asked a few minutes later, "but I wanted Beth to use my car."

"I don't mind a bit, it's a beautiful truck, nice and comfortable."

"Yes, it's not bad. I don't think that Beth has driven a pickup, at least for a while."

"We'll stop for lunch someplace," Eva commented, "and then what shall we do?"

"I suppose that I should go home and check in with Jewel. She still worries about me. But I'm doing great – most of the time."

Why did I say that? She thought, *what will he think?*

"There is church tonight," Eva continued, seemingly nonplussed. "Wednesday evening is good teaching and prayer. Maybe you can stay and go with me?"

"Yes, I'd like that. It's no fun to go alone all the time. I'll call and tell Beth and the kids."

"I see you have a barbecue on the deck, does it work?"

"Yes. It may need a little cleaning; we haven't used it yet this spring."

"Good. Let's stop and get a couple steaks,"

And so they did.

"I'll put on some potatoes to bake too. I like to halve the red ones, put a little butter and a wedge of onion, wrap in foil, start them first but they bake almost as fast on the gas grill as the steaks cook.

"Great idea!"

Brandon and Billy, the neighbors in the other half of the duplex, drove up just as they were starting up the barbecue. Eva introduced them to Alex.

"Is there room to put on a couple more steaks?" Brandon asked

"Sure," Alex answered. "Bring 'em on!"

Billie made a salad as Eva fixed a couple more potatoes and then wiped off the picnic table and put on a cloth.

"We'll have Sis and Ben join us sometime. We'll plan on it." She said.

"Guess we kind of crashed your party," Brandon said.

"I'm glad you did," Alex smiled. "I wanted to meet Eva's neighbors. I wondered how safe she is out here."

"Well, we kind of watch out for her. As a matter of fact, we wondered about you. Then, when she didn't come home last night..." Brandon stopped, looking uncomfortable.

"I called your sister at nine, and she said that you were with friends."

Eva looked at Alex and smiled, "I was."

They enjoyed the early supper on the deck, and when they started picking up, Alex caught Brandon's attention and took him aside.

"May I ask, do you have a spare room that I can rent for the night? I'm going to church with Eva this evening. I'd like to stay out here to night and not go back to town."

"We have a spare room complete with a pretty good bed, and you're welcome to stay," Brandon replies, "and you won't pay! We're glad for Eva to have a good friend."

"Thank you." Alex said. He was liking the young man more and more, as the evening progressed. "What time do you go to bed, so I can be in by then?"

"Usually around 10."

"I'll be here. Thanks!"

After the service, many folks came over to talk to them and Eva introduced Alex each of them, as well as the Pastor.

When they returned to Eva's apartment, she asked if she could make some coffee to keep him awake on the way home.

"How about some tea?" Alex suggested. "I made arrangements with Brandon and Billie to sleep in their spare room tonight."

"Oh!"

"I suppose that I could have asked if I could sleep on your couch, or on the cot in your spare room, but I was sure that you would say no," he laughed. "I don't want to go home tonight. I thought that we could spend tomorrow together. Unless you have other plans?"

"No – well – no I don't have other plans. I live a pretty quiet life. Except when I go down on the dock to paint…and then look what happens," she laughed nervously.

Yes, she thought, *look what happens. And what is happening? I can hardly think. I like Alex….maybe too much. I don't know what to think."*

"I'm glad you went down to the dock to paint," Alex laughed. "Otherwise, how would Jim and I have met you?"

The interruption of the singing teakettle gave Eva a chance to change the subject.

"Would you like some cookies or toast with your tea?" she asked, smiling.

"Toast sounds good, thank you."

Alex went to the kitchen with her and leaned against the sink while she fixed the toast, and put things on a tray.

"And some jam too," she said, "just in case we want something sweet."

Alex carried the tray to the living room.

They discussed the Bible Study lesson, finding that they had the same understanding. Eva's Bible was on a table, close at hand, so they referred to the scriptures again.

"It is very interesting and enjoyable, reading and then talking it over with someone who understands," Alex said at last, closing the Bible.

"Yes, for me too. Jewel and I get together and study and pray sometimes."

"Well, I said that I would be in before ten, and it's time," he said.

"Come over whenever you wake up. You can shower and shave here, but my razor may not be much good on your whiskers," she laughed.

"I have a razor in my pickup." He grinned. "If I wake up at three or four, can I come over?"

"Don't you dare," she laughed.

"Shall we pray?" he asked, taking her hands. At her *yes*, he prayed a short prayer.

"Good Night, Eva. See you in the morning."

"Good Night Alex."

She could hear Alex softly humming *Good Night Sweetheart* as she locked the door behind him. As she turned out the light, she found herself humming the tune too.

"Now I'm doing it. Maybe he didn't know what song he is humming."

However, she knew that he did.

As she lay in the dark, she began to review the past few days.

Let's see, Monday I went to paint – met Alex and Jim…

Monday evening, Jim came and took me to dinner with them and Alex brought me home.

Tuesday, yesterday, Alex came early and we had lunch with Sis. Alex asked me and I went with him to his house for dinner – and stayed the night.

Wednesday, today, he showed me the shop and brought me home. He went to church with me and we had a very enjoyable talk this evening. He asked Brandon and Billie for a place to stay overnight. Here in our humble little apartments, which are nice, but not much compared to his lovely home.

He is staying the night next door to spend tomorrow, Thursday, with me.

Me…Eva Mark!

Is he making up to me, or what? I don't know!

Is he interested in me? ME? Why? He apparently has money, and he knows I don't have much.

I like him- maybe too much. He can't be serious. I can't have a broken heart – again. Not for him either. He is such a nice man. We had better talk – tomorrow. Maybe I should go visit my kids for a while. Until he goes on his trip. Maybe while he's gone he'll forget me, and I can forget him. –

Okay, that's a joke, how can I ever forget HIM?

It will be a pleasant memory…but even pleasant memories can torture you, break your heart. I know that from the past.

I haven't even thought of Henry for days…and now I'll have to tell Alex…that I'm a divorced woman.

A DIVORCED woman. Tell Alex—

She groaned and, turning her face into her pillow, she began to cry.

Eva crawled out of bed to go to her knees. After crying out her heart to her Lord and committing this too, to Him, her Lord, she lay down and slept.

*

Alex reached out his hand and touched the wall.

Eva's right on the other side of this wall, he thought. *She uses the main bedroom for her studio, so she is right here."* Perhaps he felt the troubling of her heart?

Am I rushing her too fast? It's only three more weeks until Jim and I take off on the trip. I don't think that I want to go without her. Maybe I'll have to postpone the trip.

No, I can't do that; Jim is counting on going now too.

Can we talk her into going with us? Maybe if another woman or girl went with us, - but who?

No, that wouldn't look right either."

She looks scared sometimes. There is such deep sadness in her eyes. Yet she seems to be content here. I think that she likes my family, although she doesn't know us yet —

If we just had all summer to get to know each other.

Lord, show me what to do. I know that I've fallen for her. I know that I love her. I want to be with her for the rest of our lives. Lord, help me to say and do everything right!

Alex slept, knowing that his Lord would guide him.

CHAPTER SEVEN

Eva woke feeling good and happy.

"Oh, it is another beautiful day! I'd better hurry with my shower; Alex may come over any time."

She'd dressed and was just starting the coffee when she saw Alex coming along the deck. Eva opened the door, greeting him, "Good Morning Alex."

"Good Morning Eva," he answered her smile with one of his own.

I like the way that she says Alex – like she puts a caress on my name. Then he laughed at himself, *Hold on, cowboy, this isn't the right time an ego trip!"*

Still, the thought lingered.

"Help yourself to the bathroom. You'll find towels and everything…except your razor."

"I have mine from the pickup," he waved it.

"Coffee'll be ready soon, and some breakfast."

Eva turned from stirring a skillet of sizzling potatoes, as Alex came from the bathroom.

"I feel more human now. How about a real good morning, huh?"

He hugged her gently. She gasped in surprise, and then put one arm around him in the hug; the other hand still held the spatula.

"I noticed that people at church hug you, even the guys."

She got her voice under control, "Yes, they are a nice group of people, and I guess that I've them fooled into thinking that I'm a nice person too," she laughed, a bit nervously. "But how can you help but be your best when you're with such good people?"

"I don't think that you have to try very hard at that, in fact, I'm convinced."

The look he gave her started her heart to racing again.

"Keep it cool, girl!" she told herself, again.

"Come sit down, Alex. Here is juice and coffee, the rest will be ready soon."

"Good, I'm hungry."

'Will you ask the blessing Alex?"

He did.

"Ham, eggs, fried potatoes, apple sauce and coffee," Alex commented later, patting his stomach, "and we're ready for a good day! That was a great breakfast, thank you."

"You're very welcome. It gave me an excuse to fix things that I like," she smiled happily.

They lingered over coffee, talking easily.

"What do you want to do today Alex? We can stay here, of course, or what?"

"Let's do up the dishes first, then go for a drive, it looks like it's going to be a beautiful day. I'll call my house first."

Beth answered. "Dad, I was hoping that you would call, since you didn't come home last night."

"Is everything okay, Beth?"

"Yes. I just wanted to tell you that I called Tom and he said that he would like to live here in the house, if you're sure that you want to do it and fix an apartment for yourself. I just talked him and told him about Eva, that you didn't come home last night. Tom laughed and said that maybe on behalf of Eva, he should ask what your intentions are."

Beth was laughing. "Is this serious, Dad?"

Alex's laugh sounded a bit embarrassed, "I'm not sure yet, but...I hope so."

"Oh! Oh...go for it Dad. We'll love her!"

"Promise?"

"Promise!"

"Tell Tom that I would like to have you two at home. That house has been empty too long. I'll be back this evening and show you how I think we can fix up an apartment for me, and leave the main part of the house for you guys."

"All right Dad. I'll call Tom back. He said that the man he has been training to take his place is fitting in, and he may be able to leave there soon."

"That's good news...in fact, that's great to hear it! Well, I'll see you after while."

"Thank you Dad, now I won't have to house hunt."

"I'll have to tell them about me staying next door." Alex thought sheepishly, *"I don't want them think badly of Eva. I'll have to protect her better than this. Was it a dumb thing to do? Still, I just wanted to spend more time with her, and everything was honorable... Brandon and Billie can vouch for us."*

Eva suggested that they take her car, "...but you drive, if you will, Alex."

They drove up to Mount Rainier, had lunch, and then browsed through the souvenir shops.

They searched the slopes through the mounted field glasses. They walked around and enjoyed the wild flowers peeking up through the snow, where the snow was melting around the lodge.

The flowers were ready to take advantage of the short mountain season, shooting up fast, many in bloom as they popped up.

The snow was too wet to play in; still there were those who were enjoying it.

On the way back, they stopped at a small park where there was a picnic table near a small stream. Eva had a thermos of coffee and some cookies that she'd brought along. They sat enjoying the coffee and watching squirrels in the trees, and fed some of the cookies to the little birds.

The table was small and Alex reached across to take Eva's hands.

"Eva? Can we talk...seriously?"

"Yes Alex, I think we should."

Her heart jumped, and then settled, leaving a sick feeling of suspense beneath her heart.

"I know that we've only had four days since we met, really met, to get acquainted. Unless we count the accidental meeting two months ago…and I haven't forgotten that day," He grinned, then sobered.

"I think that you ran into my heart that day and I can't get you out…and, in fact, I don't want you out. I want to be with you all the time, so much so that maybe I was foolish to spend the night next door, and risk jeopardizing your reputation. I maybe should have gone home, but I wanted to stay, just to be close by, and to spend today with you."

"Eva I want to court you, like my Granddad said they did in the old days. I want to bring us to the place where I can ask you to marry me. Is there any reason why I can't do that?"

There were tears in Eva's eyes.

"Thank you Alex, you give me honor. Nevertheless, I'm afraid there is a reason. I'm so very sorry, I shouldn't let things go so far. Everything has gone so fast. I'm afraid that I was swept off my feet, and I didn't stop to think.

"Alex, I'm a divorced woman. I once heard a preacher say that a divorced woman was worse than a harlot."

Tears were slipping down her face, unheeded.

"I think that many people and preachers say things like that when they don't know the circumstances. Eva, I can see the hurt in your eyes. Tell me, can you? I want to understand. I want to help you. Even if I can never marry you, I'll still love you. Always. Can you tell me?"

"I'll try. Give me a moment."

The tears were still falling. She got up and walked away, trying to compose herself. Alex brought a blanket from the car and put it on a log.

"Come sit here; lean against the tree," he said taking her by the hand.

"It's a long story, the story of my broken marriage, and why it failed."

"That's all right, tell me what you can."

"I have to go back," she began, "so that you can understand. I started dating quite young, too young, yet they were innocent dates. He was a good boy and didn't even hold my hand, but very rarely."

Alex was holding her hand and gave it a gentle squeeze.

"We didn't see each other much during the winter, but in the summer, nearly every weekend, one day, maybe both days.

We talked of marriage and we both wanted to be virgins when we married. I was going to continue high school for two more years and graduate. He worked on his father's ranch. Maybe we would marry in the future, but we didn't set a date...there was plenty of time. We knew that we were both young, especially me.

We had been seeing each other about a year and a half when I found out that his Uncle was making 'moonshine' to sell.

One night at a dance, some men came up to us and demanded that my friend sell them some moonshine. That was when I found out about it. Although he told them to go see his uncle, they got nasty, and threatened him. I was afraid for him. I was afraid that they would turn him in to the police, and he'd be arrested.

Foolishly, I knew later how very foolish, I quarreled with him, insisting that he stay away from his uncle. He said that he couldn't do that...and so we didn't see each other fro a long time, except at a distance.

I didn't go with anyone else, but was in school and kept busy, both there and at home. I thought we would get back together eventually. I studied hard and had good grades, top in my class. I wanted a good education. I knew that it would be important in later life. Besides, I loved school.

One day a few months later, a girl that I had known since we were babies, came to my house, with two guys, and wanted me to go with them on a picnic. I didn't want to go, but the girl asked Mama. Mama said that I had been moping around the house too long, that I should go.

I had been hard for me not to see Bill, I was unhappy and Mama had caught me crying. Against my better judgment, I went.

We drove around on the open prairie for a while and finally stopped and built a small fire against a bank with some sticks they had brought with them. We roasted hot dogs that they had brought and Mama had given us a lemon pie. We sat around the fire, sang old songs, and talked.

I hadn't seen my girl friend for several years and we were catching up on what was happening in our families. I enjoyed that; it was fun...so far.

It began to get dark and I said that I needed to get home.

The wood was almost gone and the guys put out the fire and buried the ashes with dirt. We got in the car. We girls had been in the back seat so far. We drove around for a while.

I kept saying that I must go home; I usually had chores to do at home. I fed the milk cows and the horses and gathered the eggs. Mama probably had to do my chores that evening too. She helped to milk the cows.

Again, I said that I must go home, but the driver was acting silly, driving crazy-like. We were out on the open prairie, so there were no roads. Finally, he got the car stuck on a hump; high centered it and couldn't get it off.

We all got out of the car and, with the other girl to steer, and the guys lifting and pushing, they got it unstuck. When we got back into the car, I got back into the back seat, supposing that we girls would be both be back there again, but my friend stayed in the front and one of the guys got in the back with me. I knew both of the guys, but neither very well.

The driver finally said that we were lost; we'd have to wait for daylight. Lost, when you can see for miles in all directions!

He said that we would run out of gas if he kept on driving around in circles. He stopped the car and turned out the lights. It was pitch dark and I was scared.

I had reason to be.

The two in the front were making out and the guy with me began to try to kiss me. I tried to make him stop and called my friends name, but she laughed and said 'Eva, everyone does.'

"I said that I don't and I don't want to. I tried to make him stop. The car had only two doors so I couldn't get out. Slacks and trousers were not yet in style in our part of the country for girls and women, and we wore dresses.

That made it easier for him. He held my hands behind my back and forced me."

Eva sat with her heard down, tears falling unheeded.

Alex sat, biting his lip until he tasted blood.

After a bit she continued.

"I was devastated. I wanted to die. I was afraid, and very, very ashamed. I was afraid to tell anyone. Now I could never marry my boy friend, Bill. I soon discovered that I was pregnant. I felt so ashamed and scared. I couldn't get up the courage to tell Mama.

About 2 months later, that guy came back to see me. I went out with him to tell him that it says in the Bible that if a man lay with a maid, he is to marry her that no harm come of it. I told him about the baby.

He was very angry about me being pregnant. But he did say that we would get married, but that we would have to wait until his next birthday when he was 21.

Later I found out that he was 22 years old already. Even so, he put off getting married.

He wanted me to get an abortion. I wouldn't have done that, as I believe that it is wrong. I couldn't have hurt my baby; anyway, I already loved her. She was a darling baby and still is a darling. Mama found out about the baby and told my brother.

Though I didn't know it at the time, my brother threatened Henry. I didn't want to marry him, but what choice did I have? I'm sure now that he didn't want to marry me either.

We got married. I tried to make a good marriage and tried to love him. Nevertheless, he was never faithful to me, to the marriage vows, and had many girl and women 'friends' over the years.

I tried to cover up, to hide things, even from his family and mother. I tried not to let my kids know. Yet, I've found out that they knew more than I thought. He treated me with little respect and was mean at times. The only good thing from our marriage is my children. I have good kids that I love very much.

I believe that Henry tried to harm me several times over the years, why, I don't know. I had told him that if he wanted free, to just go...that I would never try to hold him back. Finally, I was afraid for my life, so I left and got a divorce...after 47 years.

The divorce has been final for almost two years, and I'm doing well now, thanks to a lot of help from my Sister.

I thank God for her help and His.

Henry tells the kids that he still wants me back. I think it's a pretense. His self-image, his ego is bruised. He can't believe that he has done anything wrong, that I would leave him.

I'm a divorced woman. I can never have a serious relationship. Divorced...it's like a brand that says, *unclean!*"

She turned to look at Alex.

"Alex, you're a nice guy, a good man. Go find a woman who lost her husband, like you lost your wife, and forget about me."

Alex sat a moment before taking a long, shuddering breath.

Then he took another before he could form the words.

"Eva," He said, looking into her eyes, "I believe that you're a victim, innocently trapped into a marriage that should never have taken place. It was a marriage that was never a real marriage. Marriage is a sacred bond.

I believe that if we understand the Bible, it means that by him breaking the marriage vows, you're as innocent as if for you, there had never been a binding marriage.

Now I'm going to stand on that. That you're innocent of breaking your vows and thus you're free, as innocent as if there had never been a marriage.

I love you, and I'm pleading my case again. May I court you and try to win you to love me? We won't get married today or tomorrow, give me a couple weeks," he smiled at that.

He sobered again. "I can understand now, the fear, the sadness that I see in your eyes sometimes. I won't ever do anything to hurt you. I only want to make you happy...and to be happy with you.

Let me prove to you that I have that kind of love.

Do you think that you could give me a chance?

Eva was weeping openly by now.

"Oh Alex, do you really believe that it is all right, that I'm free to marry? Can I believe that? That I really am free?"

"Yes, I really do believe it and you must believe it too. Will you give me a chance to win your love?"

"This is so new...it's so much to think about. Everything is happening so fast. Alex, I admire you. I do like you a lot. Very much I think. The thought that I might have someone and have love, a real love, to have the right to that love -- it's such a new thought, that I'll have to get used to, get used to thinking that way. Give me some time to think."

"Agreed. Now the first thing, while we are still alone, I want to hold you in my arms a moment. I hope that you'll feel my love and know that it is a love that won't hurt you." He held out his arms. She came to him, but he said, "This won't do." He helped her up, to stand on the log that they had been sitting on. "Now this is more like it, girl."

He held her in his arms. Her arms slowly went around his neck, her cheek against his. Her tears were flowing again. Tears of release and relief, yes maybe tears of Joy, it was too soon to know.

Alex, realizing the enormity of the battles that she'd gone through, felt humbled at the thought that God had given him the task and privilege to lead and help Eva through the last steps to freedom to love, and freedom from condemnation from the sin of another.

Tears came to his eyes and he bowed his head over her.

His heart cried out, *'Lord – Father God – help us both!'*

Slowly the healing flowed through them; the sweetness brought to his mind the phrase of 'the healing balm of Gilead.' A healing balm with a sweet fragrance.

Alex ever so lightly kissed the silky hair that he'd felt the two months before, his tears dampening it. His heart was full of words of love that he must wait a little while to say.

They returned to Eva's apartment, but the day had almost gone, and Alex did not stay long. A short prayer and he went home.

He called as soon as he arrived. "Eva? Hello honey."

"Are you okay, Alex?"

"Yes, are you? Your voice sounds – what are you doing?"

"I'm – I was – trying to pray."

"Trying? We can always pray."

"I'm...I was trying, But not me...not tonight. Alex, I...I...I'm just..."

"Tell me...what?"

"Overwhelmed, I guess is the thing - the – word. I'm trying to absorb, to grasp...to understand all this. To think...to believe..."

Her voice caught.

"You're crying," He said. "I'm coming back over there. I'll be right there."

"Oh no, Alex, not tonight. I'm fine. Really, I'm fine. Overwhelmed, but fine."

"I should have prayed a better prayer, before I left, - I just forgot. Guess I'm kind of overwhelmed too.

"There's something else that I should have talked over with you."

"Oh no Alex. What else?"

"May I come over the first thing in the morning – well, how about ten."

"Yes, but tell me now."

"No, I have to see your face and explain to you to be sure."

"Alex, now you're scaring me. Are you changing...have you decided – have you...

"It's nothing like that. I love you. It's something that I just realized it should be a decision that we make together, the two of us together. Hey, I like the sound of that, *'the two of us together.'*"

"The two of us together," she echoed softly with him. "Alex, there you go again, overwhelming me."

He laughed, just softly, "Yeah, me too. Honey girl, lets pray over the phone, and I'll be there in the morning."

"Yes, please pray. Thank you Alex."

CHAPTER EIGHT

Alex was sitting on the deck when she went to the kitchen to put coffee on. With a radiant smile, she opened the door.

"Alex, I thought that you said about ten o'clock! I'm still in my bathrobe! Good morning!"

"Good Morning Eva. Sorry, I couldn't wait. Hug?"

"Hug! Yes. - I haven't made coffee yet."

"I'll make coffee, you go dress."

"Have you had breakfast?"

"No. I'll start it – go dress. I'll find something…Eva, honey?"

"Yes?"

"Would you wear that cowgirl outfit that you wore that first night to dinner?"

"Yes, all right," she laughed. Alex was wearing his westerns too.

Her heart was beating wildly, her thoughts almost as wild.

"He couldn't wait, and he's here! It is something for the two of us to decide. What is Alex doing now?" She was trembling. *"What is the matter with me? I'm so excited! Maybe scared too. I like him. He said that he loves me!*

Hurry...I'd better hurry. Alex is here!"

"These are good waffles, what brand are they?" Alex asked, as he put strawberry jam on his second one.

"Oh, they are a special brand, a special recipe," she laughed. "My own recipe. I mix up a batch and freeze some when I make them. I can't make a small batch – small enough for one, so I freeze some. Sis comes and has waffles with me sometimes."

"I like them, they're good. You'll have to show me how."

After they had finished breakfast, Alex said, "I'd like to use the table, so let's clear things away."

He spread out the drawings of the planned changes to the house to make the apartment.

"Eva, you know how big my house is. We needed a big house when the boys were growing up, but now most of it is unused. This is what I thought we might do, but I want you to think about how you want it. If you want the house as it is, or if you would like the apartment."

"But Alex, that's not for me to decide! It's your house..."

"Remember last night? The two of us together? The two of us together will decide. I believe that we'll marry someday. I hope soon."

"All right Alex, show me – but you're rushing me again!"

He smiled at her, "I am, aren't I," taking her hand a moment. He showed her the plans and told of the changes.

"To make the apartment for us, and Tom and Beth living in the main part of the house. Now, what do you think? Shall we leave the house as it is, or do you think that you would like the apartment? Would you be happy there? Or shall we do something else?"

"Alex, I think that the apartment would be a good idea, regardless of what 'we' might do. That is if you would like the apartment, After all it is your house."

"I talked to Tom and Beth and they said that they would like the house that way. They don't need or want the whole house. I think that I would like the apartment, a smaller place. There would be plenty of room – even Jim's room will still be there. He's had a room there for years, even if he has an apartment. I wanted to be sure of what you thought."

"It seems like a good idea, Alex. Do it. Tom and Beth are moving up soon, aren't they?"

"Yes. Tom hopes to go to work here in two weeks. Of course if it should be that we don't get all the changes done for a while, we can get by."

They talked for a few more minutes.

"I'd better get back and tell Tom and Beth, and see about getting the work started. Beth would like to go back to California tomorrow if she doesn't have to look for a house."

"Alex, you should have just gone ahead with it."

"No Eva, I want to start doing things like this, the right way, 'the two of us together.' I'll call you later."

*

Her sister Jewel called.

"Are you going to be home? I'm coming out."

"Yes, Sis, come on. I'll make us some lunch."

She showed Jewel the painting. "Alex wants to buy it."

"I can see why."

"You should see the paintings in his house," Eva exclaimed.

"Now let's sit and you can tell me what's been happening. I've hardly seen you since Tuesday, except at church on Wednesday evening. Is this Alex with you all the time?"

Eva filled her in on everything.

"You told him about your divorce…and about Henry?"

"Yes. I even told him about Bill and then Henry's – forcing me into marriage."

"And he wants to 'court' you?"

"That's what he said."

"And He's a good guy?"

"He seems to be. I believe that he is, and best of all, he loves Jesus, and he prays with me."

"Well, you know they say that there is such a thing as love at first sight. Remember what you said yourself; that God would have to hit you in the face with him if there was a man for you. How do you feel about him?"

"I like him, a lot I think. I feel safe with him now. At first, I was afraid, sometimes. Scared. Now I feel comfortable, secure…but excited, too. Happy, excited…and he makes me laugh. I'm happier than I've been in such a long time."

"He's very talented in his work. The business looks like it will go well and grow. I think that he is very important in the business, but he wants to take some time away from it. That is why he bought the new boat, to take the trip up the Inside Passage to Alaska, and be gone most of the summer."

"What are you going to do while he is gone all summer? Now that you're just getting acquainted?"

"Get my feet back on the ground, I hope," Eva laughed.

He'll be gone all summer? Nooo!

"I was kind of thinking, dreaming, that we, you and I and Ben too if he wants to go with us, that maybe we could make that trip by ferry boat up that way. I know that we couldn't afford a cruse ship, but maybe a ferry."

"Wouldn't that be great fun?"

"Anyway, it's something to dream about."

"Yes, we can dream."

"Have you told your kids about Alex?"

"No, it's only been five days – we met five days ago, on Monday…and today's Friday. Can you believe it? Five days, and he said that he is going to ask me to marry him!"

"Have you talked to any of your kids? Danielle has called me every couple of days."

"No I haven't. Danielle called and I talked to her on Sunday afternoon. I haven't talked to her since. I had told her about running into a man, and she laughed at me, that I was getting desperate, waiting for God, so I tried to run one down."

They laughed over that.

"Hadn't you better call her and tell her. She can tell the rest of the kids. You know they'll be happy for you. They had told you that they hoped that you would find someone."

Jewel began to laugh. "I don't think anyone thought that you would run a guy down though. But it's your own fault, for saying that."

After Jewel left, Eva busied herself doing up the laundry, and dusting. She put out birdseed.

The little birds came, flocking around, the ground feeders at her feet. The ducks seen her and started up their raucous so she took some dried bread and went down to the dock to toss the bread to them, laughing at their antics, as each one was trying to be the one to catch the tossed bread.

When they had settled down to their quiet contented chatter and started preening them selves, she went back to the apartment.

She swept the whole deck, across in front of Billie and Brandon's apartment too. Brandon usually swept it every other day or so. She refilled the Humming Bird feeders.

There were several humming bird feeders now; there were more of the little guys around this year, more than ever it seemed. They were closer and more easily seen since Steve had fixed the feeders at the deck.

She brought her Bible out and sat in the glider swing to read.

At last, she looked up, thinking

"It's quiet, but the quiet is so full of sound. The little birds are twittering at each other. I see squirrels and chipmunks rustling around in the grass and climbing around in the trees. The ducks are always talking to each other or themselves.

I can hear the water softly lapping at the dock. It's so quiet, that I can even hear some people across the lake. Someone is singing- what is the song? 'Walking – get me off my mind – I can love others – world see Jesus in me.'

I've never heard it before. That should be the aim for us all to live, 'that the world see Jesus in me.'

What a thought! That I might live my life so close to Him that they see Jesus in me."

She raised her face, "Lord, thank you for the peace I have. Help me to understand and know that I may have the freedom that Alex spoke of last night.

"Henry departed from his vows, his pledges to me and to the marriage. I'm not guilty of the sins, so I'm not under bondage for them. I believe that your Word tells me that. We did not live in peace. I've wanted the peace, if I could not have love."

She ate some supper.

She wandered around the house, straightening books, rearranging flowers.

"What am I doing? I'm as restless as a caged tiger." She looked at her watch. "Six hours since Alex left. Alex. I like his name. Alex - Alex! – He hasn't called me, and…and…I'm talking to myself!

I wanted time. Time to think. He was rushing me. Things were going too fast. Now I'm lonesome. For a guy that I just met, five days ago.

Alex! Cool it girl. Calm down. You have got to be sure."

She put on a sweater, picked up her Bible and went out on the deck.

Billie joined her a few minutes later. "Brandon is doing dishes and won't let me help. It's a beautiful evening. Where's Alex?"

"Home, I guess. Part of his family is here from California and may have to leave tomorrow."

Billie told her about a house that they were looking at. "It's close to a good school, if we ever have a family."

Brandon brought a Bible when he joined them.

"Where are you reading, Eva? May we join you?" They read and shared their thoughts on the Word. "We haven't done this for a while, and I enjoyed it." Brandon said, closing his Bible.

"Me too," Billie added.

"Yes, me too," Eva agreed.

Brandon asked, "Shall we pray together? We'd like you to agree with us in prayer about a promotion that I'm expecting that it'll be enough so that Billie can quit work and we can buy a house, and maybe have a baby. I'm not asking much, am I? Sounds like a big order. Maybe I'm asking for too much, but we'd like to have our own home. We have been saving most of Billie's money, so we have a good down payment."

"Yes, I'll agree with you and pray. We have a great God, who cares, and if he wants you to have this, He'll arrange it for you."

*

Later, Eva turned on the television and watched the news – flipped channels – nothing good on tonight. Rescue shows – too scary tonight, so she turned it off.

"He said that he would call. He does every night when he's not here. What happened? It's eight o'clock. Well it's only eight o'clock, and his family is there; he should spend some time with them. Jim's there too. He'll call."

She put on her robe, found a book to read and stood looking at the lights across the lake, with reflected lights dancing on the water.

I like it here, she thought, *the quiet and peace, after years of no peace of a cold war. Do I want to give this up? Can I give it up? Sis says that I don't go out enough. It has been enough to see Jewel and Ben and brother Len and Alice and families…and the Church family. I love the pastor. I would like to see more of my children, though.*

Do I love Alex enough? I've never had the real love of a man. I tried to love. How much is enough? I must be sure that I love Alex the way that he should be loved.

Can I…can I marry him?

She pictured him, remembering how he looked. The way he walked. The way that he sometimes put up his left hand in a certain gesture when he talked, like he was showing a picture or revealing a secret.

His voice soft, especially his laugh, like he was thrilled to laugh! A thrill ran through her at that memory of his laugh, and she smiled.

How gentle his hands were when he took her hands, gently but firm, nothing wishy-washy about Alex! Yet, he had gentle, sure hands. No squeezing and moving the bones in her hands, hurting her like Henry did, when he grabbed her hands or arms, hurting and leaving bruises.

Henry had left black and blue marks, and thought it was funny, *you're too tender,* he'd said. She'd worn long sleeves many times to hide bruises from being too tender.

Why did she have to remember Henry now?

Probably because Alex is so different.

Alex is kind, considerate, thinking of others. Alex is a gentle man, and a gentleman. – His smile and laugh! Yes, his smile, and his laugh! Her heart did a flip-flop. The memory of Alex's soft musical laugh was so real, that she looked around, expecting to see him.

She caught her breath, "I've had it! I DO LOVE HIM! I LOVE ALEX!"

The phone rang. She answered with a trembling "Hello."

"Eva, Sweetheart, are you all right?"

"Oh...um...yes! Hello Alex."

"What's up? You sound funny."

"I'm fine, really fine...fine now that you called!" *She thought, 'I'm being rather strange, what will he think of me?'"*

"I didn't have much of a chance to call sooner. It's been rather hectic around here. Beth, Betty, and I checked out the house and projected apartment. I called a contractor to get started on Monday. Jim and I took Beth and Betty to the airport and they are on their way to California. They hope to be back here in two weeks or less. Jim went back to his place. I'm alone in this big house, and I'm lonesome. I want to see you."

"Me too, I'm lonesome...and I never get lonesome, but I'm lonesome, too. See what you do to me?"

"Good," he said with a satisfied chuckle. "What's Brandon's phone number? I want to call him." She gave him the number. "I'll call you right back."

Brandon answered. "Brandon, this is Alex. Is it too late to ask to use my bed?"

Brandon laughed, "No Alex, come on. It's Friday night and we don't have to get up early, so we are watching a video that'll last until midnight. Sort of a night out, staying at home, being comfortable."

"Good. I'll come up and spend the evening with Eva. I'll see you after while. Thanks."

He called Eva back.

"Honey, I called Brandon and my bed is available and I'm coming up. I'll be there soon."

"Oh! Okay." And he was gone.

*

Alex, as he was driving on the way to see Eva, started to sing, "I'm going to hold you in my heart 'till I can hold you in my arms, like you've never been held before."

He laughed, thrilled at the thought of holding her in his arms.

"He's coming! He's coming! Alex is coming!"

Quick shower and dress again. She put on a long skirt and blouse of sky blue with pastel flowers. She started to make coffee, and then decided to make tea. She put out a bowl of peaches and pears and a platter of sliced Granny Smith apples, green and red bell peppers and dip, some celery stalks and peanut butter. She made cinnamon toast and put in a warm oven. She pulled the coffee table closer to the couch, and then set a chair across from it. No. She moved the chair back away. Then laughed at her self.

She found some good music, turned on, playing softly. Arranged the lights comfortably.

Alex was there. She met him on the deck. "Hi Sweetheart, let me check in with Brandon, then I'll be in," Alex greeted her.

He hugged her when he came in; she hugged him back.

"I need to carry a step stool with me," he laughed.

"I have one in the kitchen."

They talked and snacked, and talked some more.

Later, Alex brought a blanket from the back of the couch, "Let's watch the moon come up over the lake." He put the blanket around Eva's shoulders.

"This love seat is a glider swing. It's kind of fun to sit in," she said, sitting down. "Oh, you'd better share my blanket or get another, it's cool out tonight." She held the blanket open so he could cover his back too. "Come share my blanket."

They had been talking nonstop inside, like they couldn't get enough said, but now, just sat quietly. The rising moon was making dancing reflections on the lake.

"It looks like a silver path doesn't it." Eva aid at last.

"Yes, a silver path, do you suppose that it is symbolic of the path we are going to start to share together? A Silver and golden path. A silver path to golden love."

"Alex, how exciting! You keep me in a state."

"What kind of a state, Sweetheart? A state of falling in love with me, I hope. Are you feeling less overwhelmed, as you said, and more secure, feeling safe, not afraid of me anymore."

"No, I'm not afraid anymore, not of you. I'm afraid that I may wake up and find that it has all been a dream."

"Alex, you talk of love and marriage, and it sounds too good to be true for me. There is one thing more I need to tell you."

"Tell me anything Jo, we'll work it out."

"Alex it's –" she stopped.

"Honey, if it's that hard to tell, then don't. I don't need to know and you don't need to remember."

"No, I must. Alex, I've hated sex for many years. I don't know if I can ever get over that, and it's not fair to you."

"Sweetheart, do you think that God would bring us together if everything wouldn't be all right? What if it were *me*? Would you send *me* away?"

"No, of course not."

"Then why should I not feel the same way about you? I love you. God will take care of that too if it is a problem, or help us with the problem. Can you believe that?"

"Yes, if you're sure, Alex, I can believe it."

"I'm sure, Very sure. No more doubts?"

"No more doubts!"

Alex stood up. "Eva, move over on this side. I want you next to my heart." He moved to the other side, sat down and pulled the blanket around them again, with his arm around her, pulling her snug against him. "Now, with you here next to my heart, maybe I can chase away all those fears. Okay?"

"Okay."

"Can you feel my heart beating next to you?"

"Yes, if mine would just quiet down a bit!"

Alex laughed at that, "So yours is doing double time, too?"

She laughed too, rather nervously. "Yes. I can hardly believe all this."

"Sweetheart, I know that I've fallen in love with you. I don't want to be away from you. I want you with me all the time. The house was so empty. I couldn't stand it. I had to come. I was so lonesome! Did you miss me? You said that you were lonesome too?"

"Yes I was, and I never get lonesome," she laughed.

"Do you think that you care for me? Do you think that maybe you'll love me someday?"

"Alex, I think that I love you now! I must be sure that I love you completely, the way love should be. Can we go a little slow, so that I can be sure, positively sure that I know my mind and heart, and be sure that I love you enough?"

"Yes. We'll just keep on getting acquainted, learning all about each other, spending time together." They sat quietly, talking, catching up on all the years that they had missed of each other's lives. Content just to be together.

After a while, they noticed that the faint sound of the TV had stopped at Brandon and Billie's apartment. Alex looked at his watch. "It's midnight! Already! Guess it's time to go in." He folded the blanket and handed it to Eva at the door.

After a short prayer – "Good Night Sweetheart."

"Good Night Alex. Come over – when ever. See you in the morning." She listened; was he humming 'Good Night' again? He was! She thought that she wouldn't sleep, but she did.

*

Eva had unlocked the door and was making coffee as Alex came to the door. She waved and called, "Good Morning Alex, come in."

"Good Morning."

"Now where is that step stool?" he asked as he came from the bath- room. Eva opened up the step stool, and stepped up on the first step.

"Good Morning!" he said against her hair, holding her in his arms.

"Good Morning Alex," she whispered near his ear. He continued to hold her for a moment.

'I'm not sure I'll ever let you go. But I suppose we'd better have some breakfast as who knows what today will bring," he chuckled.

'That could be true, the way things have been happening the last few days," she said with happy laugh.

"Can I help? What are we having?"

"Little sausages, scrambled eggs, whole wheat toast and sliced pineapple. It's almost ready."

"Let's see if I remember, cups and plates...up here? Bingo!" Alex poured the coffee while Eva dished up the eggs and sausages.

"Sit down, I'll bring the toast."

After the blessing, Alex said, "This is so much fun. I love having breakfast with you Jo."

"Yes, it's fun for me too." She agreed.

"You look great this morning. There's a sparkle in you eyes, is that for me?"

"If there is, it must be because of you, and yes, for you."

He let out a war whoop, "Yahoo!"

"Alex shush, you'll wake Brandon and Billy," but she was laughing.

"Can't help it! I'm making progress," his smile was something.

"Yes Alex, we are both making progress."

"No, not here, you'll have to go out in the hills somewhere to yell," she laughed, as he started to yell again.

"Well, come on let's go."

"Eat your breakfast first. Like you said, who knows what today will bring? You don't know when you'll have a chance to eat again."

"That's true, and it is a good breakfast," he sighed contentedly.

The phone rang as they finished the dishes; Eva patted the couch next to her as she sat down to answer.

"Hello?"

"Hello Mom, How are you?"

"I'm just fine, Honey, thank you. Doing just great."

"It's my daughter Danielle." She whispered to Alex.

"Mom, I've been trying to call you. You have been out."

"Yes, out and about," Eva agreed.

"I finally got Auntie Jewel. She said that you have met someone and are seeing him. She said to get you to tell me about it. – Is someone there with you?"

"Yes."

"Maybe I'd better let you go. Call me back?"

"No Honey, it's okay. Is everything all right there?"

"Yes. I just wanted to talk to my Mom."

"Oh Honey, thank you. I want to talk to you too."

"Are you going to tell her about us?" Alex asked softly.

"Yes," Eva whispered.

"What was that? What are you going to tell me? Who is there?"

"Danielle, remember me telling you about going down on the sound to look for a view to paint Mount Rainier and running into a man?"

"Yes?"

"Well, I finally went back and painted the picture. There was a new boat there, so I thought that I would never see that poor guy again. But guess what?"

"*He* owns the new boat!"

"Yes, that's right."

"And HE"S there with you now!"

"Yes. His name is Alex Harmon."

"YES! YES!" Danielle fairly shouted.

"Let me talk to her," Alex asked.

"Alex wants to talk to you, Honey."

"Yes, I want to talk to him. Get on the other phone, Mom."

"Hello, Danielle."

"Hello Alex! I like that name."

"Danielle, your Mom and I are trying to get to know each other, do you mind?"

"No I don't mind. Just one thing, Mom has been hurt enough; please don't hurt her any more."

"I won't, I promise. We have spent most of the days together, the last 5 days, and I've fallen in love with her. I want to ask her to marry me, but she thinks that everything is going too fast, so we are just talking and being together, getting to know each other."

"Sounds good to me. Mom, are you there?"

"Yes Honey, I'm here."

"When are you going to bring him down so we can all meet him?"

"I don't know, I hadn't thought that far."

"I've a thought," Alex said. "If we come down today, could you get the family together someplace?"

"Yes, I think so. If they are in town, they'll drop everything else, I'm sure."

"Is that all right with you?"

"Yes, I think so."

"Then we'll do it. We'll come today."

"How soon will you come?"

"Right away, I think." Alex looked at Eva for an answer.

"We should be able to leave in a few minutes. We should be there by about 1 o'clock." Eva agreed.

"Was there anything else, Danielle?"

"No, Mom. Hey, this is great! I love you Mom. Hey Alex, will you give Mom a kiss for me too?"

"Yes!"

"Mom, how about you? Do you like Alex? Does he measure up to all your requirements?"

"Yes, to all questions. He knows and loves the Lord. He knows how to pray. He's kind, a gentle...gentleman. He's tall, six-two, I think. Well built. Nice looking. Blond, blue eyes. Great smile. You heard his voice. The rest you'll find out when you see him."

"Do you love him, Mom?"

"Yes. Yes, I do!"

"Well, okay! See you soon."

"Eva– do you mean it? – Do you love me? You said that you wanted to be sure that you loved me completely, the way love should be. – Do you love me like that?"

"Yes! Yes Alex, I do love you like that!"

'Thank you Lord' he breathed within. "Then I want to kiss you once for Danielle and at least once for ME!" Which he did, and Eva responded. They're first kiss! He held her in his arms, "Next to my heart, Sweetheart." She laughed softly snuggling her head on his shoulder.

"I love this, but I guess we had better go if we are going to get there by 1 o'clock."

"Alex, we'd better plan to stay over night. Do you need to go home to get a few things?"

"No. I packed a bag. I knew that I couldn't stand to go back to that empty house. I brought enough for the weekend. I didn't want to go back."

"You did? I'll pack a few things, too. Maybe we'll stay two nights. Can we, if they want us to? I want them to get to know you."

"Yes. We can spend the weekend. Today is Saturday and most people have Saturdays and Sundays off from work. That's why I thought that we should go today. We can come home on Monday. Unless your sons run me off," he laughed.

"They won't do that."

"It may be your daughters will be the hardest to win."

"They'll love you, Alex."

"Then, what took you so long to fall in love with me?" he grinned.

"Long? Six days is long?" she laughed.

"It has seemed long to me, especially the last two days." He was still grinning.

"Alex, you're teasing me. You're hopeless." She laughed.

"That's right, hopelessly in love with the sweetest Lady, and loving every minute." They stopped about half way for a break. Coffee and a cinnamon roll. "Eva, you're not eating your roll nor drinking your coffee," Alex reminded her. "What's wrong?"

"The roll and coffee are good. Maybe it's too soon after breakfast. I have butterflies, I guess."

"I thought that you were reassuring me about meeting your family...that they are going to like me. Do I need to be worrying about it too?"

"It's not you Alex, it's me."

"It's a big step for you, for me to meet your kids?" he smiled, his eyes twinkling.

"Yes – no. That I – I – am going to say yes – when – if – you ask me- Oh, now I – I'm messing everything up!"

"Let's get out of here, my Love," Alex said with his soft laugh. He thought, *I'm going to explode if I don't get a chance to yell!*

"I wonder where I can find a high hill to stop," he said after they had started on.

"A high hill? Oh, for a view of the Columbia River?"

"Well, that will do, as long as I can give out a big yell! I don't know how long I can hold it back." He was looking soberly at her, and then burst out laughing at her expression when she realized what he meant.

She laughed too, "Alex you are a tease!"

"All joking aside, Sweetheart, I'm so happy that I could yell. And I'm going to find a place to stop for a few minutes."

"Alex?

"Yes?"

"May I move over to the middle and use the center belt?"

"Yes, Dear Heart, please do. I'll love that. In this big car, you're too far away to suit me."

"I'm sorry that I cut your coffee break short," she said.

"Are you hungry now?"

"No, not me. Are you?"

"Not for food, but I could use a kiss or two – dozen," he grinned.

"Alex!" but she laughed.

"I think this will do," he said, pulling off on an exit marked *Return to Freeway*. There was a wide place to park. "Guess I'll have to wait for my yell, there's too many people!"

He turned to her, "Recognize this?"

"My mother's ring! How did you get it?"

"Remember the day that you painted? You left it on the sink when you washed up."

"I wondered where it was."

"I kept it and took it to a jeweler to get this." It was an emerald cut yellow diamond with a yellow baguette diamond on each side.

"Eva? Will you marry me? Soon? May I put this on your finger? Or would you rather have something else?"

"Yes, Alex. I'll marry you. How soon? We'll have to think, decide about that." She held her hand for him to put the ring on her finger. "It's so beautiful! Yellow diamonds! Alex! I love it. And I'm crying again!"

"That's all right; I'll kiss the tears away." And he did.

They did make it to Danielle's by one, but just barely.

"Is this a used car lot?" Alex asked as he parked the car.

"Of course not," she laughed. "My kids and Grand kids are here, I suppose."

"OH Wow! I forgot about Grand Kids being here too. Shall we go home?" he said softly, holding the car door open for her.

"Now who's having second thoughts?" She laughed.

"Not me, my Love, I can face anything to get to marry you."

Danielle came flying down the driveway crying, "MOM! MOM!" and her arms around her mother.

"Hi Sweetheart," Eva greeted her.

"Alex, Hello," she said, including him in the hug.

"Danielle, Hello, Sweetheart." Danielle had won him completely.

"No wonder you fell for him, Mom, he's perfect."

"Now, don't go that far, I'll never be able to live up to that," Alex laughed.

"Come on in. Everyone is here waiting."

Alex did a mock groan, grinning at her.

"Alex!" Eva laughed, taking his hand.

"Oops, wrong side. I've got to have you next to my heart,

or I may not survive the test."

"I like him, Mom; he's going to be good for you." Danielle said, joining the laugh.

Danielle took charge of the introductions, taking Alex around to each one. When they came to Abbigail, he thought, "*This is the first 'darling of her heart.'*"

And, he knew that he would love Abbigail too. Her sons, he admired, meeting the clear questioning look in their eyes as they shook his hand warmly. Eva's Daughters-in-law, greeting him much the same.

It was the same with the adult grand children. The smaller children were a bit shy, but smiled at him, gravely shaking his hand. Eva was surrounded and hugged by all.

"Now that you have met everyone, do you still want to marry Mom?" Danielle asked.

"Yes, more than ever. I can see why Eva's proud of her family. I hope that I can live up to your expectations of me. With God's help, I believe that I can.""

"We've waited lunch for you to come," Danielle said. "Paul, will you ask the blessing, and then we'll eat."

After the blessing, Danielle said, "Mom, you and Alex go first. It's buffet style, help yourselves everyone."

"Sit here Mom, Alex," as she showed them to a small table. "OH my goodness! Mom! Let me see that ring! Oh Alex, I could kiss you myself!"

"Help yourself, I like kisses," he smiled back.

"You deserve a bunch for getting Mom such a beautiful ring."

"I'll remember to collect a few later," he laughed, grinning at Eva.

Later when talking to Paul, Eva's oldest son, Alex said, "I had intended to talk to you children, especially you, for permission to marry your Mom, but I got carried away."

"Well, really it should be Mom's decision, of course. I think that she has made a good choice," Paul said, reaching out to shake Alex's hand. "It is rather a shock though," Paul continued, "but we have been hoping and praying for her happiness. That is the important thing."

"Yes," Alex agreed. "I want to be a part of her happiness. I hope the rest of the family feel the same way."

"I'm sure that they do," Paul assured him. How did it happen? Danielle said that she didn't know about it either until today."

"You know that your Mother paints? Two months ago, she was looking for a view of the mountain from down on the sound. She went down on a small dock where I have a boat moorage. It started to rain suddenly and we ran into each other trying to get out of the rain. We exchanged apologies and she ran off to her car. I haven't been able to forget her.

"It was just last Monday, she came back to paint. A young friend of mine, named Jim Dugan, and I watched her and invited her to have brunch with us on the boat. I wasn't about to let her disappear again. Before I could, Jim invited her to have dinner with us that evening. By the time dinner was over, I knew that I wanted us to get to know each other. I've been with her every day since. I think that I fell in love with her the moment that I first seen her, when we ran into each other. I know that I love her, and want to be with her the rest of our lives."

"I have a home, money invested and a partnership in a furniture manufacturing business.

"I had planned to take a vacation trip with my friend, Jim Dugan, taking the boat up the Inside Passage to Alaska. We may spend most of the summer on the trip. I'm hoping that Eva and I are married by then and Eva will go with me. I know that I won't leave her. Jim and I planed to leave on the trip in about three weeks."

"I see," Paul said. "It seems rather sudden, but I can understand. I fell in love with my wife when I met her. Aunt Jewel picked her out for me, and arranged for us to meet. We probably would have married sooner, but I was in the service."

"You understand then, how I feel. I've been rushing her and we've spent a lot of time talking."

Alex continued, "My first wife died six years ago. But I haven't even thought about looking for another woman until your Mother ran into my heart." Most of the adult family had gathered around and heard the conversation. Eva was off somewhere with the smaller children.

"Have you set a date?"

"No, but I just gave Eva the ring today, somewhere on the way here. We haven't got that far yet. Here she comes."

"Hi gang, are you getting acquainted with this guy?" Eva asked.

"Yea, Mom, we've been giving him the third degree," Paul grinned. Paul put his arm around his Mother.

"Not really, Mom, just talking, and yes, we're getting acquainted. Let's see that ring." He whistled at the sight of it. "So, when is the big day, Mom?"

"Big day? Oh, I don't know. Now you guys are rushing me too." They joined her when she laughed at her own confusion.

"Mom it sounds like you have less than three weeks, if you're going on the boat with Alex, or are you going to wait until fall when he gets back? But he wants you to go with him." Paul asked. "You'd better decide and let the girls know, you know how they are about weddings."

"Alex!" Eva cried.

"It's okay, Honey, we can figure it out and decide. Shall we just elope?"

"NO!" The girls cried in chorus.

"No," Eva agreed. "I'm still not used to the thoughts of getting married. I've got to have time to think!"

"That sounds okay, five minutes long enough?" Alex laughed at her gasp. Eva laughed too, the others joining in.

"Right next to my heart, love. We'll talk about it," he said quietly. "I knew that I should have brought that step stool with me," he whispered against her hair. She gasped and looked up into his twinkling eyes. She didn't say anything; she didn't want to explain the step stool to her family too. She smiled at him.

"That's better," he said, smiling down at her.

Danielle came and taking her by the arm, said, "Mom, leave Alex with the guys and come talk to us girls. Come sit down." Danielle brought a calendar.

"Mom, Alex said a little over three weeks until he starts the trip. The Inside Passage to Alaska! Awesome! Aren't you excited about going, Mom?"

"I haven't thought about going!"

"Alex won't go without you; he won't leave you home, I'm sure of that! He wants to be married by then and you go with him."

Abbigail asked, "You did say that you love him, that you will marry him?"

"Yes, I did say that I would marry him, just today I said it!"

'I love him! I love Alex,' her heart sang. 'And I'm going to marry him! Marry Alex!'

"Then, let's decide when to have the wedding."

They talked of a day in two weeks or day in three weeks. They talked about a wedding cake.

How much time to make a wedding cake?

A wedding dress?

"Okay Mom, which shall it be? In two weeks or three? This date or this date?"

"Oh I don't know! – Alex?" he was at her side.

"Eva come with me to the car for a few minutes. I want to get some pictures of the boat and pictures of some of the furniture and plans for the shop to show the fellows."

He opened the trunk of the car to pick up the pictures.

"Honey, I would like for us to be married in two weeks or three at the latest, if that is what you would want to do.

I want you with me on the trip. I can't go without you. I know that I'm rushing you again, rushing us both.

"Another boat is going along with us. They have made the trip several times, and it would be a big help to us, if we go together. If we don't go when they do, we may have to hire a pilot to go on our boat. We can go next year. If you need more time, that's what we'll do. We can make a trip by car for a honeymoon. You make the decision. Can we be married in two or three weeks and make the trip together to Alaska, or shall we wait a while?"

"Oh Alex, that trip would be a honeymoon! A wonderful honeymoon, wouldn't it! I would love it! Yes! Yes, Alex! Let's get married now."

"Are you sure, Sweetheart?"

"Yes Alex, I'm sure!" She stepped close to him and put her arms around him. He hugged her tight.

"Let's seal it with a kiss, then we'd better go back or they'll think that we really did elope," he said bending down to kiss her.

"Sure do need that step stool."

"Alex, before you go back to the guys, look at the calendar with me for a moment, and help me chose the day. How about your family, will they come down here? The girls want the wedding here at the house."

Pointing to the calendar, Alex said, "How about this Saturday or this Saturday or even those Sundays. Most everyone has weekends off. Jim's classes end here. My family will come. I seen a motel close, I'll rent rooms. How about having the reception at the motel. The sign said 'banquet rooms available.' Then we won't have to clean up. And don't think about the cost. I'll take care of it. You decide, Eva."

He turned to the others with a big smile, "Get it worked out, girls." Then he went back to the men.

Alex showed the pictures of some of the furniture, and plans for the shop enlargement, explaining the recent increased orders for the specialized style of furniture, and the need for the new equipment.

Jason asked, "You designed and built these?"

"Yes." Alex explained how they each designed and working together and made many unique pieces of furniture.

"How often do you come up with something new?"

"That's hard to say. We have taken to keeping a pad and pencil handy, as we never know when an idea will hit us. Then again, we have people come in with ideas of their own and we work those out to please them and build what they want. Sometimes they choose something that we have made that they want with some changes. We often get ideas from working on something else."

"And there is just the three of you?"

"Yes, at this time, but my son Tom will start with us in about two weeks. My brother's son, Bill Jr. will come any day now, too. We have several orders now and need both the added space and equipment to make them. I'm hoping that they'll be able to manage without me for a month or so, while I make this trip to Alaska. I haven't had a vacation for years. I've dreamed for years of making this trip. I planned the trip, not knowing that it would turn out to be a honeymoon.

I suppose if they need me, I could fly home for a few days, but I hope that I won't have to.

"Jason, are you a wood worker? You seem to understand a good deal about the machines."

"Wood has always been my first love, but right now I'm machining metal. All three of us boys made things in shop at school and some at home, and we are not bad as carpenters. But we don't have the right equipment to do a proper job of some things we might want to make."

"Jason, if you would be interested in changing, how about going up and checking out our operation. Talk to Bill and David, and then if you're interested and would like to work with us, do it. We are going to need more on our crew. Especially if I marry me a wife." Alex laughed.

"Do you really mean it?" Jason asked. "I would like to check it out. Mom had seen some tables in Norway that she liked and has wanted one. As they aren't sold here, she asked us to build her one. I sure would like to."

"Now there, that is the kind of thing that we do." Alex said.

Allan, Eva's third son, brought a bunch of snapshots to show Alex.

"Maybe you and Mom will come rafting with Marie and me sometime. I have a 22-foot white water rafting boat that we often take rafting on the Clackamas and Mollala Rivers.

We have friends who have rafts too and we usually make a day of it and have a good time. There is usually a bunch of us and they are all good sports, game for a good time. We take plenty of food with dry clothes, as well as cameras with us. We see wild life, including deer and bear as well as otter.

We see different kinds of birds, many nests of eagles and osprey. We sometimes take fish poles and have a fish fry on some scenic beach."

"As much as I like to hunt and fish, I think that I like the rafting more. I want someday to have a guide service, taking people who want to enjoy the scenery. Maybe photographers going after wildlife pictures that are available in very few places any more. I don't want to take hunters. I'd hate to have the wild life that we get to see, killed. It is a thrill to see them."

"This is very interesting," Alex agreed. "I'd love to go. I'm sure Eva would too. What is the name on the raft? 'Bigger and Better'?"

"Yes, because every time I replace the raft, it's bigger and better," Allan laughed.

"That's a good idea," Alex agreed. "We'll plan to go with you after we get back."

"As you can see, we get some great pictures. I have lots more. Marie likes to take pictures, and catches some good shots."

The conversation continued, with Alex getting to know each one, what they did for life's work and their interests. Most were sport fishermen and interested in his new boat.

"Rebah, that's Mom's second Granddaughter, sitting in the blue chair, Rebah owns her own boat and goes fishing in the Columbia River," someone said.

"I'll bet that she is the one who owns the Yellow Viper too," Alex guessed.

"That's right, how'd you guess?"

"You can tell that she has an adventurous spirit," Alex answered.

"That's my wife," laughed James.

Meanwhile, the ladies were continuing to make plans for their Mom's/Grandmother's wedding.

Abbigail, sitting beside her said, "Mom, may I make your wedding dress?"

"Yes Honey, I'd love it if you have time."

"I've lots of time, now that I'm not working. I know just what I want you to have. Do you remember Rebah's wedding dress? It was light blue with a white lace overdress. How would you like yours made the same way? I'll make a hat to match too."

"Oh Abbi, that sounds beautiful, but wouldn't it be too fancy for an older gal like me?"

"No Mom, it would be perfect," Danielle joined in. "Will you do it Sis? You know how hard it'll be to find something now and it wouldn't be half so nice."

"Yes, I'll make it. I may need to adjust the pattern though. You aren't as tall as Rebah. Can you come over before you go back?"

"Yes, Alex said that we could stay as long as we want or need to."

"Mom, I'm so happy for you, yes for Alex too," Abbigail said, tears in her eyes.

"Isn't Alex something though? I'm so blessed to have him. It is still hard to believe what all is happening, and so quickly."

Abbigail's oldest daughter, Raylynn spoke up, "Grandma, Alex has taken us by storm too, and we've fallen in love with him!"

There was a chorus of 'yes' and 'that's right,' from the rest of the girls.

"Now you know what I've been going through the last few days," Eva said.

"Abbi, if you need me to come down for a fitting, I can do that too, just give me a call."

"Yes Mom, that would be a good idea. I'll get started on it on Monday or Tuesday for sure."

Danielle said, "Girls, let's set out salads and things for supper. Gary is barbecuing hamburgers and I have beans baking. We can have supper in a few minutes. And coffee is ready."

Alex was sitting in a big chair with wide armrests, so when Eva went to get him, she sat on the arm of the chair.

"I've been hearing stories of your hunting experiences, hunting with your family," Alex told her.

"When these guys get started telling hunting stories, they may last all night," she laughed, "...and they're all true. We've had some good times, some wonderful adventures."

"Anymore," Paul said, "we boys just hunt archery. My daughter-in-law, LeeAnna is an archery hunter too. But she is having another baby, so I don't know if she'll get to hunt this year."

Someone told of another incident, where two of the hunters had stood too close to the campfire trying to dry out, and caught their pants cuffs on fire. First, one of the guy's fire was discovered and put out, only to discover the other guy's fire, and he'd been laughing at the first guy.

As the laughter subsided, Eva said, "They sent me to tell you guys that Gary is grilling hamburgers and we can eat."

Alex took her hand, "Just a minute, Hon...did you decide on a date?"

"Yes. I remembered that Tom and Beth will be moving up in two weeks, so the first date may be a little hard for them, also for Jim. It'll be in three weeks, if that is all right for you?"

"You're right, of course, but I say, let's just elope," he said, pulling her down on his lap.

"Guess we'd better not. Everyone has gone out to eat. I'm hungry, aren't you?"

"Yes, hungry for a kiss!" She put her arms around his neck and kissed him thoroughly. "We'd better go," she whispered close to his ear, "or someone will come looking for us."

"I like this, getting a kiss now too, not just a hug."

"Yes, me too," and they kissed again. "I'm afraid that your legs will soon get paralyzed," she laughed as she got up. "Come on."

The family discussed plans for the next day, maybe to stop at a restaurant for lunch after church.

"No," Danielle said, "Everyone just stop and pick up a salad or pizza or something after church and come on over here again. I'll get fried chicken. That way we can spend more time together. I have lots of paper plates and a dishwasher."

They all agreed. Good nights were soon said, and they were gone home.

"Mom, you can sleep in Ann Marie's room. Alex, the couch in the family room opens into a good bed."

"I could go to a motel," Alex started to protest.

"Not unless you really want to," Danielle told him.

"No, I would really rather stay here, if it isn't too much trouble."

"It'll only take a minute to fix your bed."

Ann Marie had her Grandmother's hand, "Come on Grandma, let's go to bed."

"Okay Honey, but I need to get my bag."

"I'll get your things, unless you want to go with me?"

"Yes, I'll come; you'll have too much to carry."

"I'll help too, Grandma." Her bags were soon deposited in Ann Marie's room.

"Let's go see if I can help with the couch," she told Ann Marie.

"All done, now to bed, Ann Marie," Danielle said.

"Good Night, Alex."

Putting his arms around Eva, Alex bent down to kiss her. "Good Night Sweetheart."

"Goodnight, Sweetheart," she whispered back.

*

Eva woke from the nightmare crying.

The reoccurring nightmare where Henry was trying to drag her away from friends in a garden. This time he was trying to drag her away from Alex, forbidding her to walk with Alex, forbidding her to marry Alex.

She woke, disorientated, her thoughts *'where is Alex, is he gone? I've got to find him'* When she realized where she was, she crept quietly out of Ann Marie's room and went to find Alex. *'He's here, he's not gone,'*

"Alex," she said softly, touching his shoulder.

"Honey, what's wrong? Why, you're crying...and shaking like a leaf! Sweetheart, let me put my pants on."

"Now, come here, we'll sit in this chair. He held her in his arms on his lap.

"What's wrong? Honey, try to stop crying. Everything is all right, or I'll make it all right. Calm down; Honey, shush, shush. Tell me what's wrong."

"I had a nightmare," she sobbed.

Danielle came and turned on a low lamp. "Did mom have a nightmare again?"

"Yes. She's had them before?"

"Yes, but I don't think she's had one for a while. Calm down, Mom. It's all in the past. He can't hurt you anymore. You have a new life, remember? And what a life it's going to be from now on! Here's a cool wet cloth, wipe your face and eyes, it'll make you feel better."

"Did I wake Ann Marie?" Eva whispered, her voice catching on every word, "I…I tried to be quiet."

"No, she's sleeping. I heard something and knew it was you crying."

"I'm sorry that I woke you, I didn't mean to."

"It's all right Mom. I heard you let out a little scream in your sleep. I listened, and then thought I'd better come to check."

"Thank you. I'm okay now."

"All right. I'll go back to bed and leave her with you, Alex. Get some sleep. You're safe now, Mom."

"Yes, I know. Good Night."

Alex continued to hold Eva. He prayed, asking the Lord to calm her and – "give Eva peace. Lord. Help Eva to know that she is safe, that you're watching over her – and that she is safe in my love."

She lay in his arms, her head in the hollow of his shoulder. After final sob came and she relaxed, breathing normally at last. She lay quietly for a while, Alex kissing her hair gently.

'I belong here,' she thought, 'right here. I want to lay here, with my head on Alex's shoulder. I want to sleep here! Someday soon! Alex loves me. I love him, oh I really love him.' A surge of love filled her heart infusing her whole being with a warm glow, thrilling her.

Alex had been sleeping in a sleeveless undershirt, exposing bare skin. Her cheek rested there. *'I want to kiss this bare skin.'*

"Alex?"

"Yes, Sweetheart."

Her arms went around his neck, and she reached for a kiss. He kissed her tenderly.

"I'll go to bed now. I think I can sleep. I'd better let you go to bed."

"Sleep right here, if you want to. I can hold you like this all night."

"Alex? Alex, I love you."

"Oh Sweetheart, I love you! I'm going to do everything that I can put an end to those nightmares. Soon, I'll be beside you all the time. You'll be right here, next to my heart, where no bad dreams will have any right to come any more. Honey, you're safe now in my love."

"I know, Alex, and I'm so glad, so thankful. – I can't thank God enough for bringing you into my life, bringing us together. I'm so blessed!"

"God has blessed me, allowing me to have you for my own, soon to be my wife."

She stayed there a little longer in Alex's arms, the peace bringing contentment and then, Joy! At last she said, "I'm going to bed, I know that I'll be all right now."

And Eva slept quietly.

Alex did not sleep soon. Quite against his usual way of thinking, he wanted to punish the brute of a man who wasted 47 years with a woman as gentle as Eva. A man who inspired such terror as he'd witnessed tonight, a terror that lingered and attacked again after two years of safety.

Alex groaned in frustration at his inability to help her more, to erase those memories. His anger at the man was like a fire at the memory of her trembling and sobbing in his arms.

On his knees, he was asking for help from his Lord, when the word of the Lord rang in his mind: *"Avenge not yourselves, but rather give place unto wrath: for it is written, Vengeance is mine, saith the Lord. Give good for evil, my son, and go forth in a secure victory."*

Alex's anger was gone; leaving compassion for that man had lost forever a treasure. *A treasure that surely God has given to me to care for and love. Thank you Father God*, his heart cried for joy.

CHAPTER EIGHT

"Grandma?" A soft whisper, "Are you awake?" Ann Marie was anxiously leaning over her, when Eva opened her eyes.

"Good Morning, Ann Marie, Did I oversleep? Is it late? Is everyone up except me?"

"They are getting up; Mama and Alex are fixing breakfast. It's 'most ready."

"I'm up, I'm up! I'll hurry! Tell them I'll be there in a minute."

"Good morning, everyone."

"Good morning, Mom." Danielle greeted her.

Alex turned from the stove, anxious to se if there was havoc written on Eva's face, left from last night. She looked her usual self.

"Good morning, Sweetheart." He lay down a turner and came to her.

"Is Grandma your Sweetheart, Alex?" Ann Marie asked.

"That she is. She is a sweetheart, don't you think?"

"Yes, she's sweet and nice. Except when Davie and I fight. Then she frowns, and looks sad. She doesn't like it when Davie and I fight."

"Well, I guess that we had better not fight then, had we."

"Yes, it's a good idea to not fight."

"Grandma, what are you going to do with that step stool?"

"I'll show you." Eva answered.

Alex turned from putting eggs on a platter. "You found one!"

"Ann Marie, you see how tall Alex is?"

"Yes, he's tall."

"If I stand on this step, I'm just about tall enough."

Alex came and put his arms around Eve. "Now see, she can put her arms around my neck, like this."

Ann Marie laughed, "Look Mama."

"Yes, isn't that a good idea?"

"Yes. I like that idea," she laughed.

"Good Morning Sweetheart." Alex hugged her.

"Good Morning Sweetheart," Eva snuggled her face into his neck.

"Okay! Come on, let's eat."

"Joy and Hope leave already?"

"Yes, they wanted to get to church early for a special meeting for the young people. Joy and Hope are Danielle's twin daughters."

When they went to get into the car to go to church, Ann Marie asked, "Alex, may I ride in the front seat of your car?"

"Yes. Why don't we all ride in my car."

"How about me?" Davie asked.

"How about you riding in front seat on the way home?"

"Okay."

As they left the church, Alex asked, "Are we stopping at the store?"

"Yes," Danielle answered. I'm going to get something from the deli. They have a good deli at that this store."

"What shall we get Eva?" Alex asked.

"Let's see what Danielle is getting."

"I said that I would get fried chicken," Danielle said, "and fried potatoes."

"Eva here is a beautiful tray of fruits, and a tray of veggies and dip. And here are salads."

"Don't get too much," Danielle cautioned. "Everyone will bring something."

When they went to check out, Alex's cart was full, including a large floral arrangement for the table and a small bouquet for Eva. The clerk said to him, "Buying some flowers for your wife, I see."

"Yes, for my wife," with a big smile for Eva Jo. "Beautiful flowers for my beautiful wife."

The rest of the families were starting to arrive when they reached home. The tables were soon laden with all kinds of food. Alex brought the flowers to Danielle, "Where would you like this?"

"I think that we'll put it in the center of this table with the deserts. Thank you Alex."

Alex found himself standing beside Abbigail. "You girls, well everyone, are sure good at this, very efficient. And the food, there's everything."

"Well, we had a good teacher," Abbigail said. "Once Mom made a sit down dinner for 54 people, and served it with just us kids to help."

"Fifty four people at a sit-down dinner! She's an amazing woman."

"Yes, she is, as you'll find out."

"I can believe that! I think that you're all amazing, a great bunch."

"Thanks, and we have fun."

"I can see that. I'm glad to be here and be apart of all this."

"Mom taught her boys to cook and bake. Her grandsons can cook too, and they are all good cooks."

"It's the same with my boys. I believe that all men should be able to cook and take care of other house work too," Alex agreed.

Danielle came to Alex, "Alex, will you ask the blessing today, Please?"

Alex stood, with bowed head. "Lord, I stand here, overwhelmed, like Eva says. Overwhelmed to be here with this family, such a family that belongs to Eva, and to me too, if they'll let me. I give you honor and thanks. Thank you for the privilege of being here, being a part.

"Father God, I ask you to continue your many blessings to us, your children.

"Thank you also for the provision of this bountiful supply of good food. Bless it, Father. Bless it to use in our bodies. Bless our time together. We come humbly in the name of your Son, our Savior, and our Lord, the Christ. Amen"

"Amen." Echoed softly through the group.

Eva was beside him.

"Alex!" she said softly, putting her arm around his waist. Her smile was radiant, as she looked up at him through tears of joy.

"Eva, if I had known your family, I may never have dared to fall in love with you!"

"Would you have cheated me out of Love? Alex, you're a fine man. They all love you. Don't you dare back out on me now!"

"I won't. I'm just overwhelmed, like you said."

"Now you know how I felt," she laughed, the tears slipping out of her sparking eyes.

"Where is that step stool?" he said his grin coming back.

"Later," she smiled. "Come, my wonderful handsome man, let's have some food."

The family gathered around Eva and Alex to talk again. The afternoon and early evening went by and it was time for them to return to their homes. Each one had a word for them, to come back soon, how glad they were for Grandma or Mom. Glad for Alex too.

Jason said, "I think that my job will be out of work by Wednesday, until another job comes in. I think that I'll take you up on coming up, if you're sure it'll be all right?"

"Yes, Jason, do that. Can you come up then on Wednesday evening?"

"Yes, I'll plan on it,"

"Good. I'll be at your Mom's and we'll see you then. Plan to stay a few days I you can."

"I'm looking forward to it. Thank you Alex."

"We'll see you Wednesday evening."

Later after everyone was gone, Davie came to Alex and asked, "Can I see the pictures of your boat now?"

"Yes, Davie, they are over on that table. Why don't you bring them and I'll explain them for you."

Davie had lots of questions. "Is the boat as big as a car?"

"It's as big as three cars."

"Wow! Can you sleep on the boat?"

"Yes, there are little rooms that we call cabins. Each cabin has a bed or bunk beds, so several people can sleep on the boat. We are going to sleep on the boat for several weeks."

"How do you eat?"

"See here? This is a small table and a counter here to sit to eat too. This is where we cook, it's called a galley."

"It's small, not big like our kitchen."

"Yes it's small. Everything has to be smaller to fit on the boat."

"Grandma's going on the boat?"

"Yes, she said that she would like to."

"Where will she sleep?"

"Right here, this will be her bed."

"Is it a big bed?"

"Not as big as a king size bed, but big enough."

"Is it scary going on the water?"

"It might be a bit scary if a storm comes up, but it is a big boat with big motors, so it should be safe."

"I hope so, 'cause I don't want Grandma to get scared."

"No, I don't either. We have radios on the boat that we can talk to the Coast Guard to get weather reports, and call for help, if we should need to. We'll also have a ham radio that we can talk on, kind of like a telephone."

Davie stood looking at the pictures.

"Davie, if you're done looking at the boat, it's time for bed," his Dad said.

"David, would you like to keep the pictures of the boat?" Alex asked.

"Yes, I sure would! Thanks!"

Little did Davie know that he would get to see that boat in a few days, and go on it and see it all! Jim would take Davie and show him and Ann Marie the boat. The boat that was in Tacoma and Tacoma was a long ways away.

"Grandma, are you going to sleep in my room again tonight?" Ann Marie asked.

"Yes, just like last night. I'll be in soon. I'll try not to wake you when I come to bed."

"Will you have breakfast with Davie and I before we go to school?"

"Yes, I will. I'll get up in time for breakfast with you and Davie."

"Good Night Grandma,"

"Good night Ann Marie, good night Davie."

"G'night Grandma"

"Danielle, Gary, I want to thank you for these two wonderful days, opening your home so that I could meet and get acquainted with Eva's family."

"Alex, we are so happy for Mom, and you too. We all wanted to meet the man who could win Mom. You know she set some pretty high marks for you, don't you?"

"High? I wonder if I measure up to them all."

"I've been checking, and I think that you do. Did she tell you the first requirement?"

"No. None of them."

"She said that if she was to find a man, God would have to hit her in the face with him, that she would never look. I think that is kind of what happened, except that maybe she helped God out by running into you!"

They all laughed at that, including Eva.

"I'm sure glad of that! I was hurrying too. Come to think of it, I did hit her in the face. Her face hit my chest pretty good and hard. Did it hurt you?"

"No, I don't remember that it did," she laughed.

The telephone rang. It was for Alex. "Alex, this is Jim. The contractor wants to start on the house early in the morning, and I don't suppose that you'll be home early."

"No, we are staying over. It'll be towards evening when we get home."

"I'm at your house now, and it's okay, I don't have classes tomorrow and I'll be here all day. David and Bill both have to be at the shop as some of the machinery is being delivered and set up tomorrow."

"Thank you Jim, that'll be great if you can be there. The plans are on the dinning room table."

"Yes, I've been looking at them. Alex, Bill said that he and David would both be at your house on Tuesday, so if you want to stay, it'll be covered. They can't do anything until the rest of the machinery is delivered on Thursday."

"It'll be great to have their help. I'll call you tomorrow if we are not coming home, but I think that we'll be home tomorrow evening.

"And Jim, I'd better tell you, I've asked Eva to marry me and she said yes. We are to be married in three weeks."

"Wow! Alex, you sure didn't waste time did you! I'm glad! I was hoping it might happen, but I didn't expect it to happen so soon. Congratulations! I can't tell you how much I hope and pray for happiness for you both. I like her, a whole bunch. This is just great!"

Gary soon excused himself, "I have to get up early for work, so I have to get to bed."

"I think that might be a good for the rest of us, especially after Eva's short night last night."

"I'm fine," she protested, but she was soon in bed.

CHAPTER NINE

"Good morning Grandma."

"Good morning Ann Marie."

"I'm almost dressed."

"I see you are, I'll hurry."

"I was out in the kitchen and Mama said that I could wear this dress."

"What a pretty dress, I like it. You like to wear dresses don't you?"

"Yes. Come on Grandma. Mama and Alex are out in the kitchen, cooking breakfast again. Does Alex like to cook?"

"Yes he does. He cooks dinner sometimes too."

"I like Alex, Grandma."

"Me too. Tell them that I'll be there soon."

"Good morning everyone!"

"Grandma, I brought the step stool for you."

"Thank you Ann Marie!"

"Good morning, Sweetheart."

"Good morning Alex."

"Do you have a step stool at your house, Grandma?"

"Yes Honey, I do."

Alex was quietly chuckling.

"Good morning Davie, are you ready for breakfast?"

"Morning, Grandma, yes I'm about starved."

"Come on everyone, its time for school kids to eat breakfast."

Breakfast finished, Eva shook her head. "Well, David, Ann Marie, we've wasted so much time this morning, I'll have to take you to school."

"Good. Can we take Alex's car?"

"Yes, David. Here take the keys for your Mom."

"Alex! Now you're going to help spoil my kids."

"I'd like to, a little anyway," he laughed. "Don't forget seat belts."

"Mom, Alex, let's sit down and have a cup of coffee. The kids are in school and I can catch my breath."

"Honey, it's been a hectic weekend for you, you haven't had much time to relax."

"It's been a wonderful weekend! All your kids and grand kids, not only got to see you, Mom, but meet Alex too."

"Yes, it's been a great weekend for me. I don't get to see everyone very often. They all seem to approve of our plans."

"Yes, Mom, and then I think that we all put the rush on for

you. We want you to be happy and I believe that you're going to be."

"Danielle, I'm going to do everything that I can to make your Mom happy."

"I believe that you will, Alex."

"I don't need much to make me happy. Some one to love me. What more do I need?" Eva smiled through tears.

"Happy? I'm ecstatic – quit a bit overwhelmed! I have a beautiful loving family, and a lover! A beautiful, handsome lover! Who says that he is going to marry me! ME! He loves ME!"

"Eva, I think that you need new glasses – but maybe not until after we are married," Alex laughed, "and I haven't found a high hill yet, where I can let out a good yell. You once called me a poor guy because you ran into me, but I'm rich, rich in worthwhile things. I'm getting a pearl of a girl, and that is not just a cliché. The Bible calls a virtuous woman, a price far above rubies!"

"So, Mom's painting brought you together – what about that painting?"

"Yes, and that painting is going to hang in the living room of our apartment."

Abbigail called to say that she had found the fabric for her Mom's dress, "And are you coming in today or shall I come out?"

"We'll go home today and we'll stop at your place." Eva turned to Alex, when shall we go?"

"Any time you want to go."

Danielle said, "Let's go have lunch with Abbi; I want to see the fabric and pattern too."

"Yes, we'll do that," Alex agreed.

"We'll be there soon," Eva told Abbigail.

"Danielle, ride with us, we'll bring you home," Alex urged.

Making her voice sound like Ann Marie's, Danielle asked, "Can I ride in the front seat of your car, Alex?"

"Sure, plenty of room. Eva sits next to me," he laughed.

Alex asked Abbigail, "May I look at your new motor home while you girls are busy?"

"Sure, I'll get the keys."

Later as he brought the keys back he said, "I think that Eva and I'll have a motor home too. After we get back from our boat trip, we'll buy one."

"Alex! Really? Eva asked.

Éeeee-yup," he laughed. "Do you know how often you say 'Eeee-yup', Eva? And Ann Marie does too."

"Do I really say that yet?"

"Eeeee-yup, you sure do," they chorused laughing.

"Eeeee-yup, I guess I do," she joined the laugh.

"We are through with the fitting, shall we go someplace for lunch? Abbi, where is a good place around here to eat? I know that you and Leo have a favorite Pizza place, but since he's at work-"

"Yes Mom, Pizza is Leo's favorite food next to chili, but we do go some where else occasionally." Abbigail laughed.

After leaving Portland on the way home, they had grown quiet. Eva snuggled down with her head against Alex's arm.

"Tired?" he asked.

"No, just content. Happy and content being here, right here luxuriating, wow that's a good word for it. I'm luxuriating in being in love, and right here beside you."

"That's a great word, luxuriating in our love. Me too, Sweetheart."

As they neared Mill Town, Alex said, 'I suppose we should stop at your Sis's and tell her."

"Yes, let's. She'll be so glad."

"Are you sure?"

"Yes. She'll be very glad."

"Their car isn't home. Maybe they are at the Big Tree restaurant for dinner. Let's go see. They were. "Hi, may we join you, or are you through?"

"Sit down, we just ordered," Ben invited.

After they had ordered, Eva reached her left hand across to Jewel. Look Sis!"

"Eva...a ring! A beautiful ring! Really? For sure?"

"Really! For sure!" they echoed together.

"Well, how about that," Ben joined in admiring the ring.

They brought Jewel and Ben up to date with their plans, receiving congratulations and blessings. As they left the restaurant, Alex said, "Tomorrow we'll go to your brother Len, but tonight I think that you need some rest. It's been a rather exciting long weekend."

Brandon and Billie met them on the deck as they came home so they shared their plans with them too.

Brandon shook Alex's hand in congratulations and said, "I thought this would happen, but didn't expect it quite so soon. I'm glad for you both."

Billie was smiling through tears when she hugged Eva.

"I'm so happy for you!"

"We'll leave you two alone," Brandon said. Are you spending the night Alex? I'll leave the door unlocked."

"Yes. I'll be in soon. I want this lady to get to rest soon. Good night."

"Eva, shall we sit here in the glider love seat? I'll get the blanket; it's a bit chilly tonight. I want to sit here with you next to my heart and like you said,' luxuriate' in our love."

Which they did, and shared a kiss or two.

"Alex?"

"Yes?"

"May I sit on your lap for just a few minutes?"

"Yes, would you?"

"Hello, Alex," she whispered near his ear.

"Hello Darling." he whispered back, hugging her tighter, kissing her cheek. Her arms went around his neck, her cheek against his.

She thought, *'Oh! I really love this guy.'*

Aloud she said, "Thank you Father God for this guy and thank you for the love that we share. And God I really do love him."

"Father God, I thank you for his dear Lady. I too thank you for the love we share. I thank you for bringing us together, for helping us find each other. Because you have arranged this for us, we know that you'll continue to bless us."

There were tears of happiness on both faces.

"I don't want you too tired; maybe we'd better not wait for the moon tonight. It may be an hour before it comes up."

"Okay, just a few more minutes, it's early yet. Am I crushing your legs? I can move."

"No, I could hold you all night," hugging her tightly.

She turned her head, her lips brushed his, and the kiss lingered and spoke of the love that they shared. It was a kiss of love and promise that more love would come.

"Oh Alex, the moon!"

"Yes, like a benediction upon our love. 'Our silver path…to a golden love.'"

After another kiss, she slipped from his lap to sit beside him again.

Soon Alex said, "It's ten o'clock."

"Yes, we must go in. You have to get up early in the morning."

"Honey Girl, sleep in if you can in the morning. I'll try to not wake you. Good Night Sweetheart."

"Good Night, Alex, my Love."

*

Eva woke with a start on Tuesday morning.

"Oh did I hear Alex leave?"

She jumped out of bed and hurried to the front window to see if Alex's car was there.

"No, he's still here." She hurriedly showered, dressed, and was starting coffee, when Alex came across the deck. She met him at the door, "Good morning Alex, Come in."

"Now for a real good morning," he said as he came from the bathroom. He set out the step stool and reached for her hand to help her onto the step.

"Good morning, Sweetheart," he whispered against her hair, hugging her tightly.

"Good Morning, Sweetheart," she whispered. Their kiss was sweet too. "Alex, I like your shaving lotion."

"It sure beats whiskers with a kiss," he chuckled.

"I think so. You haven't kissed me with your whiskers."

"I'm going to keep it that way. I don't want you dodging me."

"Good."

As they finished breakfast dishes, Alex said, "Eva, come with me today. I know that there is going to be a mess in places, but the main part of the house will not be disturbed."

Eva hesitated, thinking, *I'll be alone all day if I stay home. We've been together for three days; I guess I'm getting spoiled. What is the matter with me? I don't want to be alone.'*

"Honey, what's wrong? Getting second thoughts?"

"No, it's not like that at all. I don't know what is wrong with me. I've been alone, by myself for nearly two years, and now we've been together most of the time for three days and the thoughts of being alone today – scares me.

I don't want to be alone all day. I should stay home and do some things. Jason is coming tomorrow and I need to move some things in that room so he can sleep there."

"Eva, come sit down a minute." He pulled her to his lap and held her in his arms.

"How about coming with me today. We'll get the men started working on the house and maybe tomorrow they won't need us and we can do the things you want done here. Will that work?"

"Okay, Alex. I feel a little silly, being afraid. I don't know why. I just feel safe when I'm with you."

"I'm glad that you're not afraid of me, Honey. We can take care of the other fears. God brings peace to his children, you know, and He is taking care of us."

"Yes, He is, but sometimes I need to be reminded of that."

"I really need you with me today; I want to go select carpeting for the apartment."

"Does it need new carpeting? It looks new everywhere."

"Well, it is maybe twenty years old, down stairs. Anyway, we'll see. One more kiss then we'll go."

As they stopped for a stoplight, Eva slid her arm under Alex's arm and hugged it.

He grinned at her, "I sure am glad that you came with me," he said.

"Me too."

"Together, Sweetheart, we belong together," he continued, "The two of us together remember! Soon we'll be together all the time."

"Together," she echoed. "We've been together most of the time for 9 days now. Today is the ninth day! I can hardly believe it. Nine days since we met, and here we are counting the days until we are married. It's a bit overwhelming, more than a bit. It's a whole lot overwhelming."

"Overwhelmingly wonderful, my darling Lady. How did you say it, I'm ecstatically happy!"

When they reached the house, they checked on the work that had already been done and Alex was pleased with the progress. Bill and David were soon there, the rest of the crew arriving shortly. Bill got the crew started.

All business, he asked, "When will the carpeting be delivered? We could use part of it this afternoon, and the rest tomorrow morning."

David joined in, "The new bathroom fixtures, we could use to day. The kitchen cabinets are here now, but the stove and refrigerator could be delivered today too, tomorrow at the latest. Here are lists of sizes and measurements."

"By the way, what's this we hear about you getting married?'

Eva was standing in awe of the men. Alex put his arm around her, drawing her forward. "Yes, it's true. In three weeks, but I wish it was sooner." Bill and David both gripped Alex's hand, congratulating him, turning to Eva Jo, "Do we get to kiss the Bride to be?"

"Yes, of course," she agreed happily, blushing a bit.

"Dad, I like the Lady," David said.

"Yes, me too," Bill added.

"Now Alex, go order things so we can get this job done."

"We're going. Come on Eva before these slave drivers decide to put us to work instead."

"Oh Dad, Jordi, Mrs. Jordan is looking for you. She's upstairs somewhere," David added.

They found Mrs. Jordan in the laundry.

"Jordi, I want you to meet my soon to be wife, Eva. Eva this is Mrs. Jordan. She has come in three days a week and has been keeping my house livable for several years."

"I'm happy to meet you, my dear. May I call you Eva or shall I call you Mrs. Harmon?"

"Please call me Eva, Mrs. Jordan. I'm happy to meet you."

"Call me Jordi, if you like."

"Thank you Jordi."

"I have some coffee ready, Alex."

"Thank you Jordi, we'll have a cup if you'll sit down for a few minutes and have one with us. You wanted to see me?"

"Yes. Do you want me to come everyday and vacuum after the men?"

"Jordi, I wanted to ask you if you could come and live here full time, and help us. I'll put you on full salary, with a household expense account. Eva and I'll be in an apartment that we are fixing. You'll have rooms down stairs. Tom and Beth will be moving home soon and have the main part of the house. They'll probably need help too. It's a big house, as you know and you may be needed much of the time."

"Yes Alex, I could do that, for a while at least. My sister, Hetti has just come to live with me and she can live at my place and can take over my other jobs. Then if you should not need me full time later, I could move home again. We'll try it and see how it goes."

"Agreed. Jordi, you know how to keep house, so just take over, If you should need help, go ahead and find someone. Let Tom or me know if you need more money."

"Yes, I can do that. Hetti can help if we need more help"

"Good. We'll leave you in charge. Eva and I are going to do some shopping; we'll see you after while."

"Shall I fix lunch for the men?"

"They would like that, I'm sure, if you want to do it. Just go ahead and make your own decisions, just don't over work. It may be rather a mess around here for a few days, if you need more help, get Hetti, if she can come.

Just do as you think best, and we'll appreciate it."

"I'm going to stop here at this bank, and put you and Beth, as well as Jordi, on the household expense account."

"Can you afford that? I've money of my own."

"Yes, Dear, I can. The money is automatically deposited and is to be used. Eva, didn't I tell you that I have a good income?"

"Did you? I don't know. I've not thought, I guess. Alex, I'm just a plain gal. – I've never had a lot. I don't know – I've never had experience like this – a housekeeper? An expense account? – What else are you going to overwhelm me with?"

"Just one thing more for right now, your own checking and credit account. We'll do that now too."

"No, Alex. No. It's too much. I can't let you do that."

"Yes, I *am* going to do this. Of course you can't go buy a new car every day," he laughed, "but you're to have money of you own to use as you please."

"But Alex, I won't need it. I've some income each month and if you're taking care of all other expenses, I don't need more."

"If you need it or not, I want to do this. It'll make *me* happy to do this." He put his arm around her – "Eva, honey, is this our first quarrel?"

She hid her face on his shoulder. "No quarrel, Alex. I'm just – just overwhelmed again. I'm used to a simple life."

"Honey, don't cry. Someone might call the police, thinking that I'm abusing you," he laughed softly against her hair. "I live a simple life too, no high entertaining or parties for me. Just family and a few friends, and Church. And now a honeymoon trip. A honeymoon trip with my darling wife! My Sweetheart! The dearest, sweetest Lady in the world!"

"Oh Alex, you're so good, so great — such a dear man. I cannot yet comprehend what all I'm getting. Just you is enough. I don't need all the rest. Just you loving me, is enough."

"Yes, just me loving you and you loving me. Come on now, we're going into the bank. Tears all gone?"

"Yes, for now anyway."

He tipped her chin, up to look into her eyes, and then kissed her gently.

"Darling!" She put her arms around his neck and kissed him again.

He laughed softly; "The bank might not allow extended kissing parties in the parking lot."

"Probably not," she laughed. "I don't see anyone coming to object yet."

"We'll take this up later, when we have more privacy and time," he promised.

They took care of the business at the bank and then the shopping, returning to the house to report the delivery times to David and Bill.

"Dad," David said, "Bill and I've been looking at the house and have another idea. Come see what you think."

"Go ahead, Alex. I want to look at the living room in our apartment again." Eva said.

"Alex wants to hang my painting here," she thought, looking at the newly painted walls.

Then she went up stars to look at the paintings there.

"I want to have a new frame for the painting. Can I give it to Alex for a wedding present?" she wondered.

She found Mrs. Jordan. "Jordi, may I ask your advice?"

"Yes Eva, of course you may. Come sit, have a cup of tea with me."

"Thank you, that'll be nice."

"Now my dear, how may I help you?"

"Alex likes one of my paintings, and wants to hang it in our apartment. Could I give it to him for a wedding gift? I don't know what else I could give him."

"Yes, I think that would make an excellent wedding gift. Are you going to give him a wedding ring too?"

"Could I? Would he wear it?"

"I'm sure that he would be very happy if you gave him one, and I'm sure that he would wear it."

"Did you see this ring that he gave me? I don't know about a wedding band to go with it. Some times they have Bride and Groom sets, but I don't know about this one."

"Ask Alex. Tell him that you would like to get him a wedding ring. You'll have to know the size too."

"I will. Thank you, Jordi"

*

Meanwhile Alex with David and Bill, were outside the garage.

"Dad, Jordi said that you want her to stay on here full time as a live in housekeeper. She was down stairs looking at the rooms to see which she could use without taking rooms that the family would use. Bill and I were talking and looking around, why don't we build a garage big enough for all the cars that you may have around here, and convert the attached present garage into an apartment for Jordi and her sister. They would be right here, yet have their own apartment. They rent where they are."

Bill added. "We can build a bigger garage over here, putting a covered breezeway across to the house. It won't detract from the house, but add to the look. There is plenty of room for it."

"We can install Jordi and Hetti down stairs until we have their apartment finished, and get them settled long before you return from the trip."

"What a plan! Let's do it."

"As soon as your apartment is finished, we'll have the crew start on the rest."

"Jim said that the last of the equipment will be delivered on Thursday, how is the shop going?" Alex asked

"Yes it is, and we should be getting everything running by Monday. New orders came in and we are going to need Tom and Bill Jr. working full time and then some."

"That is something that I wanted to talk to you about. Eva's son Jason is coming up. I'd like for you guys to talk to him. He is interested in our shop and may go to work with us. He's had experience with different machines. Right now he is working metal, but he'd like to work with wood."

"Bring him in, Alex. We'll do our best by him. We sure could more help. Our present crew is going to be overloaded, if we don't get more help. We may have a hard time getting some of the orders out on time."

"He is coming tomorrow evening."

"Bring him in on Thursday; he'll be there to see some of the machinery set up."

"I'll do that. I keep forgetting that you guys are in a time squeeze."

"That's okay, Dad, we really can't expect a guy who's in love and getting married soon, to be much help to us," David laughed, slapping his dad on the back. He continued, "Bill can be at the shop on Thursday, and I'll be here, if we are not done here. The way things are going, I think that we'll have your apartment done by tomorrow evening."

"We'll have it covered, Alex," Bill agreed. "When the crew gets done on the apartment, they can start on Jordi's apartment and the garage."

As they started back to the apartment, Bill said, "Alex, I want to tell you how glad we are that you found Eva. It's about time for you to have a life besides the shop."

"Yes Dad, she's a great gal for you."

"Isn't she though. Thanks guys. I'm so happy with her, so thankful that God brought her into my life. I'd better go see what she's doing. We are going out to her place soon. We haven't been to her Brother's yet."

"Thanks men, for all the help, seeing to the work here and everything."

"We are going to do our best to see to it that you get safely married, whatever it takes," Bill laughed.

"That's right, Dad," David agreed.

Eva and Jordi were sitting with tea, when Alex found them. The phone rang as Jordi poured a cup for him. When Alex returned from the phone, he had a big grin.

"Great news! That was Tom on the phone and they are on their way. They'll be here tomorrow by evening."

Alex leaned over the rail to call down to Bill and David, "Tom and Beth will be here tomorrow!"

Jim came in as Alex sat down to have his tea. "Join us Jim," Alex greeted him.

"First I want to kiss the bride," Jim grinned. Eva stood to receive the kiss.

"Congratulations Alex. I'm happy for you both. I know that the two of you'll be happy together."

"Jim, I wish that you were a minister now, and could marry us. Eva…that's something that we forgot to do, find a minister!"

"Oh no! We *did* forget…it's all happening so fast."

Soon Alex said, "We'd better go, if we're going to have any time with your Brother today."

In the car, Eva asked, "Alex, may I buy a wedding ring for you? I know that you must not wear it around machinery, but would you want one, and wear one?"

"Yes, I would like very much to have a wedding ring. I'd wear it all the time, except when I was around the machinery."

"I need to know the size and the jeweler where you bought my ring." Alex gave her the information. "I'll ask Jewel if she can go shopping with me tomorrow, while you take Jason to the shop."

They spent a few hours with Eva's brother, Len and her sister-in-law, Alice, receiving their best wishes. Jewel had told them about Alex and had kept them up to date on what was happening.

As they left Alice and Len, Eva said, "They like you Alex, and they are glad for me."

"Eva, I'm so glad to be accepted by your family. So readily accepted on face value. I've not had to prove myself to any of them."

"Alex, you're so real, such a good man. No falseness, no braggadocio, no giant ego, no 'I, ME, MINE', that is how you have proved yourself. You're not full of yourself. You're real. You love the Lord. And you love ME. They can know that in just a few minutes."

"Yes, Sweetheart, I love the Lord. I'm so glad that He gave you to me to love. I'm so very blessed!"

"Me too! What a great God we have. To not just let all this happen, but to bring it all about, to bring us together."

"Alex, I'm so glad your family is accepting me too. They are such nice people, and Jim, he's like family too."

"Yes, Jim is family."

Abbigail called shortly after they got home. "Mom, I've been trying to call you all day. When can you come down to try your dress on?"

"Oh! Well, maybe tomorrow. If Alex can't come, maybe Jewel will come with me. I'll call you back and let you know."

"Okay. Another thing, Mom, Danielle and I have been trying to find a minister for the wedding. Our minister is the only one free, and the only one day that HE is free, is on June first– a week from Saturday. Will that be all right?

"I know that it is setting the wedding up a week sooner, but it's the best we can do, unless we go to a mid-week date. Can you check with Alex and his family?"

"Oh! Yes, I'll check with them and let you know."

"We asked the minister to hold that date open for us, not to let anything else be set for then."

"I'll call you back as soon as I can."

Alex and Brandon were on the deck, broiling steaks.

"Alex!"

"What's up, Eva? You look troubled." Alex handed the fork to Brandon.

"Abbigail called."

"Is something wrong? Come sit down, now tell me."

"No, nothing is wrong, I think that everything will be all right - okay - it's just – rushing me again."

"Well, that sounds good so far. Now tell me what Abbigail said."

"Well, first, she wants me to come down and try on my dress."

"Okay, so far…that's doable."

"Yes, of course."

"That's first, what is second or next?"

"You remember, we had forgotten about a minister?"

"Yes, we did."

"Well, Abbi and Danielle have been checking with the ministers, and the only one who is free, is on June first, a week from Saturday, setting the wedding up a week earlier."

Alex stood up, walked out on the boat dock, through his arms up in the air, and let out a mighty whoop- "Yahoo!" and again – "Yahoo!"

Ducks all over the lake set up a ruckus in response, some taking flight, and coming.

Brandon and Billie began to laugh, "It's about time, Alex," Brandon laughed.

Alex came and grabbed Eva up and lifting her off her feet, hugging her.

"Yes! Yes! Sweetheart, that's perfect! Tom and Beth will be here and settled before then. Bill Jr. will be here tomorrow. Mike, Ray, and families will be here next Monday and are staying for a month. The Harmon clan will all be here. The house will be back to in order, except for the new wing, that we don't need just yet. I'm ready to get married. Are you?"

His whole face was lit up in a smile. "Are you ready, Eva?" he repeated.

"Yes! Well, I can be. Yes! Yes...I'll be ready!" Her face was radiant, too.

"Well, the *steaks* are ready...to eat, that is! Can you two come down to earth long enough to eat supper now?" Brandon interjected, setting the steaming platter of beef on the table.

Billie, taking them each by an arm, steered them to the table. "Love is wonderful, but food is appropriate at this moment," she laughed.

Eva asked, "Billie, Brandon, you'll come to our wedding won't you."

"Yes, we wouldn't miss your wedding."

Alex took a small notebook from a pocket, "Yes, I have you down on the list for the motel. I'll call them and confirm the new date. Better yet, let's go down there in the morning and check it out, and you can try on your dress."

"A motel? We're on a list for a motel?" Brandon asked.

"Yes. We'd like for everyone to go down on Friday afternoon or evening and meet at the Motel. We'll have a dinning room for the evening Friday and for the reception after the wedding on Saturday. The rooms and all meals from Friday evening through lunch on Sunday are furnished. We are doing that for all friends and family, so that they can get acquainted. Our families haven't met yet."

"I can understand that. You two just met a couple of weeks ago, and now you're getting married in another week. Some rush!" Brandon laughed.

"Yes," Alex agreed, "But the trip's scheduled for a departure date of June fourth to the tenth at the latest, because of the other boat that is going. We need to go when they go; they're setting the departure date. I want Eva to go with me. I won't go without her. Even if we don't make the trip, I want us to be together."

Alex smiled at Eva. Her smile was radiant and she was starry eyed.

Later, Alex asked Brandon if he knew yet if he was getting the promotion that he was expecting.

"Yes, but the pay raise isn't quite what I had hoped for."

"Are you going to be able to buy the house that you looked at?"

"No. They had a cash offer and took it. We'll have to start looking again."

Alex wrote an address on a card, "Drive over, and look at this house. The people in it are leaving as soon as school is out. They are teachers and are moving to another school district. If you like the looks from the outside, give them a call, and they'll show you the house."

"You own this?"

"Yes. It's just a few blocks from the one you looked at."

"But we would like to buy."

"I'll sell it to you. No down payment, no interest to you kids. Check it out, look it over good. If it needs anything, I'll have it done. I've ordered it painted inside and out."

Alex handed Brandon another card, "This is who is doing the work; go with him to pick out the carpeting. It is a little bigger than the house that you looked at. It's a good house. I'd like to sell it. You pay the taxes and keep it up." Alex gave the price and amount of payments. "But look it over, it may not be what you want."

"That is a good neighborhood of beautiful homes. We've been all over there, as we wanted to be close to the schools there. Alex, we aren't family – you can't sell to us with no down and no interest."

"Yes I can."

Brandon and Billie were looking at him speechlessly.

Billie jumped up and threw her arms around Alex where he sat on the bench. Tears were running down her face. "I have no words good enough – you are so good!

"You had better look at it before you get too excited," Alex said, hugging her. Alex turned to Eva, "We can claim another son and daughter, can't we, Hon?"

"Yes, we sure can. I love these kids."

Billie put her arms around Eva, tears still slipping down her cheeks.

"We don't either of us have any family," she sobbed.

"Well, you do now, Honey," Eva assured her.

"Yes," Alex said, "From now on, you're included in all our family plans."

Brandon reached his hand to Alex. "I'm speechless, Alex!" There were tears in Brandon's eyes too.

Alex clasped Brandon's hand firmly, "Like Eva said, we love you kids."

Eva called Abbigail as soon as supper was cleared away. "We'll be down as early as we can make it. Do you suppose that Danielle will come in and go to lunch with us?'

"I'll call her, I'm sure that she will. We'll see you in the morning then."

CHAPTER TEN

Eva had just come from the shower when Alex was at the door. She waved for him to come in; "It isn't locked. I've started coffee." She dressed while Alex showered, and was fixing sausage and popping frozen waffles in the toaster, when he came out.

He set out the step stool and reached for her hand. "Good Morning, Sweetheart," he said hugging her tight.

"Good Morning, my love," she said, her arms around his neck.

"Hey, I like this, getting a kiss too."

"Me too. Breakfast is ready; we'll have to be quick."

"Yes, we'll have to leave soon."

"...and we have to be back fairly early."

"That's right! Jason is coming this evening, isn't he?"

They were soon on the way and in Portland by ten o'clock.

"I want to stop at the motel and get all the arrangements made first, and get that out of the way, so that we won't have to hurry away from Abbigail," Alex told Eva.

The motel welcomed their plans for the wedding party for those three days. Alex reserved the rooms for from Friday noon through Sunday afternoon, for the rooms and all meals and the two big dinners. He gave them a list of the names of those coming. The motel manager readily agreed that they would be able to do it.

Abbigail's husband, Leo was home, so he and Alex had time to visit while Abbigail and Danielle helped their Mom to try on the dress.

"It's perfect!" Danielle exclaimed.

Abbigail agreed, "It doesn't need a thing done to it. And here is the hat."

"Oh Abbigail, it is beautiful," Eva exclaimed. "What a wonderful dress and the hat! It's a clever work of art! I love it. Abbi, I can never thank you enough!"

"Mom, you look – just radiant!" Danielle exclaimed. "Mom, just to see you happy is all the thanks I need," Abbigail answered.

"Yes Mom, that's the best part, to see you happy," Danielle agreed.

"Do you want to take the dress with you?" Abbigail asked.

"Oh no, I'll leave it here, or at Danielle's. Which ever you girls think best."

"I can take it to Danielle's, ready for you to put on just before the wedding, don't you think Danielle?"

"Yes. We can use Ann Marie's room, and Alex can use Davie's room to change."

"Thank you Abbi, for making this beautiful dress and the hat! I love you so much. I've the best kids in the whole world."

With tear-filled eyes, Eva put her arms around Abbigail and kissed her.

"I loved doing it Mom. I'm so glad, so happy for you – yes happy for Alex too."

"Yes," Danielle agreed. "It's so good to see you happy! You're all lit up!"

"Am I?" Eva laughed softly, hugging Danielle too. "Yes, I'm happy! I didn't know that I could ever be so happy. Alex is such a great guy!"

"And so are you, Mom. But let's get this dress off and hung up before you get tears on it and crush it," Abbigail laughed. "But I don't think that it'll crush easily. I think that it'll be quite durable."

"Mom, look," Abbigail drew back a curtain. "These are yours too." There hung dresses and pantsuits.

"Oh my! You made all these?"

"I made the dresses, and Danielle bought the pant suits."

"Oh, my darling girls…it's so much!"

"We'll have everything at Danielle's ready for you."

Eva admired and exclaimed over each one.

"The other girls, your daughters-in-law and grand daughters are getting some things together too, slips, nighties, robes and things. You'll only have to buy shoes."

"Oh, my dears!"

Finally, Abbigail said, "We need to go to lunch soon. Leo has to go to work at two o'clock."

As they came out of the bedroom that Abbigail had converted into a sewing room, Leo said, "Are you girls ready to go to lunch? I'm starving."

"He probably is," Abbigail laughed. "He has only had coffee, this morning. He never eats early."

"Here are my keys," Alex said, "Leo, drive my car as I might get lost here in Portland. I'll sit here in the back seat with my Eva."

"Sit up front too, Danielle, let those young lovers have the back seat."

"Right here, next to my heart," Alex said softly, bending his head close. Eva looked up at him, "Do I see tears, my love?"

"Only tears of happiness!"

"No more doubts or fears?"

"No. Not of you anyway."

"Nothing else matters if I love you and you love me."

"Oh Alex, I do love you1."

"My dear, dear Sweetheart. One day soon, I'll call you all the names that I have in my heart, and wish that I had more words, another language. Do I dare kiss you?"

"Yes!"

"Okay, you lovers, here we are at my favorite restaurant. They have both chili and pizza."

"They must have heard about you Leo, and built this restaurant for you," Danielle laughed.

"They do have other food here too," Abbigail laughed.

"Do you suppose that they have chili pizza?" Eva laughed.

"Hey," Leo exclaimed, "I'll ask them to make one for me."

That was greeted with laughter.

Still, when Leo asked, they agreed to make it for him

"Ahh," Leo admired it. "Thin Pizza crust, chili with beans, cheese, Jalapeños, fresh onions, pepperoni, more cheese, black olives. Perfect! Now how do I eat it?" It was at least two inches thick.

"*This* we want to see," Danielle laughed.

Abbigail was wishing for her camera. "It's a good thing that they brought us plates."

"That's for sure," Leo said, as he slid an overflowing piece of chili pizza onto a plate.

"May I try it?" Alex asked.

"Sure, that's why I had them make a large size."

Eva tried it too, but she took off the Jalapenos. The other girls are not great chili or pepper lovers.

They lingered over coffee and tea, talking a while.

"This family enjoys being together, making lunch at a pizza parlor an exciting time." Alex said.

A chorus of *yeses* answered.

"Life with Leo is an adventure," Abbigail laughed.

"What do you mean," Leo challenged. "Life with Abbigail has been an adventure from the moment we got married. She took me, a poor city boy, and took him camping right off. *Me*...who'd never smelled country air, I almost got drunk on fresh air...and that was only the beginning! She took me out in a boat fishing up at Timothy Lake. Then *she* caught all the fish and taught me how to clean them. Cooking over a campfire, now that was something. The things that she can do with a tarp or two.

"She can make a whole house that looks like some nomadic tribe, with a tarp, a piece of string, and some small rocks...and it stays up!"

"Then she tamed the chipmunks. They got so tame that they got right into my plate. I had to eat fast or I wouldn't get a thing to eat. Then she made a swing for them by putting peanut butter on a pinecone and hung it from a tree. They would jump on the pinecone for the peanut butter and hang on, and away they would go, swinging. Talk about adventure, I have some hair-raising stories to tell you." They were all laughing.

"I can believe that," Alex joined the laughter. He continued, "I love it. I hope that life'll be full of just such adventures for Eva and I."

"It is starting out on adventure, that trip on the boat." Danielle said.

"Oh, but it's been and adventure ever since I went down on the waterfront to paint," Eva exclaimed.

"Well now, if we are going back, let's go back to the day eight weeks and 4 days ago."

"Alex, you know that exact day?"

"Eva! Don't you know 'that day' will always be mighty important to me, one of the most important days of my life? It'll be eleven weeks to the day on our wedding day." He sat holding her hand, smiling at her.

"I think that's great!" Danielle said, Abbigail agreeing.

"Alex, Mom, speaking of weddings, what about flowers? Have you thought of what you want?"

"Flowers?" they both said.

"Oh. Can I have some or a corsage?" Eva asked.

"Yes, of course," the girls echoed.

'Yes, Dear Heart." Alex agreed. "Is there a florist near by that will deliver? Let's take care of that when we leave here."

"It's about time for me to go to work, if you'll drop me off at home," Leo said at last.

As they left the florist, Alex asked, "What else do we need to do while we are here?"

"Have you seen the minister yet? He wants to talk to you."

"Let's go do that now."

*

It was almost 5 o'clock when they got back to Eva's apartment. Brandon greeted them, "We are doing hamburgers, come join us."

"Sounds good. We'll see what we can add."

Just as they were ready to eat, Jason drove up. They greeted him and introduced him to Brandon and Billie.

"Burgers are ready, come join us," Brandon invited

"Smells good! I have an offering." He brought a melon. "I found a Crenshaw melon. I know that Mom loves them as much as I do."

They enjoyed a leisurely supper on the deck, and watched the sunset on the lake.

"Jason, I didn't get this room finished for you, but I did move most of it to the side so you can get in here. And there is plenty of room to hang up your things."

"It is fine Mom. Nothing is in my way. It's a nice room. Maybe I'll be able to see your paintings."

"I tried to get them out of the way, so they are standing against the wall. Except the one on the display easel. It's not completely dry yet."

"So this is 'the painting'! I like it Mom."

"I've laid claim to it," Alex said.

"I can understand why, not just because it's good, but the consequences of the painting of it."

"That's right!" Alex joined the laugh.

"You guys can laugh about me getting into a – situation with my painting, but someday I may do something really sensational."

"Now what are you up to, Eva?"

"I don't know yet, but I'll think of something."

"She probably will too, Alex." They were still laughing.

"Do I get a kiss?"

"Do you think that you could get out the door?" she laughed as she stepped up on the step stool.

"Maybe I'd better not try," he laughed, then kissed her thoroughly.

CHAPTER ELEVEN

The insistent ringing of the telephone woke Eva. She looked at the clock – five o'clock! Who in the world...?

"Hello my Mom, this is Steve."

"Hello Steve. How are you?"

"I'm fine Mom. Will you pray for me? I have a paper to turn in today, and it's not going well. I'm going to try to get it right this morning before class, that's why I want your prayers."

"Yes. We'll pray right now." She prayed for God to bring the right things to Steve's remembrance and that he would be able to write it all down with clarity, power, and authority.

"Thank you Mom. I'm sure that I'll get it right now. I'm sorry to wake you so early, but I was about desperate. This will make my grade."

"I'm glad that you called, Steve; it's good to hear your voice. Can you call me this evening? I want to talk to you."

"What's up, Mom?"

"It's all good, but I don't want to take your thoughts away from your paper for now. This evening will be fine, if you have the time."

"Mom, I think that I'll come home for the weekend. I don't have classes until Monday."

"That would be even better than a phone call. Yes, do come."

"I don't have classes this afternoon, so I can be home by about 5."

"Great! You have your key, if I'm not home, come on in and I'll leave you a note."

"Okay, I'll see you this evening."

Eva hurried with her shower and dressing, but Jason had coffee brewing when she came out.

"Jason, Good Morning. I woke you."

"I heard the phone, I'm a light sleeper, you know."

'Go get your shower before Alex comes in. I'll tell you about the phone call later. I'll start breakfast."

Jason had set the table, and was sitting with a cup of coffee when Alex was ready for breakfast.

"Waffles, fresh made!" Alex grinned.

"Yes, there was time this morning."

"You must have awoke early this morning."

"I had an early phone call. Steve called me."

"Steve?" Both Alex and Jason looked puzzled.

"Steve, the young man who had this apartment. He's at college in Oregon, but he comes home here, whenever he can. He's coming home this evening for the weekend. He'll get to meet you both and you'll have a little time to get acquainted. He's a dear boy; I'm fond of him. I haven't told him about you yet, Alex."

"Well, another man in your life that I didn't know about," Alex teased her.

"He is young enough to be my grandson. You'll like him."

"I'm sure that I will, Eva. I just had to tease you," he grinned.

"Mom has a way of collecting people, and they are usually good people, or are soon after they meet her."

"I can believe that."

Breakfast over, Alex and Jason prepared to leave for the shop.

"What are your plans for today, Eva?"

"I'm hoping that Sis will go shopping with me. I hate to go alone."

"Shopping? Remember to use the credit set up for you."

"No, Alex, this I'll do myself. I can, I have the money."

"I can help you, Mom."

"Thank you both, but I can and will, do this myself."

"Is there a bit of a stubborn streak in this woman?" Alex asked.

"There is a bit at times." They were both smiling at her.

"Buy the things that you want for the wedding, but you'll need clothes for the boat trip. Use the account I set up for you for that. Promise that you will, or I'll go with you! Will you?"

"All right Alex, I will."

"Shall we meet you for lunch someplace? May I call you at the shop? Maybe we can."

"Sure, call."

On the way to town, Jason asked, "You know that my Dad is alive don't you?"

"Yes. Your Mother told me about an unhappy marriage and divorce."

After a few minutes Jason continued, "Dad was not a good husband. He didn't treat Mom right."

"That was over before I met her, and I'm going to spend the rest of my life making her happy. She's a pretty neat Lady."

"Yes she is. I believe that you'll make her very happy. She sure seems to be happy now. It's about time that she'd some happiness."

"I'm glad that you can see it. The past is past. I'm the winner of a pretty special Lady. Henry was the looser when he lost Eva's love.

He is to be pitied at his loss, but it was his own doing. I just hope that all of Eva's children can let go of the past too, and let God help to bring peace, and remember the good times. I know that is what Eva wants too."

'Yes, I'm sure she does. I agree...we need to remember the good times, the good things."

Alex, smiling at Jason said, "I want my own place in Eva's family's lives, not someone else's place. Your Dad'll still be important to his family. That is the way it should be. I want to be a part of Eva's life, a part with her, with her family. Does that sound reasonable?"

"Yes. I like that way of looking at your life together. You're making Mom happy. I admire you, Alex. I think Mom is right, you're a pretty great guy." There were tears in Jason's eyes.

"Thank you Jason. I'm just a plain guy, who has given his life to the Lord and I'm letting him lead me. I'm so thankful that He brought Eva into my life. I didn't know how empty and lonely I was until she came along." Alex hesitated, then continued, "She came along and ran into me, ran into my heart," Alex said, with his smile, bringing happy light into the conversation.

The conversation turned to things of the shop.

*

Eva called Jewel. "Hi Sis, what are you doing today? Can you go shopping with me?"

"Shopping? You? It's usually me wanting to go shopping," Jewel laughed.

"*Okay…Wilma, This is Betty, come on, let's go shopping! CHARGE…it!* Isn't that the way that they did it?

They were both laughing by this time.

"Sure, let's go. How soon?"

"Let's go fairly early, if you can go. I want to take the painting and have it put in a good frame. I'm going to give it to Alex for a wedding present. I don't know how long that will take, so let's go early."

"Sure, we can do that."

"How soon will you be ready? I'll come get you."

"How will it be if I pick you up? I know that you don't care much about driving in Tacoma."'

"Thank you Sis, I'd appreciate that. Can I take my painting in your car?"

"Sure, we can put it in the trunk of my car." They dropped the painting off, Eva picked out the frame, and they were to pick the painting up on the way home.

"Where are we going? What are you going shopping for?" Jewel asked, after they were on the way again.

"I want to go to the jewelers to buy Alex a wedding ring. But first, I want to buy some shoes for the wedding."

"Only shoes?"

"Yes, then I'm going to buy some things for the boat trip." Eva explained about the wardrobe that her family was giving her.

"Alex wants to meet us for lunch. Maybe he'll go to the jewelers with me."

"Oh did I tell you that the wedding has been set up for the first of June?" they talked about that too.

Eva called Alex and they met for lunch. Jewel and Jason hadn't seen each other for a while, and were happily talking during lunch.

"Did you go to the jewelers yet?" Alex asked.

"No, we are going there from here."

"I'd like to go with you."

"Will you, Alex? I wish you would."

As they entered the jewelry store, one of the clerks came to meet them.

"Good Afternoon, Mr. Harmon, we have the rings for you that you ordered. Would you like to try them on for size? Mrs. Harmon, please sit here." He motioned for Alex to sit next to her.

"Eva hasn't seen them yet, she may want something else?" Eva looked at Alex questioningly. The clerk opened the box and held it for Eva to see.

"Please bring the rest of the tray for her to see too," Alex asked.

"Alex! These are all sets!"

"Yes, they're all sets."

"And this set you ordered special?"

"Yes."

"It's gorgeous! They all are...but..."

"But what? Don't you like any of them?"

"Yes Alex," she held out her left hand, "but I don't want to give *this* ring up! I love it."

"Honey, you don't have to give it up! It's yours. I just want you to have a set."

"A set, too...besides this ring?"

"Yes Sweetheart, a set besides. Can you choose one of these?"

"All right." Eva looked at them all. "I like this set, the set that you ordered, the best, but...isn't it too much? Too big?"

"No, dear heart. Let's try it on."

Alex reached for her hand. She didn't hold her hand out.

"Honey, what's wrong?"

"Alex, may I wear them on my right hand?"

"Yes, if you'd like to." He smiled at her tenderly. "My Mother wore her wedding ring on her right hand."

Eva's face lit up in a radiant smile. She held up her left hand. "Good. I don't want to move this one. I love it there."

"Eva, let's try these on." He put them on her right hand.

They fit perfectly.

Eva looked up at Alex, there were tears sparking in her eyes. "Alex, I didn't expect another ring. This one is enough. Alex I came to buy a ring for you."

She turned to the clerk. "Mrs. Harmon, I took the liberty to order the matching grooms ring." He brought it out.

"Mr. Harmon, you remember that you tried on a ring, and I remembered your size. Try it, see if it fits."

It fit.

"Alex, is it all right?"

"Yes."

"Do you want this one?"

"Yes."

They sat, looking into each other's faces, searching to be sure it was really all right, tears glistening in both sets of eyes. Suddenly, smiles of joy lit up both faces.

"Yes."

"Yes," softly, from both.

They looked down at the rings, still on both hands. Tears spilled over from Eva's eyes, but Alex managed to blink his away. They took off the rings, put them back into the boxes, and handed them to the clerk. Was the brightness in his eyes, tears too?

There was the same brightness in Jewel's and Jason's, standing nearby.

Alex opened the car door for Eva. "Do I dare kiss you here, Jo?"

She reached her arms up and lifted her lips for the kiss. "Thank you Alex. You're such a dear, dear man."

"Thank *you*, Eva, you are my darling," he murmured against her lips. She kissed him again before she let him go. "See you at home, Sweetheart."

Eva bought a pair of white dress shoes for the wedding, pantyhose and knee-highs, then several other pair of shoes of other colors for other outfits.

"And I need three pairs of deck shoes," she told the clerk. She bought a dozen pair of crew socks. She bought rain gear, a heavy coat and a lighter one, sweatshirts and pants.

"How are you going to pay for all this?" Jewel asked.

"Alex made me promise to use an account that he set up for me. If I wouldn't promise, he was going to come with me, and that I must buy these things."

"That Alex is something!"

"Yes, isn't he?"

"I'm so happy for you, Eva!"

"So am I."

"Where next?"

"I could go to the boat to see if there is anything else we need, but for now, I guess we'd better go home. Steve is coming this evening. Also, I'd like to have dinner started when the guys get home. How about you and Ben coming for dinner with us?"

"I'll ask Ben and call you."

"Steve said that he would be here by 5, and Alex and Jason will be here by then too."

"Do you have beds for both Steve and Jason?"

"Yes, but one is standing on end in the closet. I'll get it out and fix it." Jewel helped her to set up the bed and make it before she went on home.

"It is sure a good thing that there are such big closets in these bedrooms," she thought as she moved her paintings and supplies into the closet in her bedroom.

Eva heard Steve's car pull in, and met him on the deck with a hug. They sat on the deck a while, and Eva told Steve about Alex and the wedding. "I hope that you can come to my wedding."

"I'll come, of course. I wouldn't miss it. You're my Mom too, remember?"

"My son, Jason is here too. I hope that you won't mind sharing your room with him, this weekend."

"I won't mind a bit. I haven't met your family, your kids yet."

Steve helped to fix dinner. Sis called to say that they were coming. Eva's brother Len's family was coming too.

"Let's plan on Brandon and Billie too." They set up another table on the deck.

"It's going to be a beautiful evening for our dinner out here," Eva said.

"Are the squirrels and chipmunks still about?" Steve asked.

"Oh yes," Eva laughed. "They'll be into things if we don't keep it covered."

"If we feed them just before we eat, do you suppose that will keep them busy?"

"It's worth a try. I've spoiled them. They think that if I'm out here that it is a signal for them to come. Even the ducks on the lake come when I call."

Steve lit the barbecue, turning it down low, to keep things warm. They had made Swiss steak and had it in layers in a big roaster. All of the hot things had been transferred to the barbecue to finish cooking and wait for everyone to arrive.

Jim came with Alex and Jason. After introductions were taken care of, dinner was served buffet style with everyone helping them selves. It was an enjoyable evening, and they lingered talking, enjoying the warm evening sunshine on the deck.

Brandon asked, "Eva, have you fed the ducks this evening?"

"No, go ahead and feed them if you like."

He brought out several loaves of bread, handing a loaf to each Jim, Jason, and Steve.

"Eva, will you call them, they come best for you."

Going down on the boat dock and taking a few slices of bread, Eva began to call, "Come ducks, come ducks."

They came flying from all over the lake. She tossed some bread to the ducks, and then returned to the deck to sit with the others and watch the young men feed bread to the ducks.

Eva brought peanuts and sunflower seeds, calling, "Come Chipper, Come Chipper – Come Reddy, come Reddy."

Chipmunks came but the red squirrels wouldn't come onto the deck, so she sat on the edge of the deck, then they came to take the peanuts out of her fingers.

She soon returned to her chair.

"We hear about your wild friends, are we going to get to see anymore of them this evening?" Jewel asked

"Look." Alex quietly nodded as a Doe stepped out from behind some bushes, coming hesitantly towards the deck.

"Hold steady," Eva cautioned. She'd brought some carrot strips and apple slices. "Look, the twins are over there."

The doe looked nervously at the people sitting on the deck, and wouldn't come closer. Eva stepped off the deck towards the doe, who was watching her, then came to meet her. The twins came, cautiously to her, stepping daintily, accepting the carrot strips, flicking their tails.

The others sat in amazement, watching. The young men returned quietly to the deck, to watch Eva with the deer.

Alex was thinking, "How can I take her away from here? Will she be happy shut up in an apartment in town?"

He sat looking at the big vacant place next door.

After everyone had gone and they were settling for the night, lights out, these thoughts were taken to his Lord.

Alex stood in the dark, looking out of the window.

Tall trees in the background, with bushes, some in bloom, many soon to bloom.

"It's like a garden, a sheltered secluded spot, pleasing to the sight, and satisfying to the spirit and soul, refreshing to the mind." He thought in wonder. "A place to walk and talk to God. Eva has this same view from her bedroom. This side looks away from the lake. It is like a place where God Himself might walk to bring His beauty, to make a haven, a place of peace."

The doe stepped out into sight, and walked among the bushes, the fawns soon following, confidant of their safety, even so near the house.

It was long after dark, yet there was enough light from the waning moon to see quite clearly. He watched a while, the peace settling his thoughts. He took half-laid plans to bed, his heart longing to please and make Eva happy.

And, he went to sleep at last.

CHAPTER TWELVE

Steve and Jason were fixing breakfast, Jim setting the table, when Eva woke.

"Good Morning guys, I didn't hear you."

"We didn't mean to wake you."

"The coffee woke me; I'll be ready for a cup soon."

Alex, fresh from the shower, was pouring coffee when Eva returned to the kitchen. "These guys got the jump on us this morning, Eva. Breakfast smells wonderful."

Steve was interested in what was going on at the shop and asked questions. They talked about work in progress. He didn't say so, but Alex thought that Steve would be an asset to the crew, and the business.

"What are you studying at college?" Jim asked Steve.

"Extended math, including trigonometry, of course drafting, design and architecture, ancient as well as modern. I want to know how and why some of the old structures, hundreds of years old, are still standing, mute testimony of their designers and builders. Do you know that there are furniture and decorations inside those old buildings that are as old as the buildings themselves...and are in usable, good shape? It is very interesting to read about all that. I just wish that I could see it all."

"I'd like to see that too," Alex agreed.

A chorus of *'Me too's'* followed.

Steve continued, "Do you know that the Vikings built wooden chairs that folded, using sheepskins for seats. And tables with much the same style legs, with tops that folded or came off so that they were moveable."

"Here we thought that folding furniture was a modern idea."

"No, folding furniture was used at least a thousand years ago. The nomadic people, Abraham's people, probably had such things as well."

"That's very likely, when you stop to think of it."

"Steve, come with us today. See our furniture building. Maybe you can give us some ideas. I don't suppose that you would settle for a life's work of building furniture, when you can go on to building buildings or bridges."

"Well, I do love real wood furniture. It can be very beautiful. Yes, I'd like to see what you're doing."

"Good." Alex turned to Eva, "what are you doing today? Want to come with us too?"

"It'd be fun...and interesting, but I think that I'll let you all have a guy's day today. I think I'll go by and see Len and Alice and Jewel. Maybe have lunch with them."

They picked up their dishes and took them to the sink.

"You guys go ahead, I'll clean up."

"Okay. Thanks Mom." Jason said, kissing her.

"Yes, thanks, my Mom too," Steve said.

"I'm next," Jim said.

"Looks like I have to stand in line to kiss my girl," Alex laughed. "That's all right; I know that I'll get my turn."

He stood a moment holding her, while the others went out.

Then he kissed her tenderly.

"All day without you…"

Her arms around his neck tightened. "Think we'll survive?" she whispered.

"Barely. Then the thoughts of this evening will help," he grinned at her.

"Someone to come home to. Where you are is home, home for my heart," said, with a break in his voice.

As they walked out to the deck, Alex said, "Eva, I feel as much, more, at home here than I do at my place, anymore."

"Alex, I'm lonesome with out you too. It's like I'm halfway holding my breath, waiting for you to come."

"See you after while, Honey Girl."

He bent and kissed her again.

Eva started some laundry, put the dishes in the dishwasher, then took her Bible and sat down to spend some time with her Lord in His word.

Father, in Hebrews 4: 15 and 16, it says that we have a high priest who is touched by our "infirmities. 'Let us come boldly unto the throne of grace, that we may find grace in time of need.'

Father God, because your Son, Jesus is my savior, I come boldly to you, seeking help to settle all my fears and doubts, once and for all.

I know that you're directing my path, and helping me. I know that you brought Alex and I together, that it is your plan for our lives. I have no doubt about that.

Yet the past is there. Not that I want to forget the past completely, but parts of it still hurt. May I give that to you? Will you take it and give me peace and victory over it? I want to go into this marriage with Alex with nothing bothering me, no hindrances from the past. I want a complete and healthy break between Henry and me.

Lord God, please make the memories of the past, healthy, pleasant memories. No condemnation for me, or for Henry, that Henry may be restored to your kingdom, secure in salvation. So that he may go on with his life and have a healthy, happy life too.

I ask this, Father God in Jesus name. I believe for it to happen. Thank you Father.

Amen.

She was sitting on the deck in the sunshine. A ray of sunlight caught in the diamond of the beautiful ring that Alex had put on her left hand. She sat looking at it.

"I'll have my wedding rings on my right hand; maybe Alex will wear his wedding ring on his right hand too. I wish that Alex could have a ring, similar to this one too. Why not! I'm going to go find out if they have one!"

She dashed in, grabbed her purse and car keys and left.

"I know that I can find that jeweler," she told herself. And she did.

"Yes, we have a man's ring very similar," the clerk told her. He brought it to show her.

"I'll take it."

"Mrs. Harmon, it's quite expensive." He named the price.

"May I pay half today and put the rest on my credit card?"

"Yes, we can do that."

She was soon at home again. She found a chain to hang the ring around her neck. "I want it with me at all times, so that I can give it to Alex on a moments notice." She was thrilled to think that she would have such a gift to give Alex.

"I don't know just when I'll give it to him, but I'll know when the time comes. And I can pay for it myself, a payment each month, out of my own money until it's paid for."

She looked up to see the doe looking in the window. She took a couple of apples and a paring knife, and went out to sit on the deck and gave slices of apples to the doe.

The twins came to get their share too.

A chipmunk ran up the leg of the chair to see if he could find something on her lap. He settled for a slice of the apple too, and scampered away with it.

The squirrels set up chatter near by.

"Well, the whole gang is here, aren't you," she laughed softly. She brought peanuts, sunflower seeds, and some dry cornbread for them. The squirrels came to her when the deer wandered off.

"Guess it getting too crowded for the deer," she told the squirrels.

About that time, the ducks came to the boat dock and let her know that they were there.

"I'd better hit the bakery today for day old bread," she thought, as she took the last to the dock. She sat on the bench that Steve had built, and tossed the bread to the ducks.

As usual, others came flying, calling out the news, *'Food! Food!'*

"I'm glad that Steve will be here this summer while I'm gone, to feed you guys. Maybe Jason will live here too, with Steve and stay the winter."

The chipmunks had hibernated most of the winter, but the squirrels had been out every few days all winter. The deer were around almost every day all winter too.

"I'll miss all this," she thought. "I love it here, the peace and quiet. Did I say quiet?" she laughed as the ducks set up their ruckus, expecting more bread.

She tossed the last to them, "Okay, you guys, this is all, until I bring some more home."

She could hear the phone ringing insistently. It was her sister Jewel. "What are you doing this morning?"

"Oh, just the usual things, a little laundry, and dishes. The guys went to the shop for the day, so I'm home alone."

"Well, now that sounds sad." Sis laughed.

"Yes, doesn't it. What are you up to?"

"Well, there are things that I could be doing, but the phone keeps ringing off the wall, and it's getting on to lunch time – come meet me for lunch."

"Sounds like a winner. I'd like to stop at Len and Alice's today too."

"Sure, let's do that."

"I've some clothes to fold out of the dryer, and then I'll come. I should be there in about 20 minutes…meet me at the Big Tree?"

"Okay, see you there."

Eva prepared a pot roast and set the timer to start it.

Jewel wasn't there yet when Eva went to find a table at the restaurant. "My Sis will be here soon," she told the waitress, as she poured her coffee. "It's a good thing that I got here when I did, this is the last table available."

"Yes, it has been busy this morning and now the lunch crowd is here in full force."

The waitresses were directing people to the back room for additional seating, so Eva paid little attention to those going past her table.

She took out a list of things that she needed to take on the boat. "Have to get them ready soon," she reminded herself.

Suddenly a man leaned down and kissed her on the cheek. She looked up, startled, yet with a smile, expecting it to be her brother. It was Henry!

"Hello Eva."

"Henry! What are you doing here?"

He pulled out a chair and sat down beside her. "I came to see you of course."

"I thought that you understood the last time that you came up here, that I don't want to see you."

"That's just you Sister telling you what to do. She took you away from me when you left."

"I had already planed to leave you before she came, and I would have been gone that day or the next night if she hadn't called."

"So you say. I've tried to call you. There's no number listed in your name. I suppose the phone is in the name of that guy that you think that you are going to marry."

"No, the phone is in the owner's name."

"You know that with your belief, you can't marry anyone but me."

"Oh yes I can! You have to read the scriptures that say that if one breaks the marriage vows; the other is innocent and is free, no longer bound by the marriage vows. You did that many times. But I stayed for my kids, hoping that they would never know, and that you would change."

"I don't believe that. You're supposed to forgive and forget."

"Yes, Henry, I've forgiven you and I'm trying to forget, but I'll never forget to the point that I'll subject myself to you as I have in the past. You won't change. You don't want to change.

"Do you remember, a few days before I left when I told you that you need to forgive and forget the things that you're holding against my brothers and my Dad? You said that you couldn't forgive and forget and you didn't want to.

I knew then that I couldn't help you any more. That wasn't sins that you need to forgive, but financial losses that they suffered too. It was a venture that we all entered into and it failed. Those things happened 40 years ago.

You hate my family so much that you won't forget it. I won't listen to you throw that up to me, like you did every day - not any more. You won't change. You don't want to."

"So, you're going to marry some guy. I suppose that you had that all planed when you left me." Henry asked.

"No. I met him after I came up here. Actually, I met him not long ago."

"I don't believe that."

"I don't care what you believe, Henry. Go start a new life. Call that gal who used to call me after midnight, before you got home, to ask me why I wouldn't let you go, why wouldn't I give you your freedom.

I told you at that time, that if I wasn't the only woman in your life, that I didn't want to be in you life at all. I told you, that you could have your freedom, I wouldn't hold you. All you said was that you couldn't afford a divorce.

That was your only comment about it.

Now you're free. Go to her now. Go find her. Get out of here. Leave. I'm free of you; you're free of me. Just go!"

"Will you step outside with me?"

It was Deputy Ryan, who took Henry's arm, and lifting him to stand to his feet. Another deputy was standing near the door, waiting.

"Eva," Henry called, trying to turn back.

"Goodbye, Henry," Eva waved him away with her hand.

She could see the deputies escorting Henry to his car across the street. The deputies stood talking to Henry for a few minutes, and then Henry got into his car and drove away.

The Deputies' car was parked behind Henry's and they followed him away.

The waitress came with coffee, "Are you okay?"

"Yes. Yes, I really am! I met Henry, and I think that I handled it well."

"As long as you're sure that you're all right."

"Yes, thank you. I really am okay." She knew that she really was.

Eva sat, drinking coffee, and thinking, "I'm amazed, how calm I was, and am. Thank you Lord, I know that you're with me and helping me."

She remembered the prayer that she had prayed earlier that morning. She sat waiting for Jewel, and told her about it when she came.

The Deputies came back and reassured her that Henry was headed back to Oregon.

Eva and Jewel spent the afternoon with Alice and Len.

*

There were ducks at the boat dock, calling their greeting to Eva when she arrived home.

"Mmm, it smells good already," she said, as she put carrots, onions, and potatoes in the pot roast.

Then she took some dry bread to the dock.

Jason joined her shortly. "Hi Mom, feeding your flock again?"

"Hi Jason. You guys are earlier than I thought you'd be. Yes," she said, indicating the ducks, "these guys were waiting for me when I got home. Here comes some more."

Steve was headed their way.

"Steve, bring some more bread."

Alex joined them, sitting down by Eva. "May I interrupt long enough for a hello," he grinned.

"Of course!" She turned for a kiss, then stood up and sat on Alex's lap.

"Hello Alex, I really needed this," she said, putting her arms around his neck, to kiss him again, "Hello, Alex, my love," she whispered in his ear.

"Hello, Sweetheart. Coming home is almost worth being gone for a while," he smiled and kissed her again, hugging her.

"Almost," she agreed.

The ducks soon seemed to have enough bread to eat and started to preen themselves, contentedly talking to each other.

Jason said, "They have kind of a language, don't they? They have certain sounds when they are eating, chuckling away. They make quite a ruckus, when they put out the 'come and get it' call. And now, a quieter chatter, a happy contented sound."

"Yes, you get to know what they are talking about."

"The flock has grown since I left," Steve said. "They are tamer too. You have a way with animals, Mom. They are all tamer, the ducks, the chipmunks, squirrels, even the deer."

"I guess that they found out what a soft touch I am," she laughed. "I enjoy them all. It's great to have these wild animals living here, so close to people. I just hope that this area with the timber and brush is never taken away from them, for more houses. The animals need places left for them."

The others agreed.

"I'll show you guys something, if you'll not tell anyone."

"Now what?" Alex wondered.

She led them behind the apartment house to a clearing back in the trees, hidden out of sight. There, she pointed to three trees about six feet tall.

They had protective shields around the trunks.

"I planted these shortly after I came here. They're filberts. See, they are blooming and will have nuts on them this year."

"Filberts! Now we know why the animals trust you. They know."

"I wanted to plant them closer to the house, but I'm not sure that Owen would want them there. I thought that maybe no one would notice them out here."

"I'll ask Granddad if I can plant some more, closer to the house," Steve said. "Why not have some nuts growing here for the squirrels and chipmunks, I like that idea."

"We had filberts behind the old house, and the chipmunks and squirrels got most of them," Jason remembered.

They stood looking around at the sheltered and secluded spot. "There must be about ten acres or more here," Alex said.

"Yes," Steve said. "And actually, there is more that runs on there between the lake and the road. Granddad talked about buying it. He only owns this strip from the road to the lake, from this driveway to the next driveway. The rest belongs to the big vacant house next door."

"Then Owen owns this area where I planted the filberts?"

"Yes. I'm sure that he'd be glad, but I won't tell him," Steve laughed.

They turned to go back towards the house. "We could smell something cooking when we came home, suppose it's all right?"

"Yes. It's pot roast, and should be ready soon."

They started back to the house, Jason and Steve, soon out ahead.

Holding Alex's hand, Eva stopped and turned to look back towards the highway.

"He could easily park here and come to the house without me hearing him come."

"He doesn't know where you are. He can't find you. What brought that on?"

Eva told Alex about Henrys' visit at the restaurant.

"He didn't hurt you, or threaten you?"

"No. But I didn't see him until he kissed me." She unconsciously rubbed her cheek again. "Then he sat down beside me."

"You see, even when he came, he couldn't hurt you. You said that you talked calmly. You didn't panic."

"No, I didn't. I'm glad. A little surprised, but I'm so glad that I didn't panic."

"You see, Eva? The Lord is helping you."

"Yes. He is, isn't He?"

"The Lord will keep on helping and protecting you." He said. "That he will never leave us alone."

"That's right!" she smiled up at Alex.

Suddenly a family of birds, close by, burst into song, their throats swelling with joyous singing, their little heads looking upwards.

Alex and Eva stood, looking up at the little musicians. Two by two, the little songsters flew toward the house, and continued their sweet melody there, near the house, the song floating on in the air.

"Well Hon, the birds are escorting us to the house."

"Oh Alex, the Lord uses even the birds to speak to us!"

"Why not. They are His too."

There were tears of joy in her eyes as she watched the attending birds move on to the tree closest to the house.

Jason and Steve had the table set and dinner on the table, when Eva and Alex came in.

"Just in time," Steve greeted them.

*

"It was a good dinner, Mom, thank you."

Steve agreed. "I sure have been longing for home."

Alex asked, "Do you have more classes or are you through for the term?"

"I have classes on Monday and Tuesday, and that's all for this term, but I just couldn't wait until then to come home. I'm ready for a break from school, ready for summer!"

'When are you coming home?" Eva asked.

"I'll be home Wednesday. It shouldn't take me long to pack up and come home."

Jason said, "Mom, you and Alex go have a little time by yourselves, Steve and I'll clean up dishes."

"Come on Eva, they are trying to get rid of us," Alex grinned.

"Let's walk a bit," he said as they stepped off the deck.

They walked down by the lake, across in front of the vacant place next door.

For Sale. Shown by appointment only, Edward E. Browser Real Estate. Suburban and Summer Homes. Alex commented, "It looks like a nice place."

"Yes. I've admired it. I've never seen anyone here, though."

"The drapes are open, let's look through the windows, and see what it looks like."

"Look Eva, it is finished logs inside too. Look at that stairway leading up to the upper level. These great windows reach the second floor ceiling here in front. There is a balcony across with chairs to sit up there on the upper level. There is a big living room and a dining area here in the front, all one large room with a view of the lake. It looks like a beautiful place to live, doesn't it."

"Alex! It's beautiful! All the windows will make it bright in the winter; still the drapes are heavy enough to shut out storms. I wonder that no one lives here. It is so lovely!

"It looks like it's furnished with beautiful furniture. If I owned it, I would want to live here, at least part of the time. "

"Let's walk out the driveway and across back across through the trees."

"Steve said that there is about twenty acres."

'Look Alex, there's the doe, but where are the twins?"

"The twins maybe are hid out in the bushes; they usually don't see us over here, so maybe she is checking us out."

They walked on.

"I like this. It's like a garden here close to the house, this side away from the lake. An open space with flowers and Rhodies, azaleas, and things."

"Oh isn't this nice! Benches! Benches inviting us to sit here."

"There's baby's breath, and golden chain…and a butterfly bush! The hummingbirds will love that!"

"Look! Little flower beds. Yet looks natural - like God planted it."

"Look at this rock garden – the flowers are just starting to bloom, here's pot o' gold."

"This is what Steve should do behind the apartments."

"It is a good idea."

"Shall we rest here a while? Here where these benches are inviting us to sit."

They sat quietly, listening to the birds. "You can hear the quiet, that isn't really quiet. It's full of quiet sounds. Peaceful, because the sounds are God's little creatures, going joyfully about life."

"Man could take a lesson from that. If we would go about life with such peaceful trust in our maker, and a joyful song, it would make us happy and others that we were around would be made happy, too."

"Even when the birds aren't singing, their calls back and forth sound so cheerful."

"The chipmunks seem to keep track of each other with their calls too. If you listen a few minutes, you can tell where they all are."

"And the squirrels tell where anyone is moving about. They follow the deer and talk to them."

"Yes, they seem to tease the deer, asking them why they are here and where are they going."

Eva sniffed, and then took deep breaths. "I love the smell, it's so kind of spicy, sweet, a fragrance of many things. Clean, *out-doorsey*, invigorating smells."

"The smell of life, living things. The smells of peacefulness. It seems to add assurance to knowing that God created all this, from this tiny flower on the moss to the great trees. The tiny humming bird to the great eagle soaring, up there, soaring so high, he's nearly out of sight. The little chipmunk and the deer…all a part of His creation."

"Yes, Alex, it makes one sit in awe before God, catching a glimpse of Him, who created us, becoming our Heavenly Father. He is a loving Father, who sent His own son to become our Savior, that we may have fellowship with Him, A fellowship now and be where He is forever."

"Eva, sometimes I can hardly contain my joy to know Him. Like the birds, I want to sing and shout the joy. Sometimes I can only stand on my knees, wordless with the wonder of it. And now the joy is magnified – because of the love of God has given you to me."

He stood and lifted his face and hands towards heaven. Silent, because when we are really in thankful worship and praising our God, we do not have a language and words adequate for expression.

Alex returned to sit beside Eva. They sat quietly until a light sound told them that something was there, and there were the twins, sniffing to see if there might be a treat for them. Eva lightly touched one. It trembled a bit, startled at her touch, but stood looking at her.

She spoke softly, "Are you guys wanting a treat, or just saying hello?"

"Look, the doe is heading for the apartment."

"Well, I guess we'd better go along."

"Listen to the ducks, Steve and Jason must be on the boat dock."

The twins were following the doe.

Eva stood smiling at Alex, "Shall we go too?"

Instead, she sat on his lap, putting her arms around his neck. "The deer and the birds have all deserted us. We are alone at last," she whispered in his ear.

Alex chuckled softly, hugging her. "Alone at last," he repeated happily. They would have their few moments alone. She put her cheek against his, wanting the closeness.

"There are no reservations any more!" she thought, remembering the early Morning Prayer. Her thoughts continued, *"I'm free! Really free...free to love Alex...love him completely, really completely! Thank you Lord."*

A thrill, warmness came, filling her whole being with tingles of joy. She leaned away a bit, so that she could look into Alex's eyes.

"Wow! How I love this guy!" she thought in her heart.

"There's a new look in Eva's eyes," Alex thought. *"No more shadows, they're all gone."*

They kissed again. His arms tightened around her, holding her close. The tingling thrill passed through them both, like a charge of electricity, uniting them in the kiss as never before.

She hid her face against his neck, her heart singing. She was shocked at the intensity of her feelings.

"Me! It's like I've been asleep and waking up. It's a promise of what it's going to be —" she cut off the thoughts. *"Time for that later. For now, this is enough."*

"Eva?"

"It's all right Alex. I'm free, really free. Free to love you completely. No reservations, no fears — no inadequacy. It's all gone. I'm ten feet tall! Every fiber of my being rejuvenated, awake...awake from a bad dream...awake and healthy from a long sickness. I want to shout...to tell the world. Tell them that I'm alive, really alive. Alive and in love...in love with life, my new life with you, a most wonderful man! I'm so ready for this new life. Really ready..."

There were tears in Alex's eyes, tears of joy, and they overflowed.

"Eva...sweet Eva..." His voice was husky with emotion.

They held each other and just sat quietly, holding each other, tenderly. The ruckus of the ducks finally intruded, breaking into their quiet time together. Eva sighed, reluctantly standing up.

"Your legs must be paralyzed by now, anyway."

"Not at all, Sweetheart, I could sit and hold you like this all night." He pulled her back to his lap.

She kissed him again.

"That was a tantalizing kiss..."

"I know," she said breathlessly. Standing up, she took his hand, tugging him up too.

"Wow, there were promises in that kiss," Alex thought, *"From both of us."*

They joined Steve and Jason on the dock.

The young men had been feeding the ducks dry bread again, and now sat watching the setting sun casting glory lights in a few clouds about.

The lake, not to be ignored, was reflecting the golden-lit clouds, slowly turning to rose, then lavender. The sun continued to paint the clouds, reluctantly setting at last. The lake doing its part, until it all faded, leaving a golden rose glow, then an opalescent pearl in the west.

They sat talking quietly, savoring the last of the day. Steve and Jason discussing the day at the shop and the future projects being started.

Eva and Alex were sitting, holding hands, listening.

"Steve, come work with us a few days," Jason said. "I think that they want me to stay," Jason turned to Alex, questioningly.

"Yes Jason. Both David and Bill asked me to encourage you to stay and work with them. Eva will be moving out of the apartment and you guys can have it all to yourselves. You seem to get along well. And Steve, if you should decide to work at the shop this summer, I'm sure you'll be welcomed."

"I just may do that. It was pretty interesting today."

"Yes it is," Jason agreed, and they went back to discussing the pieces that they were especially interested in.

Brandon and Billie came home. "They're late," Eva said, going up to the deck, where Brandon and Billie stood waiting for them.

"Alex, we just came from the house," Brandon said.

"It's wonderful," Billie added.

"Alex, are you sure that you want to sell it to us the way that you said?" Brandon continued. "It's too good to be true."

"Yes, Brandon, just like I said."

"Alex, how can we thank you?"

"Just be another son and daughter to us, be a part of our family, a part of our lives."

"That'll be easy to do." Were there tears in Brandon's eyes? There were in Billie's. "You people are easy to love."

"I'm indebted to you kids, letting me use your spare room.

I just moved in, I just can't stay away from my Lady," Alex said, putting his arm around Eva, pulling her close.

"It's only a week from tomorrow," Billie said wistfully.

"When we get home from our trip, we want to see lots of you kids," Eva said hugging Billie.

CHAPTER THIRTEEN

It was early on Saturday when Eva woke from another bad dream. Unable to go back to sleep, she showered and dressed quietly.

"The guys may sleep in this morning, I don't think that they'll go to the shop today," she thought as slipped out of the door, closing it quietly behind her.

She waked down to the dock and stood looking at the lake. It was quiet everywhere. There were just a few small birds beginning to start their day.

The sun wasn't up yet and it was cool. She was glad that she'd put on a jacket.

She was restless. Hoping to calm her thoughts, she walked over past the vacant house next door, and to the garden where she and Alex had sat and been so happy the evening before. She sat down on the bench to think.

"Am I going to be a clinging vine on Alex, like Henry had said that I was?"

The dream had brought back the memory of Henry telling her that. Henry had been going to go spend the day with his mom and dad, and his brother's family.

Eva had thought that she and the two small children would go along. She had them ready to go, including a small case of extra clean clothes for them, if they should get dirty.

When Henry had seen that she was ready to go with him, he'd gotten angry and shouted at her, "Can't I have any freedom? Do I always have to have you hanging on? You like a clinging vine! A millstone around my neck, dragging me down!"

He had stormed out the door, slamming it behind him.

She stood with the year old baby Paul in her arms, with their coats on.

"Guess Dad's going without us," she'd said. "But guess what? We'll catch the bus and go down town."

They had spent the day in Tacoma and at Point Defiance Park. They went to the aquarium, seen all the fish, then the animals, later the flowers. It was good that she was used to carrying Paul.

He walked well, and had been happy to walk until he was tired.

Abbigail was good with Paul and they had a good time.

Both of the children had enjoyed seeing the fish, then the other animals. Later they looked at all of the flowers. Abbigail was entranced with the flowers, each one seeming more beautiful than the last.

Eva had found a grass area where the children could play and roll on the grass and rest a while. Paul came and sat in her lap and fell asleep and had a nap.

Eva and Abbigail had talked quietly, resting too, and watching the birds in the trees near by. A squirrel had come, running out to the end of the branches, jumping from tree to tree, until he was close, and sat chattering at them. Eva had some crackers in her purse for the children, which they shared with the squirrel.

Paul woke in time to see the squirrel come for the crackers.

Paul sat quietly watching, his face lit up with wonder.

They had eaten lunch in the park and supper in town just before they caught the last bus home. The last bus was a Fort Lewis bus that was full of soldiers, but the young men had made room for them, taking the children and holding them.

Two of the young soldiers had walked home with her, carrying the children for her.

Henry hadn't come home, so the young men had insisted on checking out the house to be sure that she and the children were safe, windows, and doors locked before they left.

The memory had come back so vividly.

Henry's "You're a clinging vine, a millstone!" Those words rang in her mind, haunting her with their hurting sound. She groaned, and putting her head down on her arms on the back of the bench, she began to cry.

"I don't want to ever want Alex to feel that way about me.

"Still, oh how I love to be in his arms. I feel so safe there, - to be hugged by him. Will he get tired of me; think that I'm a millstone around his neck?"

"Sweetheart, I won't ever get tired of you. Don't let past memory upset you. I'm not like that. I won't ever hurt you." He was pulling her into his arms.

"Oh Alex!" she sobbed, her face hid against his shoulder.

"Eva. Remember, you said that you're free, and well, and healthy. Don't let bad dreams rob you. You can trust me; I'll never hurt you. You did have a bad dream again, didn't you?"

"Yes. Years ago, Henry had called me a clinging vine, a millstone, and Alex…I'm clinging to you, hanging on for dear life.

I may get worse. I want to sleep with my head on your shoulder!"

"Well, that can't be soon enough for me. Let's just run away, elope – today. I think that we can find someone to marry us."

"But Alex, you have been alone – independent, for a long time. Maybe you'll want – need time away from me."

"Maybe we'll both need that some time, but I don't think so. If it should happen, I think that we'll be able to talk about it and not hurt each other. We are not the kind of people to want to hurt someone. Tell you what, after we have celebrated our fiftieth wedding anniversary, we'll talk about it again. Until then, I doubt if the thought ever occurs to either one of us."

He was wiping the tears away, kissing her gently. She got up and sat in his lap.

"This is what I like, what I want!" She put her arms around him, hugging him, her cheek against his.

"I guess that I'm so hungry for love, -- I've been starved for love. I just – Oh Alex, I love you! But I don't want to stifle you –smother you. I couldn't take hurting you. Losing you – would about kill me."

He nuzzled into her neck.

"I think I'll like a little smothering from you. I may never get enough. Sweetheart, I'd be the happiest man alive, if from this moment on, you were always right here, at least within arms reach. Close enough to talk and sometimes just 'luxuriate' in our love. Shall we get in the car and run off?"

"I think that I would like to do just that. But our families, what are their plans?"

"Oh, we'll come back. We could get married again, down in Oregon."

She put her cheek against his to hide her eyes from his searching look. Such a thrill filled her at the thought; she was a bit embarrassed with herself.

"The family wouldn't have to know that we were already married."

"What would they think if we were gone that long, and where – what would we -? Guess we'd better not."

"Well, if you change your mind."

"Alex, I'm sorry – for being a cry baby – for getting so upset again."

"It's okay to cry when you need to. Just remember I love you, I want to be here when you need me. I want to prove that I love you enough to go through all this with you. Don't ever do it alone anymore. If you do, I won't leave your side, married or not," he said firmly.

She giggled at that thought, and kissed him again. "You won't even make an 'honest woman of me' first?"

"Well, if you put it that way, I may not." He kissed her thoroughly.

"Oh! I think that you mean it!"

"I do, for a fact," he chuckled.

"We'd better go back."

"Going to 'chicken out' on me?"

"Never again. – So we'd better go back – or else."

"I'd rather – or else."

"Alex! You're supposed to protect me!"

"Yes, but not from me. Eva…you're blushing!"

"I know."

"Okay, we'll go back. If you're sure that you're not going to let bad dreams or bad memories upset you again."

"I won't, I promise. I'll just remember this – time and I'll be all right. I'll be fine."

"Well, keep it in mind anyway."

He swept her up in his arms and carried her.

"Just practicing, have to be ready at any moment from now on."

"Alex!" she laughed. "You'd better put me down, the boys might see us."

"It would give them something to think about, Huh?"

"No, we mustn't do that."

He was still holding her. Her arms were around his neck, looking into each other's eyes. He felt a closeness like never before.

A kiss developed. A kiss asking, a more demanding kiss, a yielding answer that also asked for more, for an answer.

Alex suddenly knew that he had awakened, as from a deep sleep. Awakened to realize that suddenly he was awake, alive.

Like Eva had said, he felt ten feet tall; alive…rejuvenated.

He was shocked at himself, at the depths of his feelings. He hadn't expected to feel like this. He was shaken to his very depths with the emotion.

"And I thought that I was in love!" he thought. *"This is far beyond that! Will I have to protect Eva from me, too?"*

A scripture that he'd read long ago came to his mind. *'Marriage is honorable in all, and the bed undefiled: but whoremongers and adulters God will judge.'*

"She'll have her marriage license first this time. That kiss tells us that we'll have a good and healthy life, a fulfillment of our love. God will bless us in every part of our life together, if we are obedient to His Word."

He set her down gently, searching her face.

"Eva! Your face is aglow!"

"Really? I'm not surprised. Just so that we don't look guilty."

"Well, that is impossible. Because we are guilty, guilty of being in love."

"Gloriously, ecstatically in love!" she agreed.

Alex wondered if she felt the way that he did. Yes, she'd said that she felt like she had awakened as from sleep, feeling alive, healthy alive.

Why did it take me so long to really wake up to the real depths of this love? He wondered.

Jason and Steve left shortly after breakfast. Steve to study for the last of the tests, Jason to pick up his things and return the next day.

Eva stood looking at the room the young men had been using, the room that she'd used for her studio.

"I've got to get my things out of here."

"Eva, it is a week today when we get married. We'll move your things to our apartment and the things to the boat that you'll use on the trip. Jim said that he'll help on Tuesday."

"I'll get everything packed and have it ready. I really don't have a lot to move. I'll leave things here for Jason and Steve."

"Let's take your painting things over to the apartment today. That'll make room for Jason's things when he comes back tomorrow."

"Yes and Steve will be back in a few days too."

"Let's stay in Tacoma tonight and we'll go to church with Tom and Beth tomorrow."

So, they took Eva's paintings and painting supplies and stored them in a closet down stairs.

"Oh, Alex, this would make a great place to paint, here with all these windows! All this light!"

"It's yours Eva, if you want to use it to paint here. I hope that you'll continue to paint after we get home again." He added.

Eva took a painting that was wrapped in brown paper. "Alex, this is my wedding gift to you," she said bringing it to him.

"My painting! Thank you. Let's go hang it in our living room."

"There, I told you that I had just the right place for it," he said, as he stepped back to admire it. "There is another of your paintings that I would like to have hanging here too. I don't want you to sell it. It's that wonderful sunset, with the Mountain and the lake."

"All right. I like that one too. It needs a frame yet."

"We'll get it framed when we get home."

Eva was to sleep in a downstairs bedroom, but she was too excited to sleep. In her robe and slippers, she quietly slid open the doors to her room and went out into the glass-enclosed hallway.

The city was lit up. She could see traffic moving on some of the streets. A faint after glow silvered Mount Rainier, standing majestically like a sentinel overlooking the hills, the valleys, and the city.

"It's a beautiful view," she whispered.

"Yes it is," Alex agreed quietly. He was standing beside her. "It's not like your lake with Rainier presiding over it, but there is the mountain."

"He is quite majestic seen from here too," Eva agreed.

There was a couch and chairs near by, and they sat for a while. Sat and held hands and talked quietly

CHAPTER FOURTEEN

Sunday after church, Beth had the joy of fixing her first family dinner since moving home. With Eva and Alex, David and Noralee, and Bill and Nancy joining in and spending the afternoon with them.

The afternoon was spent getting better acquainted with Eva, and renewing family closeness. Tom and Beth had been gone for sometime and had been missed. Close family ties were picked up and reinforced.

Eva was glad to see the love and closeness in this family, like it was in her children.

They looked at pictures and a photograph album, reminiscing of good times. Beth brought a picture of the boy's Mother to show Eva. A little silence followed as Eva looked at a beautiful woman smiling back at her.

A tender smile came on her face, "I'm very glad to meet you, Martha. I can see why you and Alex have such dear, wonderful boys and family. They reflect you as well as Alex."

Beth took the picture and put it away in a drawer, and returned to sit down beside Eva.

"I'm so glad Dad found you, Eva. He's been so alone for so long. He has needed you. We all have. We are going to love and enjoy you.

"What would you like to have us call you? Would you rather we call you Eva, like Dad, or may we call you Mom? We called our mother, *Mother*."

"You may call me what ever you're comfortable with. This has all happened so quickly, it may take time. And that's all right too."

David stood up, "I, for one, am going to call you Mom. I hear Jason and Steve calling you Mom, and I'm a bit jealous. You're Mom to me."

He walked over and bent down to kiss her, "Hi Mom."

Noralee came, "Me too, Mom," and kissed her.

"Well, I can't call you Mom, but I can sure call you Sister, but suppose that I call you Eva and think of you as my Sister." Bill bent down to kiss her too. Nancy joined him.

Beth was on her knees and putting her arms around Eva, tears slipping down her face.

"Oh Mom, I love you." Tom was on his knees and putting his arms around Beth and Eva, "Me too, Mom."

"Well I guess that settles that question," Beth said a moment later, wiping away tears.

"Thank you all, you dear, dears," Eva said tremulously.

Alex tenderly wiped tears from Eva's face. "I told you that they love you. They are a good bunch."

"They are...how could they be otherwise?" She agreed.

"We'll all be glad when you get home from your trip, but I know that you'll have a wonderful time, Alex. You have looked forward to it for so long," Bill said.

"Maybe next year Nancy and I'll go."

"Why don't you come this year?" Alex urged. "Tom and Bill Jr. will be here, with David and Jason and Steve too, as soon as he gets home from school. They can handle what orders we have now. It's time that you had a vacation too. We can call home occasionally and we'll always be able to use the radio. If we are needed, we can fly home for a day or two. Let's let the younger guys have a chance on their own, to show the stuff they are made of. A chance to develop their ideas, and give us older brothers a chance to have some time together again. We've great gals to help and enjoy. And we'll have Jim along to help too."

"That sounds like a wonderful idea," Eva agreed.

Bill and Nancy looked at each other. Bill said, "Let's do it Honey, what say?"

"Could we really?"

"Can we be ready?"

"Yes! Yes! Let's go!" Nancy cried.

"Let's see, we have this week. Eva and Alex's wedding is next Saturday," Bill turned to Alex, "You plan to leave on the boat on the following Wednesday or Thursday. We'll be ready to go won't we, Nancy?"

"Yes! Yes! We'll be ready! Oh! I'm so excited!"

Nancy jumped up and pulling Bill to his feet, hugging him.

Turning to Alex, she cried, "Oh Alex, thank you! But we'll be along on your honeymoon," she sobered.

Alex laughed, "Eva and I will have a day or two by ourselves and the boat is big enough for us all to have our privacy. We'll enjoy your company, and Jim's too. We'll enjoy having some one to share the trip and all the things that we'll see."

"Bill, we'll have to buy a few things," Nancy said.

Eva took a piece of paper out of her purse, "Nancy, maybe this'll help. Alex gave me this list."

Alex took the list and looked at it, then handed it to Nancy. "This'll help," he agreed. "Don't forget cameras."

"And remember, everyone is to be in Oregon City Friday evening. We are going have a wedding before we go to Alaska."

Later: "Dad, let's keep the tradition going." Tom brought the big old Bible to him. "Will you read a verse to us before anyone goes home?"

Alex took the Book and handed it to Eva.

"Will you read a bit? Then I will."

"Oh, yes! I've been reading in First John -*That which we have seen and heard declare we unto you, that ye also may have fellowship with us: and truly our fellowship is with the Father, and with His Son Jesus Christ.' Verse 4. 'And these things write we unto you, that your joy may be full.'* The three books of John are wonderfully enlightening. We have been in fellowship with family and friends, which we have enjoyed so very much, and our fellowship means more when we are 'of like mind' united in the fellowship with Christ, and that we may commune with Him at anytime, our fellowship with the Father assured."

Eva handed the Book to Alex.

Alex said, "I see also in the third chapter, verse 1, *'Behold, what manner of love the Father hath bestowed upon us, that we should be called the sons of God: therfore the world knoweth us not, because it knew Him not.'* *'Beloved, now we are the sons of God, and it doth not yet appear what we shall be: but we know that, when He shall appear, we shall be like Him; for we shall see Him as He is.'* Verse 3, *'And every man that hath this hope in Him purifieth himself, even as He is pure.'*

How can I add to that! Shall we pray?"

They were soon headed for home, Eva and Alex returning to her apartment. Brandon had given Alex a key, so he could come and go, as he liked. Jason was there and had put his things away.

They were soon in bed.

Eva slept, only to dream again.

She dreamed that she was in a garden like place. There was green grass and trees and flowers, a park like place. Many friends were there, talking and laughing happily.

She walked about among the flowers, talking to the friends.

There was a path that she walked on and suddenly Alex was with her, taking her hand to walk with her in this lovely place. The path led past what looked like the edge of the park, and Henry was standing there, just outside of the park.

He had a book in his hand. The book looked valuable; it had a dark red leather cover with brass metal corners.

Henry grabbed Eva's arms and said, "I want to tell you what my book says."

He pulled her by the arms, and led her away from the park-garden, out into a desert like place.

There were big rocks and a rough rock path. It was a harsh land with dead trees and little grass, all dried up.

She trued to pull away from Henry, but he held on to her arm.

"I don't like this place. I want to go back to my friends," she told him.

"You want to walk with that man, but my book says that you can not do that. It is against the rules for you to walk with any other man," he said, his voice with a hard edge.

"There can be nothing wrong with me walking with my friends," she objected.

Henry ignored that and said, raising his voice, "My book says that you'll always belong to me and you can never have someone else. Whether you walk with me or not, you cannot walk with him. I won't let you."

"I don't want to be with you any more, and we *are* divorced," she insisted. She tried again to pull away from him.

Henry was almost yelling at her, "MY book says that you can not divorce me," he laughed and it sounded mean and hard.

"When you shoved your Bible away and wouldn't pray with me, I knew that I couldn't help you anymore. We are divorced! You live your life and I'll live mine...apart!"

"But my book says-" he started again.

She grabbed the book, "Let's see that book."

The cover had big black letters, reading, *MY BOOK OF RULES*.

"Yes, it's YOUR book of rules! Take YOUR book of rules and live by them if you must, but I won't."

She shoved the book back at him, gave him a shove and jerking away from him, and ran back to the garden where Alex was waiting for her.

She had thrown the covers off in her effort of jerking away and woke up crying, "Alex, Alex!"

She went to her knees by her bed, crying out to her Lord for help and guidance.

As she knelt there, the Lord spoke to her; "*My daughter, fear not, for I, the Lord thy God will hold thy right hand, saying to thee, Fear not; I will help thee.*'

She found the scripture in Isaiah 41, 13. When she'd read that scripture, she searched and found in Isaiah 51, 16.

'*I have put my words in thy mouth, and I have covered thee in the shadow of mine hand,*' this comforted her. She turned to Psalms 63, verse 7, '*Because thou hast been my help. therefore in the shadow of thy wings will I rejoice.*' *Verse 8, ' My soul followeth hard after thee: thy right hand upholdeth me.*'

When she'd read these scriptures, claiming them for her help, she rejoiced, thanking and praising the Lord.

Comforted and with thanks and praise on her lips, she crept into bed and slept. Fear was vanquished and peace and joy filled her thoughts.

She was to recall this night to remind her of her ever-present help.

CHAPTER FIFTEEN

Eva woke early, remembering the dream and the words from the Lord.

Even in my dream, I won! I shoved Henry's book at him and broke his hold on me. Yes, his hold is completely broken. I'm free of him. I just had to be reminded again. I'm free!

She lifted her face and hands to the Lord, thanking Him for the help.

She had breakfast ready when Jason and Alex were ready to eat.

"Up early, Hon? You made your special waffles, I see." Alex said, claiming his kiss.

"Yes, Mom, I want your recipe for these," Jason said, as put yogurt and strawberry jam on his.

"The cookbook has a tab for this recipe, and I'll leave you the cookbook."

"Thanks Mom."

"Eva are you sure that you won't forget how to make them? I want you to show me too."

"I have it on some cards, and I'll take one with me, just in case." She went and got a card and gave it to Alex.

"Here's a copy just for you now, to be sure that you get it," she laughed.

"What are you going to do today? Are you going with us," Alex asked, as they were getting ready to leave.

"I'd love to go with you but I better get some sorting and packing done. Jim is coming tomorrow to take everything to the apartment that I won't need for the next few days, or for the trip. I better have it ready for him."

Jason and Alex kissed her and were soon on their way.

Soon after arriving at the shop, Alex found time to make some phone calls; one was to a real estate agent, *'Edward E. Browser, 'Real Estates, Suburban and Summer Homes.'*

Hmm, I wonder?

*

Eva soon had the washer going and things sorted into piles of boxes to go to the apartment and her things for the boat in bags.

She was folding the last from the dryer when the phone rang.

It was Jewel, "Can you come have lunch with us, Alice, Len, and I?"

"Sure, how soon?"

"Right away."

"Is there anything special that I need to hurry for?"

"No, we just want to see you."

'Okay, I'll be there in a jiffy. At the Mexican Place?"

"Yes. Hurry."

"I'm on my way."

They sat and talked over coffee. Eva reminded them that they were to be in Oregon City in time for dinner on Friday evening. She gave them cards with their room numbers. Len and Alice were going to ride to Oregon City with Jewel and Ben.

"We are going to miss you. You're going to be gone most of the summer?"

"Well, that is kind of the plan. There are places that Alex has planned to see. How long it'll take, we don't know."

"It sounds like a great trip."

"Yes, it does. David and Nancy have decided to go with us. I'm glad. I was wondering if Alex and Jim could manage the boat, just the two of them. The other boat that is going at the same time will help as they have made the trip before, but they won't be on Alex's boat to help. Of course, I know very little about boats."

They lingered a while, talking.

Alice asked, "Can you come to dinner this evening? Alex and Jason too, of course, and Jewel and Ben."

Jewel and Eva accepted, gladly.

As Eva and Alex drove home that night, Alex turned to her, "Eva, for several days I've been thinking and wondering if Jewel and Ben might go with us. They are good company, fun to be with, and Ben knows a lot about radios; it might be good to have him along. I'd like to ask them, what do you think?"

"Alex, really? I'd love to have them along too. They like to travel, and they have never been there either. I think that the work may be caught up on Ben's job for a while, and Ben may be able to get time off, and he really doesn't have to work, he just works because he likes the job and the work. The people he works for are good employers."

"Let's go by and ask them."

They followed Jewel and Ben home. "May we come in for a few minutes?" Alex asked.

"Of course, come on in." Ben greeted them.

"Ben, Jewel, I've been thinking for a few days, that I wanted to ask you, if you two could go with us on the trip. Do you suppose that you could get some time off from your job? We'd love to have you along."

"Oh! Oh Ben! Can we go?" Jewel exclaimed.

"Well, I don't know. That sounds wonderful. I don't know. I'll call them right now. I'll call the Boss."

Which he did, explaining about the trip, and would there be any possibility to have a few weeks off. By the look on his face, they hoped that the answer would be 'Yes.'

As he hung up the phone, he turned to Jewel.

"Well?" she asked breathlessly.

"Well, start packing your bags."

"We can go?"

"Yes, we can go!" Ben laughed.

"I'll make a list of suggestions for things you may need on the boat."

"Alex, - I – this is such a surprise, such a wonderful surprise! It's a dream of a lifetime. How can we say thanks?"

"Just be ready to go with us. We'll have a great time."

"Oh – won't we though!" Jewel seconded.

"It sure sounds like it'll be a fun trip." Ben agreed.

"I'm sure glad that you're coming with us." Alex said.

"Me too, I'm so glad you two are coming, Jewel. It's something that we have talked about but never dreamed we'd get to do," Eva added, hugging Jewel.

"I'll start shopping and packing tomorrow!" Jewel declared.

Later, as they said good night at her door, Eva said, "Thank you Alex. I had dreamed that we, Jewel and I, would get to make a trip, never dreaming that it would be as great as this is going to be. To think that I'll be going with my new husband too! Oh, sometimes I think that I must be dreaming, and what a dream!"

"It has been *my* dream for a long time too, but I never dreamed that I would have a brand new wife along. I've never dreamed of even *having* a new wife. I feel like giving another big yell!"

"On No! Not tonight."

"Guess maybe I can restrain myself, but I don't know for how long," he grinned.

*

Alex and Jason were had breakfast nearly ready when Eva woke. "I can't imagine why I slept so late she apologized.

"It's okay, Mom. It's our turn this morning."

"Forgot to tell you, Steve called yesterday afternoon, right after I got here. He'll be home tomorrow."

"Good. It'll be good to have him home. You two will be good company for each other after I've left; and his friends will be coming out to see him. I met some of them, and they seem to be good people. I enjoyed them. But I won't be here long now."

"That's right," Alex agreed with a grin. "I've some things to do this morning, but I'll be at Jim's and the boat by about nine-thirty. Jim is coming after your things right away, are you ready for him?"

"Yes, I'm almost ready, just a few things more. I have to leave a few things here to last me for a few days and my things that I'm taking to Oregon for the wedding. Yes, I'll have the things to take to the apartment ready as soon as Jim comes."

"You're driving your car down to the boat?"

"Yes. I'll take my things that go on the boat."

"I'll see you in about three hours then." Alex and Jason were soon off to the shop.

Jim came with Alex's pickup and took her things to go to the apartment. "I should be back to the boat by nine-thirty. Alex should be there by then," Jim told her.

"I'll be there then too," Eva said.

Eva soon had the dishes done and what little else there was to do; everything was neat and clean. She fed the ducks and birds, the chipmunks and squirrels.

"I'll miss you guys," she told the doe and fawns, as they stepped daintily away after receiving their chunks of apples and carrots.

"A few more days, but Jason and Steve will be here."

Eva was putting the last of her things into the back of her car, when she discovered Henry was standing beside her car.

He put a bag into her car too.

"Henry!"

"Hello, Eva. Are you going to town?"

"Yes, I'm going to Tacoma."

"Good. I'll ride with you. I'm going to meet a guy down town."

"How did you get here? Can't you go to with whoever brought you out here?"

"No. A guy dropped me off and I'm to meet him down town. What's it going to hurt if I ride in with you? I have to go down town, and you're going."

"All right, but I'm in a hurry, I'm meeting someone too."

"Well, let's go then."

Eva closed the back of her car. "You must be staying in town, you have a bag."

"Yes, well, I'm not sure yet, just where I'll be staying."

He didn't say that he planned to use Jason as a lever to get to stay at the lake, with Jason and Eva.

Eva sent a quick silent prayer to her Lord for help.

"Lord, I don't like this," she thought, but she remembered the reassurance she'd received from the Lord, and knew that He was an ever present help.

"So, Jason has gone to work for this friend of yours?"

"Yes. Jason likes the work."

Henry asked questions, which Eva answered with as little information as possible.

Eventually, Henry lapsed into an occasional comment on the changes in the city that had occurred in the twenty years since he'd been there.

Eva parked her car on the street above the boat dock where Alex's boat was.

"This is as far as I go down town. There are bus stops here on every corner, going in several directions from here. You can get out and catch a bus to where ever you're going."

Eva got out and opened the back of her car for Henry to get his bag, stepping out of the way. Henry came to the back of the car, but instead of taking his bag, he took the keys out of the lock, closed the back, and walked to the driver's side. "I'll be back in fifteen minutes or less," he said.

He drove off, leaving Eva standing there, utterly amazed.

I can't believe this! Even my purse is in the car!

She stepped up onto the sidewalk and stood watching her car disappear down the street.

"Of all the nerve! How dare he! He took my car – my purse – my things!" She checked her watch. Thirty minutes later, she walked down the hill to the dock where Alex and Jim were at the boat.

"Honey, where's your car? What's wrong?"

She explained what had happened.

"Alex, when I opened the back of my car, I expected Henry to take his bag and go. Instead, he took my car and drove off. He said he'd be back in fifteen minutes, but it's been almost an hour.

Alex's face was white.

"Eva, you were with Henry alone. Are you sure that you're over him, sure that you're through with him? No doubts?" Alex asked.

"Alex! I'm so disgusted with him. This is typical of him. It's enough to make me hate him all over again, to hope that I never have to see him again. Why -- do you ask?"

"I had to be sure. Your happiness comes first. The thought of you changing your mind - of loosing you – it was a tough thought. My life would be empty without you."

"Alex, I'm yours…forever. I think that I've waited for you all of my life."

Alex heaved a big sigh. His face regained color, and lit up as he smiled down at her.

"Jim, call Officer Mac. Eva, calm down. Henry's not going to spoil anything by doing this. We'll put Officer Macdonald in charge, and then we'll take the boat out for a little run."

Jim came back, "Officer Macdonald will be here any minute; he'll take care of getting your car back, Eve."

A few minutes later, "There's your car," Alex said, "and Mac's right behind him. Henry's coming down the steps. Jim, get the keys and bring Eva's car down and put it in the warehouse."

"I'll take those keys," Jim said, holding out his hand, as Henry reached the bottom step.

"These are my wife's keys," Henry protested. "I don't know what you think you're doing-"

"It's *you*, that seems to be having trouble knowing what *you* should be doing," Alex countered.

"Eva, go aboard the boat. Now, honey, please." Alex gently turned her to start her towards the boat.

"Jim will bring your things."

Jim drove Eva's car down the ramp, parking it near the boat. Jim opened the back of the car, handing Henry's bag to him. Then giving Eva's purse to her.

"I'll bring the rest." He took a bag and taking Eva's arm, helped her to the boat, returning for the rest of her things. "Just stay here and wait for Alex."

Jim put the car out of sight in the warehouse. Officer Macdonald drove down the ramp and stepped out of his car.

"Everything under control, Alex? Anything missing from the car?" he asked.

"That's my wife's car," Henry protested.

"No, It's *my* wife's car," Alex countered.

"But she can't marry...you...you're not married yet, anyway!" Henry sputtered.

"As far as *you're* concerned, we are." Alex voice was hard. "Don't come near her again."

"You have no right to tell me what to do."

Alex interrupted, "As far as Eva's concerned, I've every right to protect her and her things."

Alex remembered the Lord telling him to give good for evil, and his look and voice softened. "She's mine from now on. You lost her, due to your own faults and actions."

"I'll take over now, Alex." Mac's voice was reassuring.

"Go see if anything is missing. We'll wait right here for just a minute," Mac said, turning to Henry.

"Eva, are your things all here? Is anything missing?" Alex asked. They went inside.

"Everything's here," she said, checking the bags.

They went back out on the deck. "It's all here, Mac," Alex called.

"Do you want to press charges for a stolen vehicle?" Mac asked.

Alex looked at Eva.

"No," she said. "Let's not press charges."

"No, Mac, Eva said, no charges. Thanks Mac."

"Jim, cast off the lines, we're going out."

Alex put his arm around Eva, putting her in front of him, as he started the motor, backing away from the dock and moved out away. Alex waved at Jim.

"Eva, you can't—" Henry yelled, but Officer Macdonald took Henry by the arm to put him into the patrol car.

Eva turned and put her arms around Alex. She was safe in his embrace, her face against his chest. She stood thus, knowing that Henry could see her in Alex's arms. She was glad that Henry had seen her there, glad that she could hide there. It felt so good, so safe.

After a few minutes, she turned and looked ahead.

"Where are we going, Alex?"

"To fill the tanks with fuel first."

"But we are leaving Tacoma."

"Seattle is just ahead."

"Seattle!"

They were soon at a dock and the tanks being filled with fuel.

Eva went to the cabin where Jim had taken her things, and started putting them away. Alex came and opened a closet.

"Are you going to have enough room for your things?"

"Yes, plenty of room."

"Did you bring a dress? This will do." Alex took out the western outfit that she had worn that first night to dinner.

"Put this on Eva, please?"

"Now?"

"Yes, now please."

"Are we going out to lunch?"

"That too."

Alex took his westerns and went to Jim's cabin to change. Soon Alex knocked at the door. "Come in Alex," Eva called.

"Honey, I'm going to move the boat a little ways, so sit down for a few minutes."

She could see out, when she opened some drapes.

"How different the city looks from here! We'll be doing this for weeks! How exciting! Will we get tired of it? I don't think so; there are lots of things to see!"

Alex had soon tied the boat up at a dock and came to the cabin. He came to sit by Eva.

"Do you remember the promise I made a few days ago?"

"Promise?"

"Well, it was a promise from me, a promise to you and me.

This today, was not a dream, but a real thing that happened, where Henry upset you. I said that I didn't want you go through anything like that alone again. It has happened, and I wasn't there. No more, Eva. You're not leaving my side anymore. Not until we are in our own home and I can be sure that you're protected."

"Alex! What are we going to do?"

"What do you think about taking the boat to Oregon? Go down by boat to be married?"

"That's days away."

"We'll cruse around the San Juan Islands and out and down the coast, then up the Columbia and Willamette rivers to Oregon City. We may not have much extra time; it's quite a ways to go."

"All alone?"

"All alone, just you and me."

"You really did mean it!"

"Yes, I really did and do, mean it."

"Ooh!"

"I have a friend here in Seattle, a judge, who I'm sure will fix it and marry us yet today, or tomorrow. It's early, not yet noon. Let's go have some lunch and think about it."

"Okay."

They walked a few blocks, took a bus, and went up in the Space Needle for lunch. They sat looking out over the city.

It was a clear day and Mount Rainier stood beyond the city, shining majestically in the sun. As the restaurant rotated, they had a view of the Sound, with boats and ferryboats leaving trails of their wakes, shining in the sun as they moved about.

They talked about the view, and the way things looked different from the water.

"We'll see several cities and towns on the trip north, but none as big as Seattle or Tacoma."

"We'll get charts of the coast south and the Columbia and Willamette rivers and we'll plan our trip together. That's not as far as Alaska, but we'll get some experience before the Alaska trip."

"Just you and me? You won't need someone else? I haven't had much experience on a boat, at least never one this size, this big."

"We'll do just fine. I only need you, and you'll learn to run the boat, everything."

"Me? I'll learn to run the boat? You'll...you'll always be there close, right?"

"Yes, dearest, I'll be close."

"I'm excited, Alex!"

"Not afraid?"

"No, not as long as I'm with you!"

"Just the two of us, together!"

"I like that, Alex, the two of us, together, alone!"

"That's what we need to talk about now." He was holding her hand. "Shall I call the Judge now or wait until tomorrow?"

"What will we do until tomorrow?"

"Well, we're staying on the boat."

"But what about the wedding in Oregon – what about our families? What about all of the plans for the wedding?"

"We can't spoil it for them!" She finished.

"We'll go down and get married there too. Twice married sounds good to me, as long as I'm getting married to you."

Eva's face was radiant, her eyes sparkling. "Alex, you are such a wonderful man! I could kiss you!"

"Áha! I knew there was a good reason, besides the view, why I sat beside you."

He claimed the kiss, not caring what the other patrons in the restaurant might think. "In fact, I'll have two."

"Will there be anything else? The water had returned. "Celebrating a birthday or anniversary?"

"Anniversary – tomorrow."

"Congratulations! How many?"

"One. One day tomorrow. We're getting married today. Come, let's go, let's not keeping them waiting."

The waiter stood there with his mouth open, watching them leave.

They stopped at a flower shop and Alex asked them to make a corsage. Well, it turned out to be a little bigger than a corsage. It started with the yellow orchids.

"And add some of those white orchids, and some of those tiny white flowers. I like the forget-me-nots. Better add a couple of the Talisman roses, and a couple of the buds too. Will you put on a ribbon and streamers of this ribbon that matches the Talisman roses? Now, will you make one about like it for her hair?"

They watched the flowers being arranged. Alex carrying the box, they went back to the boat.

"Alex, what will I wear?"

"What you have on."

"This western outfit?"

"Yes. That's why I asked you to wear it. It's special to me. It's what you had on for our first date."

"There is a phone here on the dock, I'll go phone Judge Thayer."

While Alex was phoning, Eva went to the cabin to fix the flowers in her hair.

"Look at you gal," she told the reflection in the mirror. "Sure don't need much makeup. Alex does this to me! We are getting married in a few minutes! Married! Married to Alex! Alex! – We'll be alone on the boat for three whole days...and nights!"

Alex called Judge Thayer's office. When Alex gave his name and asked to speak to the Judge, the secretary told him that Judge Thayer was out of the office.

"Will you give me his number so that I can call him?"

"If you'll give me your message, I'll call him and call you back. It may take some time. He is on a cruse ship, somewhere in the islands. Will that help you?"

"Who is covering his calendar?"

"The Judge cleared his desk for a six week vacation. I'm referring calls to two other Judges. I can give you those numbers."

Alex left the phone booth at last.

He stopped and got the needed charts for the trip down the coast and up the Columbia and Willamette rivers to Oregon City.

He asked advice from the Harbor Master, and was advised as to the approximate amount of travel time between safe harbors, where they should dock for the nights.

Eva had put the flowers in her hair, and holding the bouquet, turned to Alex as he entered the cabin.

"Alex, what's wrong?"

"Sweetheart, Judge Thayer is out of town, and everyone else that I talked to, thinks that at our age, we can wait until Saturday to get married in Oregon City."

"Oh! Well. Alex, thank you for trying, but, of course, we can wait. It's all planned anyway. It'll be okay. It'll be more than okay; and we'll have this time alone together. It's exciting, being on the boat, and alone; exciting making this trip to Oregon on the boat."

"The Harbor Master suggested that we head right out. We'll hit some weather, and we'll need to catch the tides just right on entering the Columbia River, so we must be there at the right time. He told me where to stop for tonight before the storm hits. We need to leave right away.

"But you know that we don't have our wedding things with us. Someone will have to bring them down for us. Write down what you need and we'll call Jason. I'll call Beth about my things. Then they'll know where we are too."

They made the calls, calling Jim too, and returned to the boat.

"Before we change into work clothes, I'd like to say the vows that I had hoped to say before the Judge. We'll say them before a higher authority, Our Lord. Put the flowers back in your hair, Sweetheart."

Alex brought out a Bible and they knelt by a small table. Alex found the verses that he wanted and read them.

They made their vows to love, cherish and honor each other and to be as one, one with Jesus as the head and Lord over their marriage and home.

Their tear-filled eyes spoke more and they knew that the Lord was blessing them.

Alex took her left hand, "Eva, the other rings are at home, but we'll use this ring as a token of our pledge of marriage. Father, this ring is an emblem of my pledge to Eva, and to you, that I vow to love her and care for all the days of my life."

"Alex," Eva took the chain from around her neck, taking the ring off of the chain.

"Father, this ring is an emblem and token of my vow and pledge to Alex, and to you Father, that I will love, honor and care for Alex all the days of my life."

"Eva, before God I claim you as my wife."

"Alex, before God I claim you as my husband."

"This is a real as it can be."

"Yes Alex, I know that this is real."

"May I kiss my wife?"

"And I will kiss my husband."

"You're a beautiful bride. Thank you for wearing this outfit and thank you for wearing the flowers."

"Darling Alex, thank you for the flowers and thank you for the wedding. Thank you for loving me."

"Father God, I'm so thankful, so blessed to have this dear Lady as mine, my wife."

They stood and embraced. "This ring?"

"I wanted you to have one like mine, I love it so."

"But- how did you find it?"

"I went to your jewelers and he had it. Alex, I'm paying for it out of my own money as a special gift to you. I'm so glad that I did, so that I had it for today."

"Eva, it is special. You're a most dear Lady. I thank you, Sweetheart." He kissed her again, in awe of her love for him.

The sound of a ferryboat horn near by brought them back to the present.

"I'd like to spend the rest of the day celebrating, but the Harbor Master suggested that we'd better get started. We should get some distance yet today. I'll do some checking of the charts this evening and maybe tomorrow we can spend a few hours sightseeing before we go on."

They changed into other cloths and put weather coats and things near at hand, if they should be needed.

"I hope to be safely moored before the storm hits this evening," Alex assured Eva.

They were, but the storm hit as they were finishing their evening meal. The boat was securely tied from both sides, so as not to bump anywhere.

They had put up the canvas storm curtains and had them tied securely down, but the storm hit with such vengeance that Alex went to double check the storm canvas.

"All secure, safe and sound," he said as he returned. "We are 'as snug as two bugs in a rug,' as the saying goes," he grinned at her.

"Eva, come listen with me. We'll do some checking."

He turned on the radio for the weather report, then the Coast Guard report, checking the maps with each reports.

"According to these reports, there should be clearing with sunshine and a mild breeze by noon tomorrow. The seas will be down to normal by evening. We should have good weather for the next 5 days or longer. Couldn't be better for us."

He picked her up swinging her around, kissed her. They laughed happily together, their happiness bubbling up, revealed in their eyes. "We can spend tomorrow here, as long as we leave early Thursday morning. We'll make it to Ilwaco before dark and spend the night there. We should make the tide just right, with no problem, Friday morning to enter the Columbia River and up the Willamette to Oregon City before dark Friday evening."

"Really, Alex, You can tell all that by the reports and the charts? How exciting! We'll be in Oregon City Friday evening! I'm glad that we are going by boat. It'll be a great trip! I hope," she added, listening to the storm.

"Of course it'll be a great trip, and a preview of the trip up to Alaska. We'll be regular old hand sailors by then, won't we?" Alex laughed.

"Not quite old hands, at least not me, but we'll have some idea of what we are doing by then," Eva agreed.

They soon had things ready for the night.

"Eva, let's start our life together the way the Lord would have us do. Let's read a bit of His Word and pray together before we retire for the night. Would you like that?"

"Yes Alex, please. I want it that way too. He's been good to us."

Alex brought out an old leather bound Bible, well marked with many bits of ribbon and slips of paper marking special places.

"This was my Mother's," he explained. He opened it at the front where there were recorded family members.

Eva looked with him at the names written there. "Magdella Berg, Hans's daughter, Lillihamer, Norge," she read. "My Mother had a sister who lived in Lillihamer, Norway. You have Norwegian ancestors too!" She exclaimed.

"Yes. That was my Mother's Mother," Alex explained.

"So our roots are similar, our families have similar background." They read the names, tracing them down to Alex's birth being recorded there and his children too.

"Where shall we read tonight?" he asked.

"Pick a place that she marked for us, for surely her favorite passages will be something that we'll enjoy too," Eva answered.

They read several, thinking that Mother and Grandmother before her, had saved passages that would bless them in today's time, and guide them in the future too, for that is surely true of the Word of God. They prayed and asked their Lord for continued care and protection in the coming days of travel on the water.

As they prepared for bed, Alex said, "Eva, Honey, we had our own wedding before the Lord, and I'm sure it is as binding as any vows can be, but we'll wait for the ceremony on Saturday. The Lord said to obey the laws of the land.

You'll sleep in our bed, and I'll sleep in Jim's cabin, that way if anyone should say anything, we can say that we didn't sleep together, okay?"

"Oh. Alex, that's a good idea. We'll wait."

Their good night was a hug and a kiss.

The storm continued for a while, calming some, not so windy, mostly rain gusts, which lulled them to sleep, rather than disturb them.

Several hours later, the storm moving from the west, picked up with lightening. At first, it didn't disturb them until the lightning came closer.

It began to crack and crash, coming ever closer, the thunder growing louder. Finally, a close brilliant crash woke Eva. It was followed by another crack, with almost continuous thunder. Her scream was drowned out by the thunder. She jumped out of bed and ran to Alex, and crawled up behind him in the bed, pulling the covers up over her head.

Alex woke, "...what? Oh, the storm. Honey, it's okay, we're safe enough here."

"That may be," she chattered, "but I'm scarred. I hate lightning and thunder."

She waited for the next quieter moment, "besides, you said that if I was scared or upset, that you would be within arms reach. I want that arm, now."

She was trembling. Alex put his arm around her and she snuggled down with her head in the hollow of his shoulder, her arm across his chest, clinging to him. He kept talking to her, singing a bit of a song trying to quiet her, to stop her trembling.

Slowly she relaxed, as the storm passed on to the east.

At last, Alex stopped talking – she was asleep. Asleep in his arms, her head on his shoulder, as she'd said on a day not long ago.

"Now what will I say," he thought, chuckling. He too finally slept, thrilled to have her in his arms.

CHAPTER SIXTEEN

Eva woke slowly. She turned her head and lightly kissed Alex's shoulder near where her face rested.

Alex woke with a start at her movement, knowing of the kiss. He tried not to move, waiting for her to wake completely. He could tell by her breathing that she was waking.

She took a deep breath, exhaling slowly. She moved a bit, and then tensed, realizing where she was, knowing that it wasn't a dream.

Her head really was on Alex's shoulder.

She thought, *What shall I do? I've been here the rest of the night, after Alex said – but the storm –.'* Suddenly she knew that he was awake too. "Alex?"

"Good Morning, Eva."

He could hear the touch of her troubled thoughts. "It's all right, Sweetheart-" he started, but before either one could say more, the radio started: "KJF39B, calling KBC42B", a pause, then it was repeated.

"That's us," Alex said as he recognized the call. Alex went to answer the radio. Eva went to her cabin, put on her robe and slippers, picked up a blanket and went then put it around Alex.

"It's cold in here," she whispered. She went back to find Alex's slippers and brought to him. Kneeling, she lifted one of his feet then the other to put them on him while he was talking.

The radio call was Ben. "We've been listening to the weather reports. Are you all right?"

"Yes," Alex answered, "We were in port and all battened down before the storm hit. We had some rain, then later some lightning and more rain."

Ben came back, "The storm moved on past to the north of us, so we didn't hear it. Jason called us to tell us that you're on the boat. It sounds like a good connection on the radio."

"Yes, we can hear you loud and clear."

"Where are you?"

"We are in Port Angeles. We came on over here yesterday. We'll stay here tonight and go on early in the morning. We should make Ilwaco in about 12 to 14 hours from here. I thought that it would be too far from Seattle to make it to Ilwaco, all in one day. Then on Friday, we'll go on up the Columbia and Willamette Rives to Oregon City. If we don't have to wait for the tide, we should be in Oregon City by about four to six o'clock at the latest."

"Well, that sounds good. We sure wish you well. Have a safe trip and we'll see you Friday evening in Oregon City."

"Yes. Thanks for the call. We'll stand by here for a while, and then we're going over to Victoria and spend some time sightseeing, and will be back to the boat about two this afternoon. Call Jim, will you, and give him an update. Maybe we'll talk to him later."

"Okay, we'll call him, and Jason too. Have a good time. This is KJF39B clear and standing by."

"That was great, Alex, to be able to talk to them so easily from here."

"Yes. Ben was over and installed this radio, so he knew that it would work. You see, we have three radios. This is a Ham radio that we just talked on, and this one is for weather and Coast Guard to be used for that purpose only. The third has many bands and is an emergency radio, also. Here is a logbook to record all calls, also instructions for the radio use if we need to refer to them."

"I've heard Ben and Jewel use their radios, but I've never used one."

"You'll catch on how to do it. See, our call letters are right here where we can see them when we use the radio."

"That's a good idea, I'd never remember them."

"No, I might not either, yet, but we'll learn. I think that we'll use the radio quite a bit on the trip to Alaska. I'm glad that Ben will be with us to help out with the radios. He knows his radios."

"Yes, he sure does. I'm glad that they, Nancy, and Bill will be with us. We'll all have a good time."

"Thank you, Eva, for bringing me the blanket and slippers. It's cold in here this morning. I'll turn on the heat, and then we'd better dress."

"Yes, some clothes will help." Suddenly Eva was shy.

Alex stood with the blanket over his shoulders and pajama bottoms with only a sleeveless undershirt. She remembered her face against his bare chest. How good it had felt when she was afraid in the night.

She remembered that she had kissed his shoulder and felt the color rising in her cheeks, but Alex had turned and turned on the heat.

"Eva, go back to bed for a while until it warms up a bit. I'll dress." He went back to Jim's cabin.

Eva dressed hurriedly.

"Why am I trembling?" She wondered. *"Alex isn't upset at me? —I hope not. I couldn't help it. I was so scared. I hate lightning."*

They came out of their cabins at the same time.

"Eva-"

"Alex-"

They both started to talk at the same time.

"Good Mornings, first, Sweetheart," Alex bent to kiss her.

"Good Morning Alex. Are you upset with me?"

"No, my girl. Not at all!"

"Good."

Alex saw the tears in Eva's eyes, "Tears?"

"Just glad that you aren't upset with me."

He pulled her back into his arms and held her, unable to speak himself, to think that she would cry at the possibility of him being upset with her.

She put her arms around him hugging him as tightly as he was holding her.

She turned for a kiss, her eyes sparkling with tears, tears of joy, now that she knew that Alex wasn't upset at her.

"I'll put the coffee on, and then we'll talk."

"Okay."

"Now, come here and sit by me."

He took her hand and led her to the couch.

"Honey, don't ever be afraid of me. I don't know what you would do, that would upset me. I suppose there are some things, but I don't believe that you would do them."

"But Alex, you said that we wouldn't sleep together because if someone would say something. And I...I..."

"It's all right, Honey. I want you to always be able to come to me, any time, any place."

"But nothing happened, we – we didn't-"

"No we didn't." He smiled, "but, you slept in my arms for half the night."

"But we...*didn't!*"

"Sweetheart, you take things too seriously."

He smiled at her. "There was nothing wrong with you sleeping in my arms. That was the place for you when you needed me. Do you have any idea how great that makes me feel that you would come to me when you're upset? Even just to hold you, it was so important to me. I guess that I must have been sleeping sound or I would have been checking on you. I'm sorry about that. I should have heard the storm and come to you before you got so scared."

"Oh Alex!" she moved onto his lap, and putting her arms around him, hugging him for a moment, then kissed him.

"Well now, those kisses might make me think that we should have. We can go back to bed. I think that we are as married as anyone ever has been. Maybe more so."

"Alex!"

"Yes, dear?"

But, she was hiding her face against his neck. "Thank you, Alex, for being so – so understanding, so well."

"Don't put too much virtue on me, sweetheart. I'm still a man, a man who is in love with you, and a bit crazy right now. Maybe I made the wrong decision last night, maybe I should have asked you – let you say."

"You would have *me* make that decision?"

"Maybe I should have. Be honest now, are you, were you, a bit disappointed?"

"Alex!"

"Well?"

"I…oh…I don't know! I thought that I was glad, - kind of – but I – I was lonesome."

"Aha!"

She thrilled at the thought that she would be allowed to make that decision.

Her thoughts continued: *'I know that because of our wedding vows before the Lord that we are married in the eyes of God Yet, I once said 'the next time I'll have my marriage certificate next to my heart first.' I love Alex and he loves me so much, that he would have me make the decision. Either way would be all right with him. My decision!'*

"But we made it through the night," she said.

"Yes, we did. It was a little tough, but we made it."

"Alex, I –"

"Don't say it, please don't say that you're sorry, or I may misunderstand, - and take you back to bed yet."

She began to laugh. She leaned back to look at him. He was grinning, and she laughed more.

"Alex—"

"And don't tell me right now, how good I am, or how much you love me. I'm right on the edge,"

She got up, still laughing, took his hand, and pulled him up.

"Go fix me some breakfast, kind Sir, --oops," putting her hand over her mouth, she stood looking up at him, still laughing a bit.

"I'll have to learn to cook on the boat," she said, trying to change the subject.

"Well, we have two nights to go."

"Alex-"

"There you go again." He stood leaning against the counter, grinning. Finally, "All right, breakfast."

A few minutes later he said, "It's a good thing that we can laugh at ourselves."

"Yes," she agreed, not daring to make further comment, just yet.

Eva set the table and poured coffee, and breakfast was soon served. They sat looking at each other, smiling, cautiously on Eva's part.

Finally, she said, "What would be a safe subject to start a conversation?"

Alex grinned, "Well, I guess that would depend on where you wanted the conversation to go."

"Then I'll leave it to you to start -- talking."

Alex through his head back and really laughed.

"Ah Eva, my darling Eva...then I'll be good, and quit teasing you."

He poured them more coffee.

"Meanwhile back to day," he started, "Would you like to take the Ferry Boat and go over to Victoria? We'll have to walk, but I think that it might be fun to look around."

"Yes, I think so too. I've been to Victoria and it's an interesting place."

"All right, let's do it. We'll plan to be back to the boat around three or four, so we can get to bed early. We'll need to start out about four in the morning, so we'll need to have breakfast over and cleared away by then. It's going to be a long day tomorrow. We may be twelve or fourteen hours out on the ocean."

Therefore, they had a day exploring the old city of Victoria, laughing and talking, enjoying the sights, as best seen by walking hand in hand, with secret little looks passing between. They came back to the ferry dock a little early and while they waited, sat watching the water and boats going about.

"It's almost a different world here isn't it?" Eva said.

"Yes it is, kind of quiet. It's good to be away from the big city traffic."

"Yes, for me too. I'm not much of a city gal. I feel more comfortable in the country. I'm glad that your house is away from the busy streets."

"This is interesting here, watching the boats. You wonder who they are and where they are going. Do you suppose that they wonder who we are and where we are going? I'll bet no one would guess that we are going to get married and go on a honeymoon on the boat."

"I don't suppose that happens very often," she agreed. "If they wonder, we'll just keep 'em guessing. Oh, but it's been a fun day, Alex. Thank you."

"You're so easy to please. You enjoy such simple things. I enjoyed it too, just being with you made it a good day. Victoria is a unique and picturesque old town"

"My good times have been mostly with my children and family, my sisters and my brothers. I enjoy seeing new places, and seeing them again. I'm going to have lots of fun, good times. At the risk of causing – something, I enjoy being with you, very much, what ever we do."

"I'm hoping and praying that it'll always be that way for us, Eva. I believe that it will. My whole life has been changed the last few weeks. Just being with you, near you, and my whole being just sings with joy."

"I understand that feeling, Alex, and I'll be crying again in a minute, I'm so happy."

"If you do, I'll have to kiss you right here. But that's okay, I won't mind."

They had just arrived back to the boat and hung up their coats, when the radio started squawking, "KJF39B calling KBC42J."

Alex answered, "KBC42J here, that you Ben?"

"Yes. Jim and Jason are here, and want to talk to you."

"Alex, this is Jim. I called down to Oregon City to be sure that you have a moorage. It's all set, they'll be expecting you between four and six o'clock Friday evening."

"Thanks, Jim. Guess I hadn't thought that far ahead."

"Well, since it was a rather sudden decision, I thought that I'd better check to be sure. How's the boat running?"

"It's running great. I've taken it easy here in the sound. Don't know how it'll go on the sea. I hope that I haven't miscalculated the time element."

"No, I don't think so. I checked with the Coast Guard too. Your figures should be close."

"If it looks like we'll be late tomorrow evening, we can put into Westport in Grays Harbor, I think."

"Okay Alex, I'll check with them too."

"Thanks Jim. I sure am glad that you thought of all this. I guess I just took off, didn't I."

"That you did, Alex. How is Eva doing?"

Alex held the mike to her. "I'm doing just great Jim, thanks. We are having a good time."

"That sounds good, keep it up. Here's Jason."

"Mom, Alex, I just wanted to tell you, so as to relieve both your minds...Abbigail put Dad on a plane and sent him back east to his brother Earl. His plane ticket is one way, so that he can't come right back. She called Earl and asked him to get Dad to stay there, maybe all summer. So don't be afraid that he'll show up at the wedding. Just wanted you to know."

Alex answered, "Well. That's - that sounds good, Jason. Thank you for letting us know."

"Abbi was really upset with Dad for what he did up here and insisted that he leave. He should go see his brother anyway; this was a good excuse for him to go now."

"Oh Jason, I'm sorry that you kids have to go through all this again."

"It's all right Mom, it's about time that we, us kids, put him in his place. It may be a good thing that Abbi got to him before I did; I was pretty mad. He should have a good time with Earl. Anyway, rest easy about it, have fun, and enjoy the trip. We'll see you Friday evening. I think the whole gang'll be waiting for you when you get there. We are all anxious to have it all go well for you. Love you both."

"Thanks Jason. We – we are a bit overwhelmed, like Eva says. Thanks are not enough."

Jim answered, "All's well Alex, we know that our God is watching over you, where ever you are."

"This is Ben. Just want to say amen to Jim's thought there. Unless there is something else, we'll be clear and standing by."

Alex answered. "Thanks again everyone, and our love to you all. See you soon. I'll try to call you on the radio about five in the morning, if you're up."

"I'll be up and listening for you. This is KJF39B clear and standing by."

"KBC42J clear and standing by."

"Sweetheart, don't cry. Jason said that everything is taken care of."

"I know, it's just that I've never wanted my kids to be hurt by – things."

"You have protected them, now they are protecting you. That Abbi! Isn't she something?"

"That's my darling."

"Yeah, mine too. They are all good kids. The best."

"And Jim, what a guy he is!"

"Yes, isn't he? He thought of things that I just spaced out, I guess. All I could think of was getting you out of town, protect you from more hurt. To run away with you."

"I don't think that Henry will ever bother me again. Now that he knows that the kids won't put up with it anymore."

"Honey, sit down and rest a while. We've had quite a walk. I'll make us some supper. Here let me take off your shoes. Put you feet up."

"I'll sit and rest, if you'll sit with me, then I'll help later. Come."

"Sounds good to me," he grinned, sitting down beside her, his arm around her.

She cuddled into his shoulder with a contented sigh, taking his free hand in her two.

"I guess you did run away with me, didn't you, like you said a bit ago."

"I sure did."

"I'm glad."

"Are you really, Sweetheart?"

"Yes, Alex, I'm glad to be here with you. Oh, I'm sure that everything would have worked out if we had stayed. But this is so...so..."

"So...what?"

"I'm trying to find the best word. *Right*...that's the word. It seems so...right. Like we belong here, just now, right here, right now. No other place would be so right, as being here together now. Do you know what I mean?"

"Yes, I believe that too."

"It's such a contented feeling, safe secure, at home kind of feeling. Oh, I suppose there'll be storms, like last night, but we won't think of that possibility now. We weathered that storm. Let's just enjoy this, now."

"You feel safe with me?"

"Yes Alex, I do. I felt safe, content, and happy. I'm running out of adjectives, - sparkly, effervescent, excited. How many more emotions can I have? I'm running over with them," she laughed softly, tears in her eyes, as she turned for a kiss.

"You...you overwhelm me..."

She agreed. "If we are like this now, what'll it be like after we are married? Married! Alex, it's like I haven't really lived before. Like life was humdrum, and it really wasn't. There were good times. I had joy. Happy times with my kids and family, my brothers and sisters. There were even some happy times with Henry. If there hadn't been those bad times, our life would have been good. We were poor when I was a child, but we had love. We were a close family, but I've had nothing like this...because I never really had this kind of love before, the love of a man. A woman needs love to be complete. My kids love me and others love me, but it's nothing like this, this wonderful, glorious love. Such a wonderful man to give me that love."

He couldn't speak. He just held her. They sat quietly for a while; both 'overwhelmed' in the glory of their feelings.

They finally fixed supper and prepared for bed. Alex was still so overwhelmed that he didn't tease her, but kissed her good night and went to bed in Jim's bunk.

What their thoughts were, we'll leave alone.

Finally, they slept, after awhile. Each alone. All night.

CHAPTER SEVENTEEN

Alex had set an alarm, but he was up and had it shut off before it could ring. He tried to be quiet; to let Eva sleep a bit longer, but she was soon dressed and ready to help.

Alex had to remind her to eat.

She said, "I'm like a little kid, I'm so excited! The last two days have been exciting, but today! Today we go on the ocean!"

"Eva, you must eat. I don't know how busy we'll be, I've never been on the Ocean either, except on a charter fishing boat. This boat is much bigger; it'll be new experience for me too."

"I was once on a charter fishing boat too, years ago. Well, we'll be having the experience together. Together, like you said." She smiled, her happiness showing on her face, her eyes sparkling with the excitement.

They managed to eat a good breakfast, clear things away and were under way before four o'clock.

There weren't many boats out yet, so the going was uneventful. Alex was watching the compass and charts to be sure that they were traveling in the right area through the Strait of Juan de Fuca.

Vancouver Island on the north, and on the south, Hurricane Ridge and the Olympic Mountains were beginning to brighten with the rising sun. There was the promise of a clear, beautiful day.

They could see lights on the shore on both sides from time to time.

Alex indicated lights from the south shore, "I believe those are lights from Seku. We are more than an hour out, and it's five o'clock, so we'll call Ben."

Ben answered immediately. "You're coming in loud and clear. About where are you?""

"We just passed Seku, so we are about forty miles from Port Angeles."

"You're making good time."

"Yes we are. The tide is right, the breeze gentle, the water is fairly smooth, and there's been no traffic to bother us. The motors are humming along smooth. It looks like a beautiful day ahead, weather man says so too."

"Well good. You might try calling us again when you get south past the mountains."

"Yes, I've been looking at the map, and maybe we can reach you from around off Copalis Beach or Ocean Shores. We'll try then. It should be around two o'clock this afternoon."

"If I'm not home by then, Jewel will answer your call."

"Alex, this is Jewel. I'll be standing by waiting for your call.

We have some friends who'll be listening in, too, so if you can't reach us maybe they can relay for us."

"Great. We may be able to reach you from down near the Columbia River too. We'll try in the morning too."

"Yes, do that. It's good to hear from you! We'll be standing by. KJF39B clear and standing by."

"Thanks for the come back. KBC42J clear and standing by."

An hour or so had passed and Vancouver Island was disappearing behind them. The Ocean had spread to the north and west, a vast expanse of sea and clear blue sky. The water had changed from a gunmetal gray to a deep blue, with sea green on the tops of the swells.

The sun was lighting up the little rivulets running along, turning them into sparkling gems. The swells were low and running at a slow, even pace, making the Ocean seem almost flat, it was so quiet.

The breeze was gentle.

Time passed quickly for them. Alex explaining to Eva the needed navigation equipment: charts, maps, compass, and other equipment that they were to use.

Another hour saw them nearing Cape Flattery, soon to turn in a southerly direction to follow along the coast of Washington. It was all Ocean to the west.

The Olympic Mountains could be seen to the southeast, the sun lighting up the still snow covered peaks.

"How far are we from shore?" Eva asked.

"About five miles from here, but in some places we'll be closer in. If we get too close, then we would have breakers to fight and slow us down. We'll stay out where it is smoother.

We have to stay in deeper water with this size boat. There are some places where it looks deep, but it is only a few feet.

In some places, it is measured in only inches. That's why we have the charts. Then too, we have to stay in the shipping lanes, but stay out of the way of the big ships and tugboats and barges. We'll watch for fishing boats too."

"Eva, look out there, there is a big ship. I think that it is coming in to Seattle or Tacoma, probably from the Orient."

He handed her a pair of glasses. "Yes, I see it. It's coming this way." So passed several hours, seeing ships out to sea, and tugs with barges coming north up the coast.

At last, Eva went to fix something to eat.

"Alex. I've started the coffee and I'll fix us some lunch in a few, but don't you need to take a break? Can I watch for a couple of minutes?"

"Thanks Jo, that's a good idea. You don't need to do anything. There is nothing near us. I'll be right back."

He peeked out to see Eva looking with the glasses, and went back and made the sandwiches, bringing them and the coffee with him.

"How'll it be to eat our lunch here?"

"Oh yes, I'd like that. Thank you."

Alex went back to the high chair, where he could watch as they passed another ship. When they were clear again, Alex turned to see Eva looking at him. A smile lit up her face as he looked at her.

"How is it that you're looking at me so intently?" he asked, with his grin.

"I was thinking how wonderfully, handsome you are."

"Me? Eva do you need new glasses? I'm passable, but that's about all. The beauty is in my Lady."

"Maybe it's a good thing that you think that, but I know the truth. I can see the outward and the inward beauty of a very special man."

He came and got down on his knees in front of her; leaning forward took her glasses off and looked through them. "They aren't tinted and there is no pictures painted on the inside," he laid them in her lap. "Now look at me."

"I still see the same beautiful, wonderful man that I love." She smiled as she put her hands, one on each side of his face.

"Eva, I'm still the Captain of this ship. And Captains have certain rights."

"Yes, and responsibilities too," she laughed.

"It's getting to be too long a day; you haven't kissed me in ever so long."

"Oh, the responsibilities of a married man, or even an *almost* married man, a man who must be married twice to that same Lady. What a responsibility!"

"That's right, and don't let's forget it!"

"You're asking for it, aren't you?"

"Of course. Do I have to beg too? Well if I must, I must."

She put the back of one hand to her forehead, the other to her heart, - "Alex! Oh Alex! Please come kiss me before I die of starvation, neglect, and lack of kisses and hugs!" she cried dramatically.

He did kiss her, several times, until she was nearly breathless.

She caught her breath; "It's about time!"

"Eva, we're at sea and one of us or the other will have to watch out, part of the time at least, remember."

"Yes, I know. I may live a little while longer now, after that pretty good job of it. – You may go watch now, or shall I? I can if your strength is depleted too much."

Laughing, he grabbed her up, "Come sit with me then, where I can hang on to you and watch at the same time."

He sat her on the high chair, which put her at just the right height for easy kissing and hugging.

"Now, my Lady, there'll be no mutiny on this ship."

"Don't be too sure, *me bucco*; I'll not take to neglectful treatment lightly, Sir....OH! Alex! There are two ships, one going each way...and close together! Where do we go?"

"Just this way, me Darlin'."

So, there was a truce on the ship, for a while – out of necessity for navigation.

Finally, Eva said, "Alex, you have been standing quite a while, why don't you take a break, and when you get back, I'll let you have your chair."

"I'm fine, but yes, I'll take a break and walk a bit. By then, we may be in range to give Jewel a holler."

Jewel answered the first call.

"We are just passing Copalis Beach, it looks like from here. Somewhere in that area, anyway."

"Well, you're making good time aren't you?"

"Yes. It has been great, with calm, soft seas, warm. Some traffic, but I believe we are doing everything according to the book," Alex told her.

"This sister of yours is something else," he continued.

"You're just finding that out? It's a bit late now, if you can't handle her!" Jewel was laughing.

"I'm finding out that she can tease just as bad as I can."

"Well, once you get her started, heaven only knows what she'll do next. But I thought that maybe she'd outgrown that."

"Me? Never! I'll always be that same old kid." Eva laughed. "Sis, we're having a great time. It's so beautiful out here. I might not like it if it storms though. The other night – the lightning – was awful."

"You had lightning?"

"Yes. Well, Alex didn't mind it so bad, but me; you know how I hate lightning."

"Yes, I remember being in the car with you and caught in a storm."

"It's beautiful today."

"Alex, do you think that you'll make it to Ilwaco?"

"Yes. We are a little ahead of what I thought. I'll try to call you again from there."

"That sounds good. Well, continued good trip and we'll talk to you later. KJF39B clear and standing by."

"Thanks Jewel. KBC42J clear and standing by."

"Alex, would you like some coffee or something?" Eva asked.

"Yes, some coffee would be good, thanks."

Eva fixed some toast, opened some peaches, and brought it out. "Sit here, Alex, and relax a bit. I'll hold down the chair."

"Thanks Sweetheart. This is good. We won't really fix supper until we are moored, and I'm not sure what time that will be. This hits the spot. I think that we'll be at the dock about five."

"That'll be early enough to fix supper."

"Yes, but you'll be tired. It'll be a long day by then."

"I've loved every minute of it, Alex. It's been so nice."

"That's why I wanted to stay in Port Angeles last night too, so the sea would calm down. We may not be able to do that on the trip to Alaska, but we'll be between islands most of the way up there and back."

"It sounds exciting. If we do have a storm...I'll...you'll... we'll be together – won't we? I won't be alone?"

"That's right. We'll be together at last, and sooner than then, too."

There were fishing boats out around everywhere as they neared and passed Grays Harbor. They went farther off shore, so as not to interfere with the fishing. Even so, there were boats farther out, even at the horizon. A few fishing boats were scattered along the way as they progressed southward. As they were passing Long Beach there were more boats again, and more again as they neared Ilwaco. As they rounded Cape Disappointment, many of the fishing fleet was going in to the dock for the night.

They stopped at an office on the dock for directions, found their mooring spot without much trouble, and were soon tied up. It was just four o'clock, well within the time Alex had hoped for.

He turned to Eva with a sigh and a smile, "We made that long leg of the trip in record time, I think."

"I don't know how long it should take, but we are here, and it's early. Alex, it's been a glorious day!"

When they called Ben on the radio, he was waiting for their call, surprised that they were docked so early.

"It has been a perfect day, perfect traveling conditions, and a perfect traveling companion. Nothing could have been better," Alex told them.

"Do you mean that you have that girl under control, Alex," Jewel asked.

"No, far from it. She is as incredible as ever. If I hadn't loved her before, I would be madly in love with her by now, so you know what kind of condition I'm in now."

"You poor thing!" Jewel laughed.

"Jewel, do you know what she did?"

"Do we dare say such things over the radio?" Ben had joined Jewel in the laugh.

"Oh well, we didn't – we haven't – I mean – Did you see the ring she bought me?"

"The wedding ring? Yes, I was there, remember?"

"No. She bought me a ring like the first one that I gave her."

"No, I didn't know about it."

"The first night out, we had our own little wedding. Just the two of us, and the Lord, and she brought out this ring to say our vows with, and we used the one that I had given her. She was so incredibly sweet. She is the dearest, most wonderful lady. It's not surprising that I love her...but that she loves *me!*"

"Alex, after all that, you ---? You have my blessing, Alex." Jewel was laughing, and they could hear Ben laughing in the background too.

They could hear Eva's, "Alex!"

"I better go – hang up. Clear."

"Alex, do you know what all you said and over the radio?"

"Did I? Well I wanted to tell Jewel about you and this ring you gave me, and tell her what a wonderful darling you are."

"Well, you had your big yell, and over the radio, louder than the *wahoo* at the lake." Eva was laughing.

"...and here I've been out on the ocean, where I could have really given out a big yell, and didn't do it. See what you do to me? I can't even think straight sometimes."

"Alex! Darling! I think that maybe we are in love with each other."

"No kidding? I'm wild about you, lady!"

They were tied up inside at a far end of the dock, but other boats going by caused waves that rocked the boat some.

"It's a good thing that this boat is as large as it is, a smaller boat would rock more," Alex said.

"Maybe all the boats will be in and docked soon and it'll quiet down."

"We'll hope so."

They fixed dinner and had their quiet time with the Good Book. Alex checked on the boat, before going to bed.

"It all looks quiet around now," he said as he came back. He kissed Eva good night and went to bed in Jim's bunk again.

Some time later Eva heard noises. She pulled back a drape to look out. There were two men, one on the dock and the other on a boat not far away. They were not using lights and were moving around quietly.

She went to Alex. "Alex," she whispered. "Shh, there are some men out there. I don't know what they are doing, but I don't think that they should be there."

"Where?"

"Come look out my window," she whispered.

"Let's be quiet," He whispered. Alex watched for a few minutes. "Eva, be real quiet." He went and put on his pants and slippers. "I'm going to look from on the deck. Stay out of sight, Honey."

Alex could see a car without lights move and stop at the access to the docks and another car at the other end of the dock. *"Police cars!"* he thought. He went back to Eva.

"Honey," he whispered, "come here and stay low, but when I say 'lights,' flip this switch on. There are police on the dock, so something is going on."

"Alex, be careful," she whispered.

"The police will handle it."

Eva sat with her hand hovering over the switch, waiting, it seemed a long time. At last at Alex's soft 'lights,' she flipped the switch, and lights came on flooding the area around the boat with lights.

The Policemen were there, close to the two men. "Put your hands on top of your heads." They soon lead the men quietly away. One of the Officers soon returned to thank Alex for the timely light.

They soon said good night again and went back to bed.

Eva had gotten cold and couldn't seem to get warm again.

At last, she gave up and went to Alex. "Alex, I'm frozen. I can't get warm."

"What?"

"I'm frozen. I can't get warm." She crawled into Alex's bed.

"Sweetheart, you *are* nearly frozen! Turn your back to me, that's the fastest way to get warm." He put his arms around her, pulling her against his chest.

"Alex?'

"Shh, not one word. Go to sleep."

A moment later, she gave part of a giggle, not quite. Alex felt it, and grinned, but didn't say anything. They were both getting warm and soon were asleep. Sometime later, Eva dreamed that Alex had taken his arms away. She woke up and he had, he'd turned his back to her in his sleep. She turned slowly, and put her arms around him.

He moved a bit, but she said, "Shh."

And they slept.

CHAPTER EIGHTEEN

Eva woke, again with her head on Alex's shoulder.

She turned a bit and kissed his shoulder. How she got there, neither one knew. *"Is this a dream, or just remembering?"*

Now she was fully awake, she knew that Alex was awake too. "Good Morning, Alex."

"Good Morning, Sweetheart."

"I know, not one word," she said, and crawled out of bed, taking the covers with her, taking them clear into the bathroom.

"Hey!" Alex called, but it was too late, both doors were closed.

He had coffee going when Eva came out. She'd made both beds, and Alex had breakfast ready.

"Good Morning, my Darling Husband," she said, coming up behind him and putting her arms around him.

"Good Morning, my Darling Wife," catching her up and kissing her thoroughly, her arms were around his neck.

"Oh Alex, I wish that we were going to have weeks and weeks alone. Aren't I awful?"

"You know, I've been thinking that too. Not awful, wonderful." He put her down at the table.

"You know there is a place in the Bible where it says that a man didn't have to work for a whole year, when he married. Maybe I'll take a whole year to marry me a wife."

"Do you suppose we'll be thoroughly married by then, or like this? Ecstatically in love!"

"We may be thoroughly married, but I think that we'll still be ecstatically in love, Darling Eva."

"On the trip, we'll enjoy the others and still have our time alone."

"You won't sleep in Jim's extra bed and make me sleep alone?"

"See what I mean, I can't quite catch up with you..."

She laughed, "I'm going to keep it that way!"

"I bet you will."

"I know I'll have to be good, when the others are around, but when we are alone..."

"Eva," he laughed, "I hope not too 'good.' If this is what you call bad, I love it."

"Am I – too naughty, Alex - am I – too much -? Or..."

"Not at all. Almost too much, I just don't know what to expect next, but I love it. Keep it up. I'll catch on soon."

"I warned you. I never know what I'll do next myself."

Her eyes sparkled, twinkling with a challenge, her smile mischievous.

"Yes, you did warn me," he chuckled.

"I'll try; really try to be good on the trip. After all, the trip was for you and Jim in the original planning. I'm just an afterthought."

"And what a thought! God's thought, a blessing from Him that I can hardly believe that He would bless me with such a lovely, loving Lady as my wife."

They continued the talk of their love, bantering and laughing; yet managing to eat their breakfast at the same time.

"This is fun, but unless we want to miss our wedding, we'd better get going," Alex said.

"I'll clear things away, while you get the boat ready," Eva said.

"I want to fill the fuel tanks before we leave here, and check with the Coast Guard."

They had to wait for some of the fishing boats to fuel up, before they had their turn.

Alex talked to the Coast Guard. They told him that they should have no problems, "just stay away from the Peacock Spit. You have your charts?"

"Yes we do, but having never been here before; I wanted to check with you."

"Where are you from?"

"We're out of Tacoma, headed for Oregon City. Alex Harmon and Eva Marks Harmon." Alex gave the registered number of the yacht.

"Good luck 'THISN SMINE', have a safe trip."

Leaving the harbor was slow as other boats were moving about.

"Let's call Jewel before we get too far."

Jewel answered, "Well, good morning you two. How is it this morning?"

"Doing great so far. We are just leaving Ilwaco. We are a little late getting started, but we should be timing it about right for the tide at the Columbia. The Ocean is still quiet, so we shouldn't have any problems. We should make it to Oregon City by five. The traffic in the rivers will slow us some, very likely. I hope not too much."

"We are leaving here in a few minutes too," Jewel said.

"You just caught us. Ben has a radio in the car too, so if you should have any problems, you can probably reach us. After we get to the Kelso area, we should have clear radio contact from then on."

"Maybe we'll call you after while. KBC42J clear and standing by."

"What do we have to watch for, Alex?"

"We watch the chart and instruments for depth, the compass for direction, it all fits together. We should have no problems."

"I'm sure glad that you know how to do all that."

"There are buoys and marker lights too in places to help guide us. You'll get used to it all. Jim knows all the rules and how to read the charts. He'll be a big help, and help the rest to learn too. Jim or I'll have to be close by at all times that we are traveling on the water. We had to take classes before we got our license and permits. We'll be responsible for the boat and passengers."

"Be sure to tell me, or us, if we do something wrong, or if we might need to know something. I want everything to go right, and as safe as possible."

"We will. We are going to have a wonderful time, Eva."

"Yes! It's so exciting even to think about. It was exciting out on the Pacific Ocean and exciting here on the river, the mighty Columbia River! It's been exciting just being with you, Alex."

"It would have been a dull trip without you."

"Honey, go put on that cowgirl outfit, will you please. We'll go directly to the restaurant when we get there."

Eva had put the flowers in bags in the refrigerator. She took them out and they were nearly as nice as the first day. She put on the western outfit and put flowers in her hair, some of the others she fastened on the front of her blouse. Breathing in their fragrance, she put her lips to them, "Oh you beauties, you're still glorious!"

Alex was standing beside the tall chair, and Eva climbed up on it to be beside him. He turned to look at her with shining eyes, eyes full of love.

"You're beautiful, my love. Thank you."

"You're welcome, my gallant lover." Her smile was tremulous. "I won't bug you now, I know there is no auto pilot, you have to do it all yourself."

"Yes, from here on to the dock in Oregon City, I'll be busy to put this boat through the traffic."

They passed a ship going in and two going out. There were a number of yachts, some smaller, and some about the same size as the 'THISN SMINE' on the river, as well as a number of smaller craft.

The going was slower as they went through Portland, then south and east to Oregon City. They pulled in to the dock in Oregon City at four o'clock.

There was a bunch of people crowded along the walkway, all friends and family, waiting for them.

Jim helped to tie the boat up, and then jumped aboard to grab Alex's hand, then hug and kiss Eva.

"Come on, the gang is all here waiting for you."

Alex took a moment to put on his western boots, having put on his western shirt and pants that morning.

Such a clamor! With everyone greeting them.

"The restaurant is about two blocks, or there is a car to take you up," Jim said.

"I'd just a soon walk, how about you, Eva?"

"Yes, let's walk. It's been a while since we've been on land. I may have to learn to walk again," she laughed.

Most everyone had walked down, so they had quite an escort up to the restaurant, there to find the rest of the family and friends gathered and waiting to have dinner a little later.

They were greeted with many hugs, kisses, and laughter.

The two families had been introducing themselves and getting acquainted. Jason, having met most of Alex's family, was doing his best with introductions.

Eva and Alex were separated in the press to talk to each one. Jim was in the group of men around Alex.

"Wow, Alex, that ring!" Jim exclaimed.

"Eva gave it to me the first night on the boat. Judge Thayer was gone, so we couldn't get married, but we had our own little ceremony. I used the ring that I had given her for my vows, she had this on a chain around her neck, and she used it for her vows. She'd bought it for me."

"You had your own wedding, just the two of you?"

"Yes. It was so – so special, so real. We knew that the Lord was there with us, and we included Him in our pledges."

"You're getting married again tomorrow?"

"Yes, of course. We must have that marriage certificate. We didn't sleep together – well not really."

"Not really? What do you mean, or should I ask?"

"There was a storm…then the storm got worse with lightning. Eva's afraid of lightning. We had gone to sleep, and I didn't hear it, but it woke her. She was so scared that she came and crawled in bed with me. I held her in my arms with her head on my shoulder. I had to keep taking the covers off her face. I talked to her until the storm went away and she fell asleep. She slept there the rest of the night. But that's all, - we didn't—"

Jim laughed, "Alex, if it was anyone but you, I wouldn't believe that story!"

The other men standing around were laughing too.

"I wonder what the guys are all laughing about, looks like they are laughing at Alex."

Eva looked over.

"Oh no! I think I know. I'll be right back."

"Alex, you didn't!" Eva exclaimed.

"Yes he did, Eva. He told us about the storm. *All* 'bout it," Jim laughed.

"Did you tell them about last night too? Now I'll have to tell the girls, so they'll hear my version."

She went back to the girls.

"Well, Alex, no more storms?" Jim asked, "What about last night? You might as well come clean. Eva said 'last night too,' tell us about last night."

"No more storms, but last night, she was nearly frozen and came and got in bed with me."

"Well, since you have started all this, you'd better explain."

"Well, we had gone to sleep –"

"In your own beds, not together?"

"...and Eva heard a noise. She came and got me. There were two men on the dock, messing around. As I watched, wondering what to do, I saw two police cars by the dock. I thought that maybe some light would help them, so I had Eva stand by the switch to turn the light on when I called to her. The police caught the men and hauled them away. We went back to bed, but Eva couldn't get warm again, so she came and got in bed with me, again. She said that she was frozen, and she was real cold. I had her put her back against me and I held her in my arms to get her warm. We both fell asleep. Again....again...we didn't..."

The men were roaring with laughter.

Bill laughing, wiping tears away, "Alex, you probably could have gotten by without all this confession, especially in front of Eva's sons....but it makes a great story."

"She'll probably get even with you later for telling all," someone said.

"I agree, you can just about count on it," Paul said, wiping tears away, hardly able to talk.

"Is it really that funny?" Alex asked. "I really didn't think that it was funny at the time," but he joined in the laugh.

"I was a bit – well – maybe confused!"

That set off another round of laughter.

"At your age, Dad, you're confused?" David joined in the ribbing.

"Well, now wait, I was determined that Eva would have her marriage certificate first."

"We understand that."

"She is so sweet, so wonderful, so much fun, too. And I never know what to expect next."

"That's Mom, and she'll get you when you don't expect it, too." Alan warned.

"She did this morning. When she got out of bed, she took all of the covers, clear into the bathroom." That was greeted with more laughter.

Meanwhile, Eva was trying to explain to the girls, and having as much difficulties as Alex.

"I was so scared, I hate lighting. Alex talked to me, and sang to me. He has a good voice. I was worried that he would be upset with me, because we weren't going to sleep together – but we didn't – didn't, we just fell asleep. He wasn't upset. But when I was going to say I was sorry that I had caused us to sleep together when we weren't going to, he said not to say it, or he might misunderstand, it would be better to not say a word."

Every one was laughing. "And last night, I was freezing."

"Last night? Last night too?"

So, she'd to explain that too.

"He didn't sing last night?"

"No, he just held me and warmed me up."

"Explain! Explain!"

Finally, she told both stories.

"...and this morning when I woke up on his shoulder again, I – I said good morning," she began to laugh, knowing how funny it would sound, "then I said, 'I know, not one word.' I jumped out of bed and took all the covers with me into the bathroom."

The girls were in gales of laughter.

"But we didn't...we haven't...our wedding is still...okay?"

The girls were still laughing.

"That Alex! He said that we just wouldn't say anything about sleeping together or not sleeping together. Then *he* said it."

"I think that you have him pretty well shook up, Eva!" Jewel said.

"Me! How could I shake him up?" That started the laughter again.

*

They had dinner in a banquet room, Eva and Alex sitting together. "Alex, you told them," Eva said.

"I don't know how it happened," Alex confessed. "I think that Jim some how got it out of me. He asked me about this ring, and..." He shrugged his shoulders, "it all came out."

That started the laughter again.

Jim sitting with Jewel and Ben across from them, "Don't blame me for your wild stories," Jim chimed in.

"Eva, I'm sorry..." Alex started.

"Not one word or the next time you'll lose more than covers," Eva said frowning and looking at him sternly, then she broke out laughing too. She relented, "Alex, my darling husband, it's okay..." she reached over and pulled his head down to hers and kissed him. "I love you, remember, I love you ecstatically," she whispered.

He put his arms around her, pulling her close, and kissed her again. "I never know what you'll do next."

"I know, isn't it fun? You've been warned!"

"I'll not warn *you* next time," Alex said with his grin.

She put one hand to her heart, the back of the other to her forehead and cried, "Promises! Promises!"

The others were laughing uproariously. How anyone was ever able to eat, it was never known, with all the talk and laughter. They lingered until nearly eleven o'clock.

Finally, Danielle stood up and said, "People, if we are going to have a needless wedding tomorrow, we'll have to call a halt to all this fun and get the Bride and Groom to bed... *separately*. I'm taking the Bride with me; some of you guys can put the Groom to bed. That's your responsibility. We'll see everyone here at eight o'clock tomorrow morning for breakfast. Right?"

"A chorus of *okays* answered between the laughs.

"Good night, Sweetheart. See you in the morning."

"Good night Alex, my darling."

Eva slept in Ann Marie's room. She woke from a dream that Alex was somewhere else...and, of course, he was.

"Alex," she whispered, "I just want to be close to you."

There were tears before she slept again.

CHAPTER NINETEEN

Eva woke with Ann Marie leaning on her elbows on the bed, her chin in her hands, looking at her.

"Good Morning Grandma. Are you getting up?"

"Good Morning Ann Marie. Yes, I'm getting up. Is everyone up?"

"Yes. Mom said to come see if you're getting up yet. She said that if you're going to go have breakfast with everyone, you'd better get up soon."

"Oh, it's almost seven. I'll hurry. It won't take me long."

Danielle came and brought one of the new pantsuits for her to wear. "Put this on, Mom."

"I love it, thank you."

It was a medium light blue, with sweater and shoes to match.

She showered and was ready by seven forty-five.

"I'm ready at last," she said as she came out. "Guess that I overslept some."

"It's okay, Mom. We have plenty of time to get down to the motel restaurant. We are all ready."

Alex was standing outside waiting for her.

"Good Morning, Darling. Do I dare kiss you?"

"Good Morning Alex, my love. You'd better."

She reached her arms up to his neck, and he bent down to kiss her.

"Where, oh where is that step stool!" he whispered in her ear.

"Come on lovers, let's go eat. If we have a day like yesterday, we'll have a hard time getting through breakfast."

"What do you suppose Danielle meant by that?"

"I can't imagine. What was wrong with yesterday?"

"I thought it was perfect, myself."

Danielle laughed, "I can see that we are on the same wave today." Someone called, "Well, did you get any sleep?"

"No" In unison.

"Well, we should have let them sleep on the boat again."

"Alex, are they trying to give us a bad time?"

"That could be. I can't imagine why. Everything seemed to me like it was just right."

David let out a whoop. "I can see that Dad is still...*confused*."

The food was served buffet-style. Eva and Alex, being first in line, were first to sit down, with a few minutes by themselves.

"Did you sleep, Darling? No waking or crying?"

"Well I slept, but woke knowing that you weren't close by."

"And you cried?"

"A little, does it show?"

"Maybe, just a bit, or maybe it's from the sun yesterday."

"Am I burnt? I didn't notice."

"Well, maybe just a little, you're a bit pink. You look natural; maybe it's just a glow. I think that's it, you are *aglow*."

"Really? I'm not surprised. Today! Today, Alex!"

"Is that a new suit?" He asked, "I like it. Have I told you that you're very beautiful this morning, my Dear Darling Love?"

"Alex, you're going to make me cry..."

"Because I think that you're beautiful? You really are."

"I may cry that you think so and love me, and I'm so happy, so deliriously deliciously happy."

"That is what it is, delirious, delicious happiness!" Alex exclaimed.

They were soon surrounded, and included, in conversations. Jim came and sat close. "Alex, before I forget, the Bransons' called, and they would like to start on the trip on Friday, next."

"Say, that sounds great. We were supposed to start on Wednesday. I don't think that we could make it back until afternoon on Wednesday. With getting everyone's things on the boat, it would make it pretty late to leave on Wednesday. Friday...yes, we can make that."

Jim continued, "He said let's leave at dawn on Friday. So we'll have to get all our things on board on Thursday, and spend the night on the boat."

"We'll be ready," Bill and Nancy said together.

"We'll be there, ready too," Ben added.

"Eva and I are pretty well settled," Alex started.

"Oh no you're not! You aren't going to sleep in *my* bunk," Jim exclaimed, "even if I do have two."

That got them started again, and they kept up a constant flow of teasing, first one and then another.

"Time's flying," Danielle, said at last. "We've got to break this up, if we are going to have a wedding at two o'clock. Whoever wants to, come on out to the house, the rest be there by one-thirty, at the latest. Alex...are you going to dress at the house?"

"No, I'll use the boat, and someone will have to take me to the house."

"All right, we'll see everyone at the house."

Alex put his arms around Eva.

"Honey Girl, this may be the last kiss before we are legally married. Next time you'll be my wife, legal, and on paper."

"Alex, I'm overwhelmed again."

"Yes, me too. I'll see you soon, Sweetheart."

"I love you, Alex!"

At the house, Danielle said, "Mom, we are going to set your hair and do your nails, and you should rest for a while. Why don't you lie down for a half hour or so, then we'll get started."

Eva went to Ann Marie's room to lie down.

"Are you going to sleep, Grandma?"

"No dear, I'll just lie here a little while."

"Can I sing some of the songs that I learned at church, to you?"

"Yes, I'd like that, Ann Marie."

Ann Marie sang and talked to her Grandmother.

"Have you kept Grandma entertained, Ann Marie?" her mother asked.

"Yes. I sang some songs to her."

"They were good songs too. It was very nice, Ann Marie. Thank you so much. I loved every minute."

Abbigail came, "Mom, I made these little pillows for the rings; I thought maybe you'd like to use them. Ann Marie can carry the ones that you have for Alex, and Davie can carry the ones Alex has for you. What do you think?"

"They are beautiful! I'd love it, but you had better ask Alex too."

"I'll do that, just as soon as he gets here."

When asked, Alex approved, heartily.

They put Eva in a tub with lightly fragrant oils, rubbed her down, and massaged her. Washed and set her hair, and while it was drying, they gave her a manicure and pedicure. They helped her dress in the new clothes that were waiting.

At last, put on the dress that Abbigail had made. Joy and Hope very carefully arranged flowers that matched her bouquet on the little hat, making it look almost like a crown.

Raylynn opened a box containing a necklace and earrings of Sapphires and put them on her grandmother.

"Grandma, we, your grand kids, got together and bought this for you. It's something new and blue too."

Rebah gave her a beautiful old lace handkerchief, "Something old and borrowed. You know how I love antiques, and I know that you do too."

Rose brought her a blue garter, and put it on her.

Joanna brought a little white dove and a tiny yellow bee and tucked them in her bouquet, "For lasting love and sweetness of life, Gram."

Ann Marie and Davie brought and put a shinny new penny in each shoe.

With hugs and kisses, her granddaughters and daughters-in-law left. She was ready.

"Paul is coming to escort you out. Danielle and I are both going to stand with you, and Ann Marie will be close with her pillow with the ring. Davie will stand with Alex and Jim."

Abbigail kissed her Mother, "You're just beautiful, Mom. God Bless."

Danielle kissed her too, "My lovely Mother, I wish you so much happiness." They went out, letting Paul in.

"Are you ready, Mom? You look lovely." He put her hand on his arm and they went out to the landing, with two steps up from the living room level.

Jim and Davie were there by Alex; Paul stepped along side them. Abbiagil, Danielle, and Ann Marie stepped beside Eva Jo. The Minister was standing before them. The landing was open on three sides, and the family and friends were seated around so all could see.

"Heyya, sweetheart," Alex whispered. "What would you have thought if I had worn my western boots?"

"I would have thought, 'there's my beautiful, handsome man," she whispered back.

The minister heard the exchange and grinned, putting his hand up to his mouth to hide it.

Jim snickered, then nudged Alex, "Alex, be serious," in a loud whisper.

Alex jumped, nearly knocking Eva down.

"Alex!"

"Sorry Honey, Jim poked me." There were no more whispers. He turned back to Jim, "I'm serious, Jim. This is serious, getting married."

By this time, the minister himself was tittering aloud. Jim had been holding his breath, trying not to chuckle, but it came out in an explosive laugh the he couldn't stop. The minister doubled over, trying to control himself.

Alex looked at Eva, raised one eyebrow, and nodded his head, as though to ask, *what's with them?*

Eva raised her eyebrows and shrugged her shoulders...

Who knows?

The minister, and Jim, and most of the crowd could see it.

The minister roared with laughter, Jim grabbed hold of the railing and really hee-hawed. The whole crowd started to laugh. The minister reached into his pocket for a handkerchief, which wasn't there. Someone brought a box of tissues to Jim; he passed them to the minister, than sat down on the step, continuing to laugh.

"What did I do?" Alex whispered to Eva.

"Just being your self," she whispered back, giggling.

The crowd tried to be quiet when trying to listen, then roaring by turns.

Someone said, "I'll bet Jim nearly wet his pants."

Abbigail whispered, "Shh Leo!"

Jim and the minister couldn't stop laughing but for a few minutes at a time, then would start again. The crowd was having the same problems. The minister's wife brought him a glass of water.

"Thanks Honey," he said in a falsetto voice. That started the whole crowd again.

"William, get a hold of your self," his wife whispered, through her giggles.

The minister tried to take a drink of the water, but succeeded in spilling it down the front of his jacket and shirt. Jim was standing by then, and that started him off again.

Abbigail and Danielle were laughing so hard that Danielle was poking her finger in her eye, trying to catch her contacts, and keep them from running down her face in the tears.

The minister finally said, "This is the most unconventional ceremony I've ever performed."

Ann Marie protested, "This isn't a *confentional*, it's a wedding!"

Davie poked his head around Jim, Alex, and Eva and said, "Hush, Ann Marie."

The roar was on again.

Alex turned to Eva, "Honey…let's elope!"

"Guess we'll have to if we are going to get married," she answered.

"What's elope, Mama?" Ann Marie asked.

"That's when you run away and get married," Danielle answered.

"Well, that's what they did, they ran off and came down here to elope and get married," Ann Marie affirmed.

Alex looked at Eva, "Guess that's what we did, didn't we, Sweetheart?"

"Well, we're trying to, any way," she answered through her giggles.

Davie let out a snort, "Well, is anyone going to get married today or not?"

Ann Marie paid him back by leaning forward and saying, "Hush yourself, Davie."

The minister cleared his throat and started to say, "Dearly Beloved," but it came out in such a high-pitched voice, that he stopped, while gales of laughter drowned out his further efforts.

"I'll be okay...I'll make it in a minute," he said, holding his hand up, trying to get his voice back under control.

"Take your time," Alex said, "We don't have to leave here until Monday morning."

The minister started to laugh again, the rest following.

"Alex!" Eva said, shaking his arm.

"Just trying to help."

"Yes, you're very trying," she burst into laughter again.

Gradually everyone quieted.

"Dearly," he cleared his throat. Dearly bel-" he tried again to clear his throat.

He took a deep breath and started again.

"Dearly beloved..." he continued on through the ceremony without any more difficulty. Until, "Do you – I've forgotten, what's your name?"

"Alex. Alex Harmon."

"Do you Alex, take – what's your name?"

"Eva Mark."

"Do you Alex take Eva to be your lawfully wedded wife?"

"I do."

"Do you – a- a?

"Eva," she whispered.

The minister was chucking between times. The tittering began again, but not in such volume.

"Do you Eva take Alex to be your lawfully wedded husband?"

"I do."

"Do we have rings?"

"Yes. David?" Alex reached for the ring just as Jim pulled the ribbon, untying and releasing the ring. It bounded away to the floor; down it rolled, between the minister's feet.

"Catch it!" Alex exclaimed, "Don't let it get away."

Davie dived for the ring as it rolled between the minister's feet, nearly upsetting him. The minister staggered backwards, nearly falling. Jim came to the rescue. He jumped and grabbed the minister's arm, knocking the book out of his hand.

It was sent flying and someone in the crowd caught it as it went passed. The crowd was roaring again.

The ring was restored, and they proceeded.

Ann Marie said, "I'm not going to let this one get away," and she didn't.

It came time for the minister to pray. The prayer was punctuated with soft giggles and chuckles. When it came time for the Amen, Davie added a loud 'AMEN.'

"Now, you may kiss the bride."

"I've practicing for this!" Alex lifted her off the floor and Eva, caught by surprise, threw her arms out, unintentionally tossed her bouquet.

Jim caught it.

He stood, staring at it, while Alex kissed his bride. He put her down at last.

"Now let me introduce the newlyweds, Mr. Alex – and Mrs. Eva Harmon."

The minister was off again, wiped out in laughter. The crowd was in an uproar.

*

Jim carried that bouquet around with him all day, and no one ever knew what he did with it.

But, I'll tell you the secret…

Late one night, while on the trip to Alaska, Jim took that bouquet out, and standing praying, "Father, somewhere it is said to cast our bread upon the water. Father, I think that I love Betty, and as sort of a fleece, I'm casting the bouquet of the traditional next to be married, on the water.

I trust you to lead me and show me my way. If my way includes Betty, I know that you will lead me and show me. I'm not in a hurry. I know that I'm to be a minister of your Gospel and need teaching, both by teachers and by you. I'll wait until you nudge me, if that time is to come for Betty to be in my life forever."

And so, Jim cast the flowers on the waters.

*

After he'd kissed Eva thoroughly, Alex turned to the minister and asked for the certificate. The minister getting it duly signed by the witnesses handed it to Alex.

Alex turning to Eva, "Here Sweetheart, now we are legal," he said with his usual grin.

"Yes, Darling, legal at last."

Jim was denying that his signature was legal because he was still shaking with laughter.

Paul agreed that maybe his wasn't either, "Maybe we'll have to go through all this again."

"Oh no, not today anyway," the minister said laughing.

"Shall we try again tomorrow, Dad?" David asked.

"I'm beginning to think that it was a mistake to include these people in our wedding. We did just as well without them."

"We did, didn't we," but she, trying to keep a straight face, was not succeeding very well.

"Ah well, we have the certificate, legal or not, it'll do just fine for our purpose," Eva said, tucking it down the front of her dress.

Alex couldn't hold back any longer, and threw back his head and had a good laugh, joining the others.

Although the friends and family gathered around to kiss the Bride and congratulate the Groom, the laughter held full swing, making it difficult for anyone to be serious in their wishes and blessings.

In a lull, Alex sat down and pulled Eva to his lap, "We made it, Sweetheart, we're married!"

"*Eeeeyup*, we sure did. We made it."

"No more fears about the future? About us?"

"No Alex, no more fears about anything. I'm sure that we'll be just fine. I think that there is a saying, 'love conquers all,' and we have love."

"That we do, my darling Wife."

The minister, who had collapsed into a chair, was trying to apologize.

"I don't know what came over me; I've never done anything like this before. But the boots – it just set me off, and it snowballed from there."

Jim sat down near by, "Pastor, you should have been here yesterday. That would explain everything. I'll tell you about it. You deserve an explanation. It really wasn't your fault at all."

Danielle blew a whistle, "Come on everyone, we are to go back to the motel for the wedding cake."

Everyone started to leave. Alex stopped Jim. "Jim, your keys, please. I want a few moments with my wife, alone."

"You're not going to run off again are you?"

"No. We'll be there soon."

Joy and Hope caught Jason and Steve; "Jim will help us. We want to take most of these flowers over and put them on the boat."

"Yes, let's do it."

Jim asked Danielle if he could take Ann Marie and Davie with them to the boat. Betty joined them, and they took the flowers and decorated the boat. Jim showed Ann Marie and Davie all over the boat. Ann Marie discovered the washer and dryer.

"Look! Look! They have a washer and dryer too!"

Jim had made a big sign on canvas and hung it up on the back of the boat, 'JUST MARRIED.'

Alex driving away turned a corner that he knew did not lead to the motel.

"Where can we stop for a minute, Jo?"

"There is a view point overlooking the falls and the river, turn here."

"Well, let's look while we are here. A little fresh air will help too. What is this?"

"This is the Willamette Falls. There is a paper mill on each side of the river. The river used to power a woolen mill that used to be where those buildings are now. The river still runs a power plant that powers the mills part of the time."

Alex had turned to look at Eva. He leaned one elbow on the top of the wall.

"What? My hat is not on straight? I'm not surprised, after what I've been through," she laughed.

"I'm just admiring my wife."

No one was around; he turned back towards the river, threw his arms up in the air, and shouted, "Hey world...this is my wife!"

He turned back to her. "My wife, Eva. I like the sound of that. *My Wife.*"

She laughed softly, stood up on her toes, and reached to kiss him, putting her arms around his neck.

"Hello, Husband Alex."

"Hello, Wife Eva!"

He crushed her in his arms, kissing her again and again, leaving her nearly breathless.

"Now your hat *is* falling off," he laughed as he released her.

She took it off.

"We had better go; they'll be waiting for us."

"Yes, I know, but I just had to have a moment with you alone. Alone with my darling Wife."

Jim and David were waiting outside for them. Abbigail and Danielle met them inside.

"Is my hair a mess? My hat came off."

"No, it looks good." Abbigail ran her fingers through a little of her hair. "Let's leave the hat off for the rest of the pictures."

"Come this way, the cake is over here."

"Darling, look at that cake! I've never seen anything like it. And a water fountain under it!"

"It's beautiful girls! Just lovely. You did a beautiful job. Thank you, darlings," Eva exclaimed.

"Do you mean that you made this cake?"

"Yes, Alex, we made the cake," Danielle laughed. "We've made cakes before, but this one is special."

There were pictures taken of them with the cake. Unknown to Eva and Alex, there were pictures taken at the wedding too. There were pictures that would remind them of that 'unconventional' wedding.

Danielle's twin eighteen-year-old daughters, Hope and Joy, had set up chairs and a table just at the entrance of the banquet room that they were using this afternoon. The girls were making nametags for each one as they came, "because it's hard to remember every ones name, and we want to be sure to get to know each other."

Jason stopped to help.

Steve pulled up a chair to sit and talk.

"Here I've been so lonely at school, when I have family so close. Did you know that I've adopted your Grandma for my Mom?"

"You have? Oh, you're the Steve that Grandma lives in your apartment."

"Yes. Jason and I live there now. I'll be there for the summer, and I'll go back to college this fall, down here in Oregon."

"Are you a *Duck* or a *Beaver*?"

"A *Duck*. Will you come to one or so of my games? I'll send you tickets."

"Yes, we'd like that, if we can get Mom and Dad to take us." They continued to talk, getting acquainted.

The Minister and his wife had been persuaded to accompany them to the motel for the rest of the afternoon.

Jim, true to his word, seated the minister, and told him the story of yesterday.

Several others gathered around to put in a word of two, and the day was lived over again, with much laughter.

The minister finally said, "I still don't see why it should have struck *me* so funny. I knew nothing of all the preceding."

"Well, laughter is contagious," Alex chimed in, "so is a yawn," he opened his mouth and yawned a great yawn.

"Not yet, Alex," Jim shouted over the laughter. "We've got hours yet, with dinner and everything. Besides, anyone can tell that was a fake yawn." That was greeted with howls of laughter.

It finally quieted down as they ate dinner. Billie and Brandon came and sat with Eva and Alex to share their news, "We are moving next week into our new home," Billie started, "And Brandon asked me to give notice that I'm quitting my job. I'm taking a few days off to move, then work two more weeks, and then I'll be a housewife!"

She leaned over and whispered in Eva's ear, "I think that I'm pregnant!"

"Billie, how wonderful!"

Brandon added, "Owen and Naomi are moving into our apartment to live, permanently, and that beautiful place next door has been sold. Owen and Naomi are going to watch it, be kind of caretakers for the owners until they return from an extended trip. They are going to have it thoroughly cleaned."

"I'm glad that it'll be lived in. It looks so lonesome sometimes." Eva said, a bit sadly. Brandon continued, "The owner said that since it is such a big place and such nice grounds, that it could be used as a family gathering place and a retreat for family and friends."

"What a good place for that use. It is so beautiful there," Eva added. "So much happening and we have only been gone for five days. We'll have a lot of catching up to do when we get home again. You'll come out and see us when you get home? We'll miss you, and the lake and the animals," Billie said, a bit wistfully, "but I'm excited about our new home."

"There is a good church close by, as well as the school. I know that we'll be happy there." Brandon added.

Eva called Abbigail and Danielle over, "Girls, I hope that you have had a chance to get to know these kids, my neighbors next door in the apartment."

"We've met, but it's been so busy around here, we've not had much time to get acquainted. Maybe you can come down some time this summer; we'd love to have you come. I have a big house, please come," Danielle invited.

"Thank you, we'd love to come," Billie answered.

Abbigail added, "Do you get a vacation? Come go to the lake down here with us. We sometimes spend two weeks at Timothy Lake, up by Mount Hood. Sometimes we go to the beach for two weeks. We'll figure something out. We haven't decided where we'll go this summer. I would like for our families to get together again. It would be such fun."

"That would be great," David said, "and maybe you can come to Tacoma. We could use Dad's place while they are gone. There's lots of room."

"That's true." Tom chimed in. "We have lots of room at Dad's. May have to put some in sleeping bags, but we have a big hall down stairs that'll hold all of us."

"We'll make some plans and check with each other and do get together." Beth added. "And remember, Billie and Brandon, you're included in all our plans."

"It sounds like they aren't going to miss us much, Eva," Alex said.

"It sounds like they'll have a good time too. I'm glad."

"You know that we'll all miss you, but you'll have a good time and come back to us with lots of stories and pictures for us to enjoy!" Bill Jr. said.

David interjected, "You have to remember they are married now, the stories may have to come from Uncle Bill and Nancy or Ben and Jewel. Or maybe Jim, the lone wolf of the pack, will be the big story teller."

That brought a laugh.

"We'll keep a log book and copy it for you and send you a copy every few days," Alex said.

"Yeah, but who is going to keep the log? Did you write down your 'scepades on the last few nights?" some one asked, and that brought another big howl.

Jim waited for his opportunity to catch Eva fairly alone.

"Eva, I want to apologize for starting the riot. I don't know what got into me...it's just that when Alex whispered about the boots! I...I just couldn't help it. I knew that he'd worn them when you had your little ceremony, and then after everything, the way he talked and told things, I just came unglued. If the minister hadn't started – Here I am, blaming it on everyone else, when I started it. Will you forgive me, Eva?"

"There is nothing to forgive, Jim. I'm happy the way it went. It was kind of the way with Alex and I on the way down here. We were either serious or cutting up teasing. We are so excited, so emotional over all this, getting married and everything.

I think that we are rather shocked, amazed at falling in love at our age. We are worse than teenagers," she laughed.

She continued, "I'm amazed at the emotions that I have to have the love of a man like Alex. It's still so hard to believe that Alex loves me. *Me!* He's the greatest, like you said that first day we met."

"Eva, may I call you Mom too? I'm rather jealous of Steve and the others, and I'd like to call you Mom as well."

"Yes, of course you may, if you like. I love you, and would be very proud to claim you as a son. You'll always be special to me."

Danielle came up and asked, "May I hug my new brother? Thank you Jim for helping carry this wedding along. You know we are all so happy over this wedding, that it would have been tears soon, tears of happiness. It couldn't have been better!"

Alex had slipped his arm around Danielle as he joined them.

"How wonderfully put, Danielle. I know that I've been deliriously happy, and got worse every day. You give me an excuse for acting the way that I did."

"Yes, Alex, we can believe that," Jim laughed.

"That's all right Ol' Pard, your day is coming. And this day will not be soon forgotten." Alex laughed.

"When, and if, ever I get married. I'm going to elope," Jim declared.

"You may elope, but we'll be sure that the bride doesn't." Alex threatened.

"This day will long be remembered by me," the minister spoke up.

"I've never been to such a wedding. I was supposed to be in charge of the ceremony and I never was less in charge of anything in my life!"

They all laughed with him.

"Just one thing more; Jim, may I call on you to come help me sometimes when it might be a difficult wedding?"

As soon as the laughter died down again, Jim said, "Pastor, it may be hard to believe it, but I'm really a rather serious guy. I'm going into the ministry myself. I've no excuse. I really thought that I had brought Alex up better, but it's better to admit failures."

The laugh was on again.

Jim sat down by the minister, "Pastor, thank you putting up with us and being such a good sport, and doing as good as you did. It just snowballed, never completely out of control, and never completely in control."

The minister said, "I haven't laughed so much for a long time, and all clean fun. So much love shown in such a large group."

"I want to invite you all to come to my church tomorrow. Or do I?" he grinned. "Jim, you're to sit on the platform with me. That way you'll be behind me and I can't see your face, to get me started laughing."

"I'll wear my boots." Alex said. That started it again.

*

Eva and Alex found themselves alone for a bit.

"Sweetheart? You look a bit dewy eyed."

"Alex, I'm still – it's so incredible, all this…and that we're married!"

"It is isn't it?" He pulled her to his lap. She put her arms around his neck, her cheek against his.

"You know, it's been ever so long since you hugged me and kissed me," she whispered.

"Oh, the responsibilities of a married man," he chuckled softly in her ear.

"Yes, and don't you forget it!" she whispered back.

He kissed her tenderly. "Sweetheart, I love you."

'Alex, you are my darling wonderful, dear man. It seems that I love you more and more. I'm just overflowing with love. It amazes me that I can feel this way!"

"Yes, Darling Wife, we are soul mates as well. I'm glad that we are going to have most of three days alone again."

"Yes! I'm glad too. It'll be more incredible that before. I'm anticipating – well-"

"Yes, me too. Like you said, our love just seems to grow and grow."

"Alex, I'm so glad! So glad that I can love you like this! You deserve to be loved like this."

Allan came.

"Mom. We want to get some generation pictures. Benny and Kenny both want pictures of you with their kids and new babies." So, he took Eva away for a little while.

Alex sat down beside the minister, "Pastor, I should apologize for the disruption that I started. The thing is, I'm not sorry about how it turned out, and you carried it off very well. Thank you for that."

"Alex, I enjoyed it all very much. It was a unique wedding, unique in several ways. And very precious too, that God would bring this all about."

Alex explained about trying to get married in Seattle before coming down alone on the boat.

"The boots, Pastor, we both wore western clothes on our first date, and I wanted us to wear them for our own private wedding on the boat.

We made our vows and dedicated our marriage to the Lord. It was a special time, but later, I thought of Jesus saying to 'obey the laws of the land.' I knew that we should wait for this wedding.

I believe that Jim told you some of the rest."

"It sounds like a wonderful experience, Alex. I admire you both. You're very unusual people. I'm glad that I don't know how many couples do not wait. God will bless you both. I believe that He has already blessed you."

"Yes, we know that God is blessing us."

The Minister stood. "It's time for me to go. Thank you all for including me in this afternoon. It is refreshing to see such happy people. To see the love demonstrated in the family."

"Is it time for me to yawn yet?" Alex asked.

"Yes, Alex," Paul said, "it's time for you to yawn. We'll all go and be back at eight o'clock in the morning for breakfast, then on to church. After church, we are to have lunch back here again.

Pastor, will you pray before we go?"

He did, a prayer for thanksgiving and blessings for the newly weds and for all the family.

They crowded around to shake the minister's hand and say a word of thanks.

Eva and Alex slipped away to the boat, knowing that they would not have to say good byes until after lunch tomorrow.

And so, we leave them...Alex and Eva, to their privacy, and leave the goodbyes for tomorrow, knowing that they'll be said with love and best wishes and God's blessings on all.

A safe and happy trip ahead, and happy years ahead as well.

Oh yes, Alex did wear his boots to church...but we won't say any more.

The End

A SILVER PATH

List of Characters

Eva Jo Mark
> Sister; Jewel, husband Ben
> Brothers; Len, wife Alice
>> Cal
>> Sven
> Children; Daughter, Abbigale, husband, Leo
>> Daughters; Raylynn
>>> Rebah, husband, James
>>> Rose and Jo Anna
> Daughter, Danielle, husband Garry
>> Daughters, Hope and Joy, twins
>> Son, Davie
>> Daughter, Ann Marie
>> Sons, Paul, wife Ruth
>> Jason, single
>> Allen, wife Marie
>>> Sons, Benny and Kenny

Alex Harmon
> Brother, Bill, wife Nancy
>> Son, Bill Jr.
> Children; Sons, Tom, wife Beth
>> Daughter, Betty
>> David, wife Noralee
>> Mike and Ray, families unlisted

Harmon housekeepers; Mrs. (Jordi), Jordan
> Hetti
Friends;
> Jim Dugan
> Steve Owens
> Owen, wife Naomi Owens
> Brandon wife Billie

Ex husband, Henry

About the Author

I'm the seventh child of parents who emigrated from Norway. My father's name was Paul, Ole's son Heimark. Emigration officials dropped the Heimark so our last name became Olson. I am Emma Johanna Olson and I married John A Renner.

Thus: Emma Jo Renner.

I married young and my oldest daughter was born a week before my 17th birthday.

Now I find myself with nineteen great-grandchildren and one great-great grandchild. All are beautiful, wonderful people.

I went to college at eighty-two. There were four generations of my family in college that year, my youngest daughter, her daughter and a great grandson. I took computer and writing and loved every minute of it.

I read a lot, three or more hours each day, and my chain-reference Bible has hundreds of highlighted places in it where God has shown me and taught me.

Alone with God, that thought gives me a thrill that cannot be found anywhere else.

"His grace is sufficient unto me."

-   Emma

-

For more on Emma's upcoming books, or to purchase additional copies, please visit: www.emmajorenner.com.

Made in the USA
Charleston, SC
03 July 2011